What's Left

Book Two

James Fuller

Hello again.
It's more of a lake
then pond.

What's Left

Copyright © 2019 – James Fuller

Formatting by Rik – Wild Seas Formatting
http://www.WildSeasFormatting.com

The scope on the .303 rifle was damaged; two distinctive hairline cracks marred the upper left side of the outer glass. It only truly affected the shot when facing toward the direction of the sun; the light formed a strange prism within the scope, throwing off the distance and visibility of a target. If bullets were easier to come by it would have been a challenge happily accepted to learn to perfect a shot with such a handicap. But bullets were scarce, more so for a gun she wasn't even allowed to have; undamaged scopes even more so. But this was life.

Auska grinned, patting the side of the scarred-up rifle as if it were alive and would understand the affection. It was a hard-won trophy from nearly two years ago. She had killed its previous owner while his pants had been down around his ankles. He had thought he had cornered a helpless woman, lost and alone in the woods. He had promised to spare her life if she allowed him to ravish her body with little resistance. Playing the part perfectly had made him drop his guard. He had died too quickly for her taste, but she couldn't afford to risk him getting the upper hand again. The fact that she had been caught off guard for him to sneak up on her in the first place angered her still to this day.

Her lithe frame and youth were one of her most valuable assets in the dark, hardened world she had been born into. As much as she detested playing the weak and helpless maiden, it was a skill set she had used several times and to which she owed her life. She liked to believe *he* would have been proud of her for her resourcefulness. "*Any weakness one can exploit to stay alive is one you should use. Honor and heroics will get you killed.*" Words he had left imprinted on her very soul in the time they had travelled together.

A flood of fresh guilt and pain assaulted her momentarily, for honor and heroics had proven his downfall... for her. She pushed the guilt away quickly, knowing it would do nothing to help. The past was done, over; only the future remained. Survival and seeing tomorrow; nothing more. To put too much hope beyond that would likely end in disappointment for many.

Looking through the scope again she scanned the narrow area ahead. Two infected staggered about in the shadows of the trees, ever searching for living flesh to consume. They would find nothing at this time a day. Animals had learned their scent long ago and knew to stay far away from these devilish creatures. Only if an unprepared traveler happened by would they have a chance at feasting during the day.

Travelers this far north were few and far between now. Most thoughts of a safer place had long faded into myths and legends, and so people accepted whatever life they could find. But when night came, that was their time and she had no doubt they would find a bedded down deer or elk, or some other helpless creature that didn't stand a chance in the dark of night.

Glancing up at the afternoon sun she knew it was too late to make it back without her absence being noticed. Hopefully, Barry would look the other way, or maybe she could bribe him again. Either way, she didn't care. Bring on whatever punishment they found fitting for breaking their stupid rules and laws again. She wasn't hurting anyone. She almost wished they would leave her behind, lock the doors and refuse her entry; at least then she'd only have one thing to worry about... herself. She grinned; not like she couldn't still get over the walls unnoticed if she wanted.

Auska slowed her breathing, waiting for the shot to come; it would only be a matter of time. The weight of her knife on her belt reminded her she could save a bullet if she wanted to live dangerously. But she didn't want to risk it, not today of all days. Today was important to her, today she had to live. Tomorrow was another matter entirely.

A cool breeze picked up and nipped at her face and bare hands, but she ignored it. Over the last eight years, she had become accustomed to the cold weather the north gave out. With winter quickly approaching, it would only get worse in the weeks to come until winter's grasp squeezed them in tightly and trips outside the walls were almost nonexistent.

Auska's finger caressed the worn trigger delicately, her heart quickening as the two infected lurched and stumbled closer together. She had to be ready, she would likely only get one chance at this and it had already been near an hour. She hated waiting, but patience was important for survival. *He had taught her that and often*.

"Come on you mindless fucks, I don't have all bloody day," she whispered, knowing it would take her at least an hour or more to get back to the others if they even waited for her. She really didn't want to end up getting caught out here at night again. It wasn't the danger that bothered her. It was the lying as to why she hadn't returned with the group that was the hard part. Of late her rogue activities were frowned upon more and more, with punishments more hindering to her lifestyle.

Sanctuary was, for all intents and purposes, safe and livable and for most more appealing than life outside the walls, regardless of the strict rules and crooked politics. For Auska it was almost worse, for her entry had been founded on a lie, one that at the time she didn't even know about. Yet the council and many of the folk within still held her in contempt for it. The only reason they hadn't been discarded was that Vincent and Kelli had promised to work themselves to the bone and do whatever was required of them. The first year had been brutal, but soon they had earned their place within Sanctuary, made a handful of friends and even a life if that's what one could call it. But they seemed happy, fulfilled in a way, but she never had. If anything, she just felt emptier each passing year.

Her body tensed as she knew the moment grew closer. *His* words echoed in her mind once more: *'Never tense up, stay loose, a loose body reacts faster to a possible change in a situation.'* Licking her lips, she rolled her shoulders a few times, trying to unwind them.

They were so close now; once again she ensured her aim. Three feet... two feet... "Come on you bastards," she cursed silently. One foot... Her finger tightened dangerously on the trigger... Half a foot... So close... She had to remind herself to breathe.

The rifle kicked in her arms, but she knew how to absorb it with ease. The bullet cleared a hundred yards in a blink, entered the first skull and exited through the second, dropping both infected to the forest floor, unmoving.

"Eighty-six." Auska grinned, shouldering the rifle. She retrieved her pack and made her way down into the small clearing.

If any other infected were within the area they would come to the sound of the gunfire, but she was confident that she had scouted well and there was nothing around for a few miles.

Before going to the rusted-out car she checked on her kills, making sure her shot was true and there wouldn't be any unwelcome surprises. They were both dead and would no longer be a threat to anyone. From the look of them, they had been mindless creatures for some time; barely more than a few strains of matted hair remained on their rotting heads. Their clothes were nothing more than moldy strips pasted onto putrid flesh. Eyes milky and dead, yet their sense of smell and hearing were impeccable; it was one of the reasons they were so dangerous. That and their seemingly endless strength and stamina. They never seemed to tire, nor did pain affect them as it should.

Auska went to the corroded, half-buried shell of a car. The kind of car it had been she had no idea. The time where vehicles were plenty and knowledge of them widely known were long gone; she was a child of this world, had never known the world before. Anything of use had decades ago been stripped cleaned and likely traded a hundred times over by now.

Now it served as nothing more than a landmark or a place for a traveler to spend the night if they were desperate enough. The car offered little protection from the elements and even less against the infected. There were no doors or glass in the windows, leaving the rusted shell wide open. But that wasn't why she was here.

She unclasped the silver chained necklace she wore and fingered the worn key a moment before pushing it into the lock. With a little work, she got it to turn again and it popped open. A musky odor seeped out but not nearly as bad as other times. The hinges creaked loudly in protest as it was forced open the rest of the way, allowing fresh air and sunlight into it after months without.

Tears stung her eyes and she stared down at the trunk's contents. Contents she herself had put there three years before after an extremely dangerous endeavor that had almost gotten her killed several times. But there was no regret and she would have done it a hundred times over if she had to.

The bones were dirty and grey, dried pieces of what had once been skin or flesh resiliently clung onto their owner. Only the skull was clean, stripped down to the pure bone and washed thoroughly. She had considered cleaning the rest but knew he would have scolded her for wasting time on something that mattered so little. But it did matter; at least to her it did. One day, when she had more time, she would clean the rest in honor of him. To preserve what was left for as long as she could or until the time came when she no longer needed him; then she would find a spot he would have liked and bury him. Somewhere he could be alone, as he had liked.

Sitting on the edge of the car Auska picked up the skull and moved it back and forth between her hands casually as if it were a ball. "You know, I'm still mad at you for lying to me all those years ago. You knew the cure was fake, you should have told me, I could have handled it. I would have handled it." She sniffed back her emotions, this was a conversation she had had with him now several times. "You would have made me like you made me handle everything else that came at us. You would have slapped me and told me this was life and to fucking deal with it. You would have said a cure was a fairy tale my parents had created to give purpose to all this misery, to shelter the innocent girl I had been. I would have argued, and you would have slapped me again, told me the fairy tale was dead and an innocent girl I was no longer." A long paused ensued, with a mournful sigh she continued, "It would have been better that way. You might even be alive to scold me still. To teach me all the things you didn't get a chance to. I miss you, even more each day that passes. I hate how things are now. Sanctuary isn't what we thought it would be... not at all how I dreamt it would be or even how my father promised it would be. It is a horrible place. I hate it, I hate them and all their rules and laws. They are stupid and corrupt, almost no better than what's left out here in the wild. At least out here there is an honesty to it. No falseness to what needs to be done or how it's done. I want to leave, but where else would I go? What else would I do? Sanctuary is the safe place that everyone wants to be. I should be thrilled I get to live there while others suffer worse than I, day after day, and yet I hate it there. Each year that passes I feel like I am even more of an outcast than the day I arrived."

She stood and began pacing around the car, still holding the skull out before her as if looking into the vacant eye sockets would make the skull understand her better. "It would have been different had you survived and come with us. You would have made them listen, would have made them do things better, smarter." She nearly laughed at the thought. "No, no you wouldn't have, you would have told them to fuck off and just left them to their delusional world after taking what you needed."

Tears stung at her eyes and she quickly wiped them away. He had hated tears and would have reprimanded her for such weakness. "But you would have taken me with you. You would have told me to stay, that I would be safer there," she smirked, "but I know you would never have left me behind... things would have been better."

Auska slumped down on the trunk again. "I don't belong there, I don't fit in. I have tried to, but I just can't, and I no longer even want to. I hate it. I'm so lost without you, without..." she sighed, "I don't even know anymore... purpose, maybe."

A cold breeze reminded her that it was getting late. "I will be back when I can get away again." She placed the skull back in the trunk and closed it, making sure it was locked and would not be easily disturbed if someone did happen by.

With one last look at the car, she started north-east back towards Sanctuary and the others she had left behind. She would have to stop by her stash spot and hide the rifle. If she turned up with an unauthorized weapon, it would become Sanctuary property and she would never see it again. She wondered if they were looking for her yet, or if they had just left.

The rusted can bounced off an ancient tree trunk,

propelled by growing frustration. "Goddamn it! Why does she always have to do this? We should be on our way back home by now, you know where it's safe and warm! Not waiting around for her to casually stroll on back like it was no big deal putting all our lives at risk, AGAIN!" A handful of the others murmured their agreement, while others just rolled their eyes at the typical outburst.

"Calm yourself, Nick, before you blow that vein in your neck," chuckled Barry, the leader of the Eighth Division. He was the youngest of the Division leaders, at only twenty-eight, but he had proven himself time and again capable of getting the job done and keeping those around him alive.

He had taken a different approach to the leadership of his scavenging unit, one that had worked perfectly until the new addition had been thrust upon him. Rumors had come to him about Auska beforehand, so he had been aware of her. But when the council had assigned her to his unit, he had been shocked that she had even been allowed to join a Division after all he had heard. Then one morning there she was, in his command for better or worse.

Some days were better; others like now made for the worst, but there was no denying she was capable and deadly. If only she listened to anyone else but herself.

The tall girl of the group chuckled loud enough to draw everyone's attention.

"Is something funny, Jennifer?" Nick growled at the tall brunette.

Her crystal blue eyes locked on him and he almost took a step back at the intensity. "Very, actually." Standing up she jumped from the stump she was resting on and started to pace the clearing casually. "What real danger have we been in this trip? Hell, what real danger have we been in since Auska joined us? Let me think...," she tapped her chin, "...well there was that one time... hmm nope, Auska killed those ones... but then there was that other... wait no, she killed those ones, too."

"What about the infected we came across today?" Jordon replied nervously, instantly feeling a fool.

"That is a very good point, Jordon, what about the infected we came across today," Jennifer said. "I am assuming you mean the three that we came across today that were already dead, clearly by the hand of our ever so vigilant forward scout. I mean it is true, they certainly were ugly... dangerous, sure, but that was before she got to them."

"Yeah, but what if there had been more?" Nick pushed his grievance, though he had lost some of his edge. It was true; Auska had been the best forward scout anyone had ever seen before. Even several of the other divisions often joked about taking her off Barry's hands.

"Then I expect there would have been more bodies for us to find," Jen countered with a cocky smirk. "Bottom line is we have yet to ever be in danger when Auska has run off. The worst thing we have to ever endure is waiting a few extra hours for her to return, which she always does and normally brings back things we all benefit from." Several in the group voiced their hearty agreement. "If anything, she's making the damn job boring as hell now. But you know what is good about boring? It's safe."

"I've been with the Eighth now for seven months," Jordon put in quickly, "I haven't even seen a living infected yet. I figured by now I would have killed at least half a dozen by the way the other Divisions always talk."

Jennifer slapped him on the back. "I am sure your mother sleeps soundly knowing that you haven't even seen one."

"Those other Division guys are full of crap anyway," Michael added, scratching his unshaven face. "Maybe years ago there were that many, but now? Shit, if there were more than a dozen within a twenty-mile radius, I'd be surprised."

"They are still out there," Dan replied. "I've been doing this for three years and I've killed nine of them myself so far."

Nick turned his irritation back to Barry, ignoring the others who he was losing. "It's your fault you know. You let her get away with it. You let her do this shit every goddamn time! Gods, if you would crack the whip occasionally with her maybe she would be so inclined to follow a fucking plan!" He kicked at the ground again. "That mouth of hers better be as good on your cock as it is fabricating a bullshit story to save her ass," he muttered, but loud enough.

"Stand down, Nick!" snapped Tony, a normally

quiet, grimy-faced Sanctuary veteran who was also second in command of the Eighth. Tony wasn't overly tall, nor overly big, but he was a survivor; one look at him and you knew he had made it this long by doing whatever it took.

"Well, holy shit, the relic speaks," Nick growled back, his voice losing some of its power in the process. "Surely you have something valid to say about our rogue scout and her behavior? A man of your experience should be able to say with ease that Auska is causing a problem and it will only get worse if it isn't dealt with!"

Barry patted the veteran on the back before he could reply. "It's okay Tony, Nick here has every right to express his opinion. Knowing each other's minds and feelings is what makes a strong unit and helps us work through potential problems that could result in disaster when danger strikes."

Nick snorted in disgust. "Yeah, like one of our scouts always running off, leaving us potentially blind to what's ahead, behind or to the sides of us!"

Before Barry could reply, a calm, sweet voice cut through the trees with a response. "You wound me deeply, Nick. I would never run off if there was still danger around." Auska smirked coolly walking into the clearing as casually as the rising sun. "I always kill everything that needs killing before doing what I need to do." She walked right up to Nick and patted his shoulder like a big sister would an annoying younger brother, even though Nick was older than her by a few years. "Because I know how scared you get when I'm not around to protect you."

Nick pulled away. "Look who decided to grace us with her ever-absent presence for nearly this whole five-day trip." He spat by her feet. "Might have been better if you hadn't returned for once."

"Curb that shit." Barry pointed a stern finger Nicks way before turning his attention to Auska. "Where'd you go this time, scout?"

"And I even brought you back a present Nick as compensation for making you wait for me again." She ignored Barry's question, a full pack of cigarettes appeared in her hand and everyone's eyes bulged a little at the rare find. "It's all yours if you'll forgive me again."

Nicks hand instinctively twitched to grab them, but he quickly steeled himself. "You can't think you can just bribe us to forgive and forget your bullshit every time you do this, Auska. This is a serious job, that can have serious consequences if we aren't all on the same page and know we can trust one another when the time comes."

She grinned, knowing his eyes betrayed him. He wanted the cigarettes badly and who wouldn't? Whether he smoked or not, the trade value on a full pack of unopened smokes was golden. But he still wanted to try and save face in front of everyone else for the sake of his rant.

As much as she wanted to continue to toy with him, she decided it would serve her better to play it differently. "Wasn't a bribe, more a gift for a squad member to show that I care about the team even if I am tardy from time to time." It was a lie, but it sounded pretty good. "Plus, I found enough for everyone." Reaching into her pack she pulled out the carton of cigarettes and handed the other seven members of the Eighth a pack. It pained her to do so, that many packs would have gotten her a new scope for her rifle and at least twenty rounds. But it was better than someone ratting her out to the council and her getting kicked off scavenging duty. This was the one job she almost enjoyed; it gave her some freedom to do as she wanted. Also, it gave her the ability to find things to keep for herself.

Nick grabbed the pack bitterly and shoved it into his pocket. "You're off the hook in my eyes this time, but seriously Auska, stop this shit, it's getting on my nerves." He looked around their surroundings with a shiver. "You know how dangerous it is out here; not all of us are hardcore like you. Not to mention it's starting to get fucking cold out."

Jennifer walked up to Auska's side and casually placed an arm around her shoulders with a cocky smile. "You are always good in my books, girl, if you keep bringing gifts like this." She lit the cigarette in her mouth and inhaled deeply. "Hell, a gift like this has got to redeem you for a few offenses in the future, too, I'd wager." She winked at her as she strolled off.

Tony hid the pack of smokes in his jacket lining. "Next time take me with you kid. You're having all the fun out there and I'm sitting here getting rusty with age." He smiled at her. "Your good kid, ain't no denying it, but I'd bet an old-timer like me could still teach you a thing or two out here."

Auska was touched by his words and wondered if it was because of the day it was. "Next time, you can come, so long as you can keep up."

Tony smirked. "We will see who can keep up with who kid."

"Alright now that we are all accounted for, time to move out, double-time," Barry ordered. "We got a few miles to cover before we get home. Let's not be late for dinner!"

The group gathered their packs and set off, but Barry held back, motioning for Auska to hang back with him.

Auska rolled her eyes. "I'm sorry, it'll never happen again. I lost track of time. Thought I saw something worth looking into..." She stopped. "Any of these working for you?"

Barry held up his hand to stop her. "We both know none of that is true, nor has it ever been." He handed her back the pack of smokes she had given him. He wanted it, for it was a bartering chip that would get him much, just like all the things she had bribed him with. As always, his moral compass cut at him.

She sighed, slipping the cigarettes back in her pocket. "I know, but those excuses used to work on you. At least, you use to pretend they did."

Shaking his head, he chuckled lightly. "Where the hell do you go all the time? What is it you feel you have to do alone out here?" He knew he wouldn't get an answer, he never did. "We are a team, a family...

a dysfunctional family, but what family isn't? We need each other, need to work with each other, need to trust each other."

"That's my business, as it always has been."

"And the squad and everyone in it when we are outside the walls is MY damn business, and you'd do well to remember that from time to time!" he'd retorted more harshly then he had intended, yet Nicks words had struck a chord. He had been too forgiving with her; he knew of no other squad leader who would put up with such behavior.

Auska's eyes darkened. "Then you had better punish me! Want me to carry everyone's packs? Maybe do extra cleaning of gear and chores around the barracks? Or maybe just go straight to the council and tell them of my rogue outings? Tie myself to the lashing pole and count the twenty?"

"All fitting punishments for your insubordination. I can assure you any other Division leader would have had all of those things done to you already," he shot back dangerously. "Do you know what would happen to you if I told the council what you do out here?"

"Lock me up in solitary again for a few days, maybe a week," she replied as if it was no big deal. She had spent time there before in the dank little room, with naught but a single candle to give her light and the grating noise of a food tray being push under the door twice a day to keep her company. "It's rather peaceful. Maybe you should tell on me yourself; I could use the peace and quiet. Maybe it will give me time to reflect on my callous ways."

Barry moved in front of her and stared her hard in the eyes, making sure she was looking at him before he spoke. "Oh yes, you would spend at least a week if not more in solitary, but you'd also feel the bite of the lash as well." His voice darkened. "I've seen others get fifteen to twenty strikes for transgressions half as bad as yours."

"So be it then!" she spat and tried to walk around him, but he grabbed her arm and held her firmly.

"Damn it, Auska!" he cursed, drawing her eyes to his again. "You need to understand that this is serious. Every time you do this, it puts me and everyone else in our squad at risk of possible punishment for not reporting it. This isn't just your ass, it's all of ours. Hell, I could be stripped of rank and expelled from Sanctuary because of this," he confessed with a hint of fear in his tone. "So, this shit needs to stop, or at the very least not happen every damn time we come out here. Because it's only a matter of time before someone talks. Your "gifts" will only keep them silent for so long before greed takes over and they start wanting more and more to keep quiet. I don't know where you keep finding this stuff, but you're bound to run out sooner or later." Her eyes softened and he knew at least some of his words had gotten through to her.

"Okay," she replied, barely more than a whisper.

"Okay? Really, that's it?"

Auska rolled her eyes at him. "I fucking said okay already."

He sighed, not willing to give up yet. "Look, I can't even begin to understand what goes on inside that head of yours. Why you feel compelled to be alone all the time, or why you seem to enjoy pushing the limits of my leniency, even with the threat of such harsh punishments knocking at the door each time. But something needs to give, even if it's just a little at a time."

"You're beating a dead horse again."

"You are one of the best scouts these people have ever had," he told her truthfully. "It would be a shame if Sanctuary lost such a talent due to you not applying just a little more of that skill for the greater good and not just yourself."

Auska rolled her eyes again and tried to sidestep him but he would have none of it and his hand held firm.

"I know you have had a hard time since getting here. I have heard the talk and rumors. You can talk to me, about anything, you know that, right?"

Her eyes hardened again. "I don't need a therapist."

He released her arm. "No, you don't, but a friend might not be such a horrible thing for you either."

"Are we done here?" Her tone left no doubt that she was.

"Think about it."

Vincent looked down at the large aluminum tray

and the thirty scrawny rabbits he had just finished preparing. They had looked so much bigger with their fur and guts but once he stripped the meat from the bones there wouldn't be much to work with. But this was what had been rationed for the night and he had worked with less before over the years and always surprised himself how far he could stretch the ingredients he was allotted for each meal.

It was a tough system, ensuring there was enough food for everyone that lived there. Two hundred and nine mouths to feed was a chore under the best of times. But the people who rationed the supplies worked hard at what they did, and he did his part to ensure it was enough.

Though a good handful of those people were allotted special treatment for their stations and services and did not eat with the commoners from this kitchen. In truth, only a hundred and seventy-three would rely on what he made tonight. But as a rule, Vincent always tried to push that number to the maximum just in case. That way serving sizes for those who did require it could be that little bit more.

There had been hard times where things were tougher than normal, but still, they had all managed. It was this skill set that he had that made him nearly invaluable to Sanctuary's cause, even making him and Kelli among the few that were given slightly better treatment and resources, though they seldom took advantage of it.

Picking up the small boning knife he went to work; he needed to get the bones in the boiling water soon so the broth of the stew would have as much flavor as possible. There was next to nothing in way of spices anymore and those were only allotted a few times a year for special occasions. So, he had to make the flavors of the foods he used work for him to their fullest, a talent he had gotten good at over the last few years since being stationed in the kitchen.

It was a job he much preferred to what he had been doing before, even if it was harder. He shuddered at the memory of the first two years he and Kelli had spent emptying the bathroom waste and carting it out to the massive hole dug half a mile outside the walls. A primitive and disgusting method, but with no real plumbing, it was the only way to discard it and keep the filth from causing disease. They had done so with little complaint, knowing if they didn't they would be kicked out of the safety of the walls, and they would endure whatever they had to make certain that never happened. Memories from their time within the wastelands still to this day plagued his nightmares regularly.

Everyone in Sanctuary had a role to play, everyone worked and did their jobs, and for that, they had a safe place to live and enough food to stay alive. Those who didn't pull their weight were given only a few chances before they were banished back into the chaotic, dangerous world beyond. There was no room for those who didn't contribute to the greater good of all who lived there. It was far from a perfect system, but had there ever been such a thing even before all this?

When they had first arrived, they had been brought in under false pretenses. A cure that wasn't real, was nothing more than saltwater in a little glass vial. But it had gotten them in and once in he had explained themselves in full and all they had been through to get there, being sure to leave nothing out, in hopes for pity. They had almost been thrown out but had managed to convince the council of their worth and so they had been given a chance.

It hadn't been easy. They had had to prove themselves and work twice as hard as the others already there, often working fifteen hours a day for weeks at a time. Harder still, Auska had been young and not in a good way with the loss of Archer, and hearing that the cure was fake had almost destroyed her. Her whole world had been a lie, but Kelli and himself had pulled together and did her share of the work as well until she had accepted it and was ready to accept their new life.

Vincent shook his head dolefully. Eight years later and she still hadn't fully accepted it. But they were making it work; it wasn't easy, but it was better than the alternative. Auska was a woman now at twenty-one and, for over a year, was part of Eight Division's scavenging team. Even though neither Kelli nor himself liked what she was doing, it was by far the longest she had ever managed to hold a work position. For Auska, her options were running out, as was the council's patience.

It was by far some of the most dangerous work

anyone could do, and yet she claimed she enjoyed it and, from what her squad leader had told him, she was excelling at it, though rumors were circulating that she wasn't always a team player and often returned late.

In the eight years they had lived here, Auska had been punished more than anyone else, spent more time in solitary than most of the others combined, and had even had to endure the lash once before. Her will against them was unbreakable and yet it would only one day spell unchangeable disaster for her.

Vincent shook his head. "You left a big imprint on her that I don't think she will ever be free from, Archer. As much good as you did for her, you left equal damage."

"What was that?" Kelli asked from the other side of the counter.

He looked up at her and smiled. She was busy chopping the meager amount of carrots and potatoes for the stew. At least they worked together now and were able to spend more time together because of it. "Nothing, was just talking to myself."

"Well, as long as you don't start answering yourself, I think you'll be okay," she teased playfully.

"What if I need expert advice, though?"

"Then ask me," and she winked at him.

"Have I told you how beautiful you are today?" Vincent asked her.

Kelli stopped cutting and regarded him with a childish smirk. "No, not today. I was wondering if you had forgotten or had found someone else to catch your eye."

"I doubt such a woman even exists." He paused and pretended to think. "Well, she might have, but likely she got eaten by something out there."

"After all this time you still know just what to say to make a girls heart flutter."

"With you as my muse, how could I not?" he joked.

She waved her knife at him. "Well, you just cool your smooth tongue right now, least we find ourselves in the cooler again and we have too much to do still to be acting like horny teenagers at our age."

"But when we are done," he winked at her, "maybe those locked away teenagers can find some time."

"You are insufferable!" she laughed, returning her attention to the vegetables.

"Pretty sure he's been called worse." A reply came from the back door.

Both turned to see Auska strolling in, her dark grey jacket and faded jeans travel-stained with dirt and grime from her perimeter check with the Eighth.

"I know you aren't planning on tracking mud all across this kitchen again!" Kelli scolded her sternly, looking down at the boots she wore, happy to see them surprisingly cleaner than normal.

Auska threw up her hands in defense. "I wouldn't dream of doing it again," her tone dripping with sarcasm. "Not after the thirty-minute lecture I got last time."

"How'd it go out there?" Vincent jumped in, knowing if the topic didn't change it would turn into another fight. These two could never seem to hold a conversation for more than a few minutes before they were at each other's throats. "Anything interesting happen? The section cleared, or are the infected finding their way through the forest again?"

"Same old same old. Safe as ever," came her curt reply as she looked around the counter for something to eat. "Is there nothing ready yet?"

"No, you'll have to wait and eat with everyone else tonight," Kelli said, her tone bordering on annoyance.

"That's okay, I'll just grab a small loaf and some cheese." She made way to grab at the tray of freshly baked loaves, but Kelli was quick to intercept her.

"I said no, Auska!"

Auska took a step back, confusion clear on her face. "What the hell? Why not?"

Before Kelli could reply Vincent was there. "We've been getting a lot of heat about how you never eat with the others and always have your food before anyone else. They're not stupid. They know where you get it from and it has been told to stop. This isn't a place we can just free-range and do whatever we want. There are rules in place and we all need to follow them." He looked at her remorsefully. "That includes you Auska. The special treatment we are allowed can only be played with for so long before it needs a break."

"Seriously? This again?" She folded her arms

across her chest.

"It's been eight damn years, Auska! EIGHT! You've had more than enough time to grieve. Move on and accept this new life as everyone else has," Kelli barked at her.

"Don't you dare!" Auska growled, her arms falling to her side defensively, her fist balled up.

"He's dead."

Auska took a step back her lips quivering. "Don't you fucking dare do this, not today!"

"He's dead, Auska. He died so you could get here, so you would be safe and have a chance at as normal of a life as one can hope for now. And your behavior and attitude are a mockery to the sacrifice he made for you!"

Auska's eyes widened and burned dangerously with acrimony. Before she knew it, her fist lashed out, connecting with Kelli's jaw and causing her to stagger backward several paces and into one of the cupboards.

Vincent threw himself between them as Auska advanced for another swing. "Enough!" he yelled, "both of you!" He caught her arm and forced her back a step. "That's enough, Auska! Violence isn't always the way!"

Auska snarled, pulled back and left without a word.

Kelli rubbed her jaw. "Damn, she hits a lot harder now than a few years ago. I wonder if I could still take her in a fight."

"Did you really need to push those buttons

tonight?" Vincent scolded. "She's likely not to talk to us for a month or more now and God only knows what trouble she will get into."

"She needed to hear it," she countered. "She's not a child anymore, Vincent, hasn't been for a while. She needs to accept reality and learn her place here."

"I know... but not like that she didn't. And not today of all days." He sighed going back to his work. "Definitely not today."

"Shit, I didn't even realize that was today." Kelli slammed her hands down on the counter. "Damn it all to hell, I am such a fucking idiot! I should go after her and apologize."

Vincent rested his hand on hers. "It'll have to wait, my dear, we need to get dinner done. Besides, she is going to need time to calm down. Going to her now will only further the fight."

The target dummy stared at her blankly. It's non-expressive features almost felt mocking to her; she launched into another series of feints, jabs, and strikes upon its upper body and head. A quick pivot and she dropped down and kicked, slamming into the dummy's knee and enjoying the cracking sound of the aged wood. Had it been a real leg, it would have snapped the knee, but the wood held, at least for now.

It had been over two hours already since the fight with Kelli and Vincent; she was dripping in sweat, her muscles burned, and her breathing came in labored gasps. The skin on her knuckles had worn through the callouses, leaving light bloody prints every time her fists connected to one of the three targets she was attacking.

But still, her temper had not cooled. So she pushed herself harder, diving into a forward roll and coming up to the next target. Several strikes and kicks and she launched herself at another, repeating her rounds between the three leather-wrapped dummies, always moving, always changing her attack patterns. On so many occasions she had watched others, their repetitiveness, their weakness of being predictable. So, she strived to never repeat her attacks too often, changing her movements, her angles, her strikes.

Auska was about to launch herself at another target when suddenly it moved launching its own surprise attack. She was caught off guard but managed to block the first two punches for her face, but the third slammed into her side. She turned with the hit and swung around kicking low, sweeping the feet from her opponent as they moved in. Before her attacker hit the ground Auska was on them, forearm pressed to their throat.

"You win!" Jennifer croaked out, but still managing to chuckle despite the lack of air. "You win, I said!"

Auska pulled back and wiped the sweat from her eyes. "What the hell were you doing, trying to get yourself hurt?"

Jennifer sat up and rubbed at her neck. "Well, after watching you beat on targets for twenty minutes, I figured you could use a real target to change it up. You know like Tony always says, 'Be ready for anything. A surprise out there is a death sentence'. Must admit I didn't expect to end up on my back, given how tired you looked. Guess old Tony's other favorite saying plays true here too: 'Never underestimate your opponent or you'll wind up dead.'"

"Why were you watching me?" Auska stood up apprehensively and after several moments took the outstretched hand of her adversary and helped her to her feet.

"Seen you storm off from the kitchens earlier and then when you didn't show up for dinner, figured you must have got into a fight with your folks."

"They're not my folks," Auska growled back instantly.

"Right, well those people who you showed up with who have been taking care of you the last eight years then."

Auska caught the slight smirk Jennifer tried to hide. "They were just people I met along the way."

"I know the story. So, does everyone else here most likely."

"So, what do you want? Why are you here?"

Jennifer shrugged and walked over to the doorway to the training room where she had watched Auska's fighting display. "Thought you might be hungry." She lifted a tray from the floor and brought it over setting it down on a table. There was a bowl of thin rabbit stew and a thick chunk of flat bread.

Auska hadn't realized she was still hungry until the smell of food hit her and her stomach growled in response, but she held back from sitting down as she eyed her fellow squad member. "Why would you care? You never have before, nor have I ever given you any reason to."

"Shit, are you always so suspicious of everyone's motives?" Jennifer laughed.

"Yes."

Jennifer looked over her shoulders to make sure no one else was around. "Sit." She pushed the food tray further towards Auska.

Intrigued now, Auska sat and before she could stop herself, hunger betrayed her as mouthful after mouthful of stew disappeared behind chunks of bread.

"Look, you're someone who knows her shit out behind these walls." She licked her lips nervously. "Someone who isn't afraid to go against the grain of how things are supposed to be done around here. I'm sure you catch my meaning."

Auska stopped eating. "I don't like where I think this is heading."

She looked around again before continuing even quieter this time. "We found something yesterday... something big."

Pushing the finished tray away, Auska wiped her mouth from the grease of the stew. "Then tell

Barry and a plan can be made."

"We will, of course," she grinned, "after we take a little peek of our own first. You know, finder's fee and all."

Auska folded her arms. "So, you want to be the first there to steal what you want before it gets noted and becomes 'property' of our wondrous leaders."

"Well being honest hasn't really afforded me much in way of 'extra's', like it seems to have for so many others." Jen went quiet for a moment, then her eyes changed; grief and sadness were apparent. "The truth is, this isn't something I want to do, but something I need to do."

"Need to do?" Auska asked with a raised brow. "Risking life and death, punishment or banishment, there has to be a pretty big 'need'."

"My little brother is one of the ones that caught that strange sickness going around. I figure Dr. Brown is likely as corrupt as everyone else here. Maybe if I can get something he needs or wants I can persuade him to give a little extra attention to my brother. You know, pay the 'hidden' tax in this place to get what really can be gotten, instead of just what can be spared."

Auska hadn't known Jen's brother had been one of the people quarantined in the last week. Though she doubted she could name a third of them. "What you are proposing is against Sanctuary law, and comes with strict punishment, even banishment if they deem it a great enough offence." Not that Auska cared, she had broken this very law many times before; so had nearly every scavenger that went out.

"Ah, that is very, very true, but only if we get caught. Which I, of course, have no intention of allowing to happen."

"Famous last words by anyone who has ever been caught," Auska said flatly. "Where is this place?"

"Come now, you don't think I am just going to tell you that do you? So, you can sneak out of here and hit it yourself," Jennifer answered calmly. "But I will say this: it's surprisingly not far."

"And pray tell how you happened to find such a score so close to home when we have searched nearly every inch around Sanctuary for thirty plus miles."

"To be honest I don't know, but it doesn't look like it hasn't been there long," the taller girl admitted. "Couple of days at most, but it looked like more was being brought in."

This really got Auska's curiosity piqued. Supplies being moved in close to Sanctuary... Could it be a group moving supplies in hopes to buy their way in behind the walls? It had happened several times in the past, but not often. "What all did you see for supplies? Weapons? Food? Gear? What?"

"So, you're in?" Jennifer asked eagerly.

"What all did you see?"

"Foodstuff mostly it looked like, but there were some guns, likely ammo, propane, clothing, and God knows what else. Most of it was in wooden crates."

Auska looked at her suspiciously. "Really? You have seen all that? Must have gotten really close."

"I shit you not, that's what I saw being moved off the truck."

"How many men did they have?"

Jen grinned. "I can tell by your tone you want in on this."

It was true; a score this big, if they could hit it before anyone else knew about it, would set her stash up for a good few years, and with a few new guns and boxes of ammo she might even think about leaving. "I haven't said yes or no yet. But you have my attention, at least for now, as long as you don't bullshit me. If it sounds doable, I might be interested."

"I don't actually know how many were there, I saw four outside unloading and it looked like another two were inside," Jennifer confessed. "But once the unloading was done the truck drove off again. So as long as the truck isn't there, I am thinking two, three, maybe four guards' tops."

"A stockpile that big would be guarded by more than that," Auska muttered, rubbing her chin, running risks in her mind.

"Likely true, if it had seemed like they were at all worried anyone knew they were there." Jen countered. "They didn't seem to have a care in the world. No sentries, no one on watch, almost like it was all routine and they'd done it all before. It was really kind of strange, really, but their arrogance can be our reward."

This surprised Auska even more. She knew what life was like outside and knew supplies like Jennifer was talking about weren't cheap and weren't casually moved around without purpose. The more she heard, the more this sounded like something Barry needed to know about and soon. What if it were staging for an attack on Sanctuary? Or one of the many gangs finally deciding on move closer to pick them off when the Divisions went out? "This is sounding like more than a simple score that two people could pull off, and it might even be a serious threat to everyone here. It might be best to tell Barry about this and hope for a reward."

Jennifer seemed baffled. "Really? This, from you? I thought out of all people you would be the easiest on board for this, and yet here you are sounding more like Barry or Tony rather than the famed badass Auska, the no-fucks-given queen of Sanctuary."

The words were a slap in Auska's face and pricked her pride deeply. It truly wasn't like her to think that the higher-ups ever needed to know anything, let alone something that could be of benefit to her first. "How many others do you have onboard and when are you planning to make the hit?"

Jen slapped the table with an excited laugh. "That's the Auska I wanted, the Auska I need! I've got two others, Matt from the Eighth and Ross from perimeter patrol, that'll be coming with us, and Nick just so happens to be watching a section of the wall tomorrow night. So long as we give him a small cut, he said he will turn a blind eye to us going over the wall and coming back. All we've got to do is make sure we are back before shift change."

"Do you really think Nick can be trusted?" Auska didn't like the sound of Nick knowing anything about this. He already had his balls in a twist with her; something like this would be all he needed to really cause her problems.

"Believe it or not, Nick is solid so long as he gets a share. I know you two have something against each other, but I think that's more to do with his being jealous of you. Or maybe he likes you. Tough to say. But I trust him in this. Plus, if he fucks us over on this, I'll make sure he gets it just as badly."

Auska drummed her fingers on the table in thought. She didn't like the thought of working with so many others. Having to depend on other people to do their part or keep quiet always led to trouble later. But if there was half of what Jennifer claimed there to be then it would be worth the risk and might even be the final piece she needed so she could leave this place. "Fine, I'll be ready to go tomorrow night."

The taller girl's grin lit up her face. "This is going to be a hell of an adventure! With sweet rewards for all!"

"We will see."

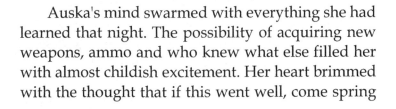

Auska's mind swarmed with everything she had learned that night. The possibility of acquiring new weapons, ammo and who knew what else filled her with almost childish excitement. Her heart brimmed with the thought that if this went well, come spring maybe she would finally abandon this place and roam the wastelands in solitude like Archer had done. It had been a fantasy of hers for years now, but she just never had enough supplies to make it real.

She had to steady her overworking mind. One step at a time. Who knew how accurate Jennifer had been in her scouting, what actually might be there or how many guns and guards might be protecting it? She would go with them and look; if it looked like something they could handle, fine. If not, they were on their own. Risking her life was only acceptable if the risk was going to be worth it and the odds weren't impossible.

Stopping at a fork in the hallway, she looked down the right towards the medical center of the large facility and a faster way to the exit that would lead her to her bed. To the left was the longer route, by nearly fifteen minutes. The long day and brutal exercising she had done in anger that evening had her exhausted. She didn't like the prospect of going near the medical area with so much buzz going around about some sickness that had affected a dozen or so residents, but her legs felt like lead beneath her.

"Worst off, I get sick and die." She shrugged, deciding to take the risk and turned down the faster route. If she didn't get enough rest, she might die tomorrow night anyway. Every day was a gamble in this world now; some foolish risks just seemed worth it.

She stalked down the hallways as quickly and as

quietly as she could. Though the rooms would be temporally sealed to prevent anything airborne from escaping, it was still a tendency to move hastily through possible danger zones. Nor would it be uncommon for guards to be about, protecting the medical supplies from anyone who might think of stealing them, though things like that were a rare occurrence nowadays. The punishment for stealing medical supplies was death.

Coming to the corner of the hallway that would take her to the side doors leading outside, she overheard voices. Auska stopped; she wasn't sure why this wasn't a restricted zone and she wanted nothing more than to get to her bed. But instinct told her not to present herself just yet.

"Is everything ready?" a male voice said in almost a whisper.

"Yes, everything and everyone is set to go." The voice of a female replied in the same hushed tone and Auska was sure it was Dr. Brown and Nurse Whitney. "I've given all the patients a stronger dose, which should keep them sedated until it's time."

"Tomorrow, inform the families that things have gotten worse and that visitations are canceled until a later time."

"If they ask, should I tell them how bad it's getting?" Nurse Whitney asked.

Dr. Brown sighed remorsefully. "No, it's too dangerous. This is already getting harder every time. We can't risk it, not with winter knocking on our doors. One slip-up and it'll all go to shit, and we will be at the front of it. It's not worth the risk. The council can tell them when it is time."

"Understood, doctor." She turned to go back into the lab.

"Get some sleep, Whitney. Tomorrow is going to be a long stressful day and I need you a hundred percent for this."

"I shall, just as soon as I clean up a few more things."

Auska heard the door to the lab close and the fading footsteps of Dr. Brown. She slipped around the corner and made her way for the side exit. The news she had overheard was devastating. Everyone that was sick was going to die. How could that be? What kind of sickness was this? There had been viruses and illnesses in the past that had claimed several lives from time to time, but always a handful pulled through. And from everything she had heard everyone who had been affected had been under the age of thirty. Surely there were some of them strong enough to pull through?

Opening the side door, she slipped out into the crisp night. The fresh air washed over her and pushed some of the exhaustion away as she made her way home, if one could call it that. Though it could be worse; at least she had a place to call her own, somewhere she could escape people.

A good portion of Sanctuary's less privileged population resided in several dozen large shipping containers that had been stacked three high to save room within the limited compound. The 'higher classed' citizens lived in the apartment buildings and a handful of houses that had been within the compound when the world fell apart.

The old shipping compound and containers had been abandoned when the infection had broken out nearly three decades before. It had been a large riverside shipping port for coal and lumber, though the once mighty river that ran adjacent was now a third of what it once was and would no longer be suitable for the large barges that carried the containers downriver to the towns beyond.

The compound had been a diamond in the rough when the two dozen original founders of Sanctuary had come across it. The mountain woodlands were remote and secluded from heavy populations of infected and raiders alike, making it an ideal place to try and live. The abandoned compound and small town that had been built for all the workers and their families had made the perfect start.

With the equipment and building supplies that had been left behind, the wall had been built around the whole of Sanctuary, leaving only one way in through the southern gate, though rumors said escape tunnels had been dug, but none had ever been found.

The wall was impressive by rights. It stood thirty feet high and was two feet thick in most places, with an eight-foot walkway that encompassed nearly the whole thing. It was made mostly from thick lumber, steel plates, and a cement, stone mixed base. After nearly three decades, repairs happened almost monthly to ensure the impressive structure remained ever the beacon of safety to those who resided within.

Auska worked her way through the maze of housing containers to her own near the back of the compound. Just over a year ago, she had finally been permitted to move out of the unit she had shared with Vincent and Kelli since nearly the day they arrived. Housing was sparse but due to her job undertaking in the Eighth and the long hard hours she often had to work at all hours of the day and night, she had been granted her own unit. That and the older couple that had lived there had frozen to death last winter, due to the horrible cold snap they had gotten.

At the time she had been annoyed that she had gotten a bottom unit, the view from the top looked over the wall and was breathtaking during the sunrise or sunset. But as time wore on, she was glad to be on the bottom; it was easier for her to sneak in and out of without alerting the neighbors of her coming and goings.

Auska pulled off her boots, undressed and poured some water into her washbowl and quickly scrubbed the last several days' worth of dirt and grime off her slender, firm body. Tossing on a nightshirt she fell onto her pallet bed, which was softer than most due to the several animal hides she had smuggled in to use as a mattress.

Her thoughts went back to what she had heard. Jennifer's younger brother was one of the people who fell ill and was going to die. The whole reason for tomorrow night's excursion was in hopes Jen could steal enough supplies to bribe the doctor to take better care of her brother. No amount of bribery would save him now.

Should she tell her about what she had heard? Auska quickly dismissed the thought. She would find out soon enough and it wasn't her problem. Besides, if she told Jennifer then she might abandon the attack, seeing no point to it now. Auska was too interested in what might be there to lose out on this opportunity.

She closed her eyes and sleep quickly took her…

…her eyes shot open as an unnatural feeling of falling washed over her, yet she was standing perfectly still though no ground could be seen beneath her. All around her was an empty ancient fog. No breeze could be felt and yet it swirled and danced around her, caressing her skin in a disturbing yet familiar way.

"Where the hell am I?" she called out, her voice getting lost within the emptiness as she turned around to see if anything changed. "What is this place? What the fuck is going on? Where am I? Hello!"

Auska started walking, but no matter which direction she went nothing seemed to move or alter. She tried running, and though she could feel her muscle moving, her blood pumping, her breathing increasing, nothing around her moved.

"I must be dreaming, none of this is real," she

growled, finally giving up and stopping.

She closed her eyes tightly. "Wake up, wake up you idiot!" she pleaded with herself, which she found strange. She was in no danger as far as she knew, no discomfort, no anything and yet all she wanted was to not be here. Something about it made her uneasy.

"You will wake up when it's time to wake up and not a moment before," a familiar, long lost voice said behind her.

Her heart cramped in her chest at the sound and she spun around, eyes wide open, "Archer?" There he stood, but where there had once been fog was a wooded clearing, with tall waving grasses and wildflowers, a place she remembered far too vividly. "This can't be real, you're... you're dead..."

Archer rolled his eyes. "Of course, I am dead, and this isn't real, and yet here I am standing before you."

"Am I dead, too?"

He stepped forward and his hand lashed out, slapping her across the face firmly. "Did you feel that?"

Auska had seen the attack coming but hadn't the wit to move and the sting of the slap was somehow reassuring. "Yes." She rubbed her face.

"Then you're not dead. Not yet anyway."

His tone was hard and patronizing just like it had always been. She smiled girlishly and finally stepped forward and threw her arms around him, surprised that it truly felt like he was there in her arms. "I've missed you so much."

"You've gotten soft, kid, I'm not even real." He grumbled, but his arms folded around her in return anyway.

Finally, she pushed herself away and looked at him, wiping the fresh tears from her eyes. "What is this place? Why am I here?"

"It's a dream, and you and I are here because you wanted it."

Auska's face screwed up. "I have wanted to dream like this since the day you died. Never have I been able to. Why now?"

"How the hell should I know, kid," he replied. "Maybe you need to now. Maybe this is your way of working through the things bothering you in your life now."

"Why this place?" she whispered looking around. Everything was exactly as she remembered. "Why the place I lost you? The place that hurts the most?"

Archer shrugged and looked around, his eyes stopping at the place his body should have been. "Not sure. Maybe because this is the greatest emotional moment between us, and so it was the only place your mind could pull us together like this? It's your dream, not mine."

"But why now and never before, when I was a girl?" she pleaded for an answer. "I needed you far more then than I do now."

"Are you sure about that?" he said, but it was more of a statement than a question.

"I don't understand."

Blood formed around the corners of Archer's mouth; a thin line slowly dripped down his chin. "I have to go now, kid," the line of blood thickened.

"No!" Auska protested stepping closer, but for every step she took closer, he seemed to move further away. "No, this is my dream and I'm not ready for it to end yet!"

"Some things are in your power," he said as his form

started to fade away, "and some things aren't."

Morning came far too early for Auska's liking. Her body protested the hard exertion she had put it through the night before. Staring up at the roof of her apartment she wondered if she should just roll over and go back to sleep. The rumble in her stomach forced her hand. If she was doing anything tonight, she needed to eat and have her strength and wits about her.

As she stood in line to be served breakfast, she went over every detail she could remember of last night's vivid dream. It had felt so real, like nothing she had ever experienced before, yet it had only been a dream, a bittersweet dream that she had awoken from in tears or both joy and sadness. She had prayed, wished and begged for dreams such as those for years after he had died, and never more than regular glimpses or playbacks had she ever received.

The next two days were the Eighth's off days, where another Division took their place on patrol in search of much-needed supplies and keeping the infected population thinned close to home. She had noted on the schedule that none of the patrols would be going anywhere near where Jennifer saw the men and supplies, which was good news for them; no one would happen upon it before they had a chance to get there.

The line seemed to move slowly as Vincent and Kelli dished helpings of scrambled eggs and hash browns to each person. Auska kept her eyes downcast, not wishing to make eye contact or conversation with either of them. Last night's fight still had her blood simmering and she was not ready or willing to forgive them yet. But her wish was short-lived.

"Morning, Auska," Vincent said cheerfully, his tone hinting at nothing from the previous night, yet his eyes searched desperately for amnesty.

She tried to pretend she didn't hear him and held out her plate, not making eye contact, knowing full well how stupid this must look to anyone paying any attention.

"I'm not going to give you anything until you look at me," Vincent told her, matter of factly.

Auska rolled her eyes and did her best to suppress a sneer. "Are you happy now, I've made eye contact. Now can I have my food?"

Vincent leaned closer to her and kept his voice low. "Come and see me later. We should talk after last night, and hopefully more calmly and without flying fists."

"I have nothing to say to either of you right now." Auska pushed her plate forward more aggressively, hoping that would be the end of this.

"Well, we have things to say to you," Vincent said remorsefully, looking over to Kelli who merely shrugged with indifference.

Auska's eye flashed with fresh anger. "Oh, she's said enough already and if she says more, she'll have more than just a sore jaw next time!"

Vincent was about to say something else when Jennifer butted her way behind Auska, completely ignoring the mutters of complaints behind her.

"There you are," Jennifer beamed energetically, her ice-blue eyes dancing with life, "I've been looking for you all morning." She pushed her plate out to Vincent. "Got something to talk to you about."

Vincent sighed, knowing the moment was lost and filled both their plates. "We will catch up later okay, Auska."

Without a word, Auska turned away and went for the furthest table away from anyone else, with Jennifer right behind her.

"Still fighting with the folks...erm... the kitchen staff?"

Auska dropped her tray down at on the stained table and sat. "What do you want?"

Jennifer sat across from her. "Well, good morning to you, too, sunshine."

"I'm not much of a morning person," Auska replied digging into her eggs, "nor a people person, anytime."

"Oh, as if the whole compound didn't already know that little bit of information." Jennifer grinned starting in on her own food. "But I have something important I need to talk to you about," she leaned in closer, "about tonight."

"What else would it have been about? Getting

together and doing each other's hair and nails?" Auska grumbled back more venomous then even she had intended, but her mood had soured further.

Jennifer nearly choked on her food trying to suppress her laugh. "Someone clearly woke up on the wrong side of the bed." She wiped her mouth. "You seem to have more bite than normal. Must be something really bad between you and your folks."

"They're not my folks."

"Right, right, we covered that last night, didn't we? Though that's not a bad idea," Jennifer said staring at Auska.

"What's not a bad idea?" Auska asked confused.

"Getting together to do each other's hair and nails. You clearly need to do something with that mop of yours and judging by the look of your hands I am sure you've never had a manicure in your life. I bet I could make them look so pretty, maybe even as pretty as mine." The taller girl grinned nearly ear to ear.

Auska just shook her head and kept eating, wondering if she just ignored her, if she would go away.

"Oh fine, I'll get to the point, but you know you really need to lighten up a bit, I'm just trying to be your friend."

"I don't need any friends," Auska replied sharply, "now out with it."

Now Jennifer's face grew serious. "I was hoping you'd lend us the use of a few of your guns or other weapons for tonight. It'd make things a little safer if we were all packing a bit of firepower."

Auska's face screwed up. "What makes you think I have anything like that?"

"Come on, don't give me that shit. A badass like you has got some heat stashed. Besides, I heard the gunshot the other day. The others were too far away but I wasn't and that wasn't the sound of that handgun they let you use when out. That was a rifle shot."

"Could have been anyone that might have been out there."

"Except it wasn't, it was you," Jennifer pressed. "Look, I'm not stupid, nor am I a snitch, and if we are gonna pull this off we should use all the advantages we can. Plus, if you help with this, you can have the first pick of any weapons there."

The offer was a good one, not that Auska didn't already intend to do just that. But not having to argue and have ill feelings from others who might betray her at some point was a comforting thought. "I don't have enough firepower for all four of us, at least not in the way of guns and ammo. Is there anything you can bring to this table?"

"Old Harris has a revolver stashed between his container and the one above him. But it's only got three bullets in it, and they are looking worse for wear, so I don't know if they'd even fire."

"Better to have it, even if only one of the shots fires it might mean the difference between life or death."

Jennifer's face turned grave. "You don't actually

think things will work against us, do you?"

Auska finished her food and pushed the plate aside. "Yes, I do. But I always assume the worst and hope for the best. It's how you stay alive out there."

Pushing her half-eaten food away Jennifer asked, "So, what do we do if things do turn sour?"

Auska grabbed the taller girl's plate and finished it off before she could protest. "We run and fast, or at least those of us that are still alive do so."

Jennifer leaned back in the chair. "I was afraid of that."

The day wore on slowly, and Auska found herself back in her quarters, resting at her crudely built cinder block and plywood desk. Most of her weapons stash was out beyond the walls, for several things she possessed she wasn't authorized to have and they would have been confiscated.

She honed her two knives and her throwing hatchet. Grinning, she put the final edge on the axe. By design it had been just a regular hatchet when she had been given it, to help cut through the undergrowth when scouting. But over the course of several months, she had altered its handle and head and found a way to create a balance. Now she could hit a foot round target from twenty feet away almost regularly, after countless hours of practice. She often drew a few spectators from the different Division squads and, while she hated the attention, she had to admit the praise and clapping when she began to score hit after hit felt good.

Flipping it between her hands she took a few practice swings and blocks, getting her arms used to the weight and feel. She had never actually used the weapon in the field yet and she hoped tonight she wouldn't either. Not that she was afraid of a fight, but still hoped to manage without one.

"If we don't have to fire a single shot tonight that wouldn't hurt my feelings at all." She muttered, putting the axe down on her desk. But she knew the reality of that hope wasn't very likely. These would be hard men, killers, murderers, and raiders. People that wouldn't hesitate to kill or worse. Auska's biggest hope was that Jennifer's numbers were correct. If there were only three to four guards, then it should be a simple enough task to take them out quickly and quietly if their guard was down.

But there was another issue with the plan: Jennifer she could trust, knowing the taller girl was well trained, and even had tasted some action against infected and a few raiders before; Matt and Ross she knew little about but knew neither of them had any real experience. Matt had basic training like all scouts in a Division, but that didn't mean he would use it or could use it when the time came. Killing infected was easy; killing people... that took something else. Matt had spent his whole life in Sanctuary; he was soft to the real world outside. And Ross? She knew next to nothing, which made him even more of a dangerous variable.

A loud knocking on her door pulled her from her thoughts. She cursed inwardly, knowing whose knock it was. *If I just stay silent maybe they'll go away...* that thought was quickly dashed.

"Auska, I know you are in there," Vincent called out. "Please open the door, we need to talk."

Cursing, she pulled the latch and slid the door open. "I really don't have it in me to do this shit right now."

Vincent stepped in and closed the door; his eyes surveyed the weapons on the desk. "Preparing for something?"

"Every moment that I can," she countered. "Preparation is the key to survival."

"I know, I know." Vincent rubbed at his face and leaned against the cool, metal wall. "Barry told me a while back that you were quite good with that axe. Told me he won a few good pieces on wagers while you were practicing."

"Well, I guess I should tell him to give me a cut. Either that or I'll start missing on purpose."

"He also told me you're one of the best forward scouts he's ever seen."

Auska rolled her eyes, though the compliment wasn't lost on her. "He's only a handful of years older than me, so it's not like he's seen much to compare."

Vincent ignored the retort. "But he also told me some other things. Things that worry me and Kelli about your behavior out there, and the risks you take."

Again, her eyes flashed with annoyance. "Well,

I'm twenty-one now and not even your kid, so you needn't *worry* about me and what I do any longer. That burden can be lifted from your weighed-down shoulders and forgotten."

"Goddamn it, Auska, don't do this again," Vincent pleaded. "You know damn well we care about you. No, you're not our kid, but out there we went through hell and back to get here." He threw up his arms. "And shit even here hasn't been all we had hoped it would be! But we did it together, as a family, even a fucked up different pieces to different puzzles kind of family like we are. I mean I know it hasn't been great, but has it really been that bad? Are we really that bad?"

"If she cared so much, where is she now?" Auska replied cruelly.

"I told her not to come. You are both too much alike, hot-headed and quick to cut with your words," he grinned, "and fists."

"We are nothing alike," she shot back.

"Funny, she said the exact same thing with that exact tone." His smile was warming and even a little infectious.

"What do you want Vincent? To reminisce? To change me into something I'm not? What? I'm not a little girl anymore who needs protecting. I'll never be that person you two want me to be, it's just not in me."

"All I want is to keep a promise I once made to a man we all owe our lives to more than once," he said solemnly.

The words cut deep, and Auska could feel the moisture forming around her eyes. "You kept it, you got me here, you saw me become an adult. Your conscience can be guilt-free from here on out. You know as well as I do that would have been more than enough for him."

"But it's not enough for me."

"Then that's on you, and you have no right to expect anything from me in that regard."

"Why can't you just let me in Auska?" Vincent said in frustration. "Why can't you just let me be there for you, let me care about you? Talk to me, tell me what's going on in that head of yours! Your thoughts, your feelings, dreams, goals, fears any of it! I just want to help. I just want to be a friend, someone you can rely on, a shoulder to cry on, someone you can confide in."

Auska stood up straight. "You want to know why? Really know why?"

"Yes."

"The more people you care about, the more people you let in, all just equals more pain and suffering when it's all taken away and destroyed. I lost too much, saw too much, suffered too much as a naive young girl out there." Her voice went bitterly cold. "I have cried all the tears I intend to shed for anyone ever again. The world is a cold dark place now, and the best way to stay alive is to be just as cold."

Sighing, Vincent opened the door and turned to her. "I hope you know we will always be there for you, even if you don't need us or want us. We will always care because you are wrong; the best way to stay alive is to care. I knew a young girl once not so long ago that taught me that... I miss that girl." With that, he left.

Auska ran her hands through her hair and cursed loudly in frustration. She almost wanted to yell down to him to come back and to apologize but couldn't... or wouldn't. It wasn't that easy for her, why couldn't he just see that? Why couldn't they just let her come and go as she needed?

"FUCK!" She kicked the rickety chair across the small room and watched it break on impact with the wall. Why did people have to make things so complicated?

The night was brisk, with a northern breeze that promised the arrival of winter within the month. The sky was littered with patchy slow-moving clouds that obscured stars and moon alike for several minutes at a time before allowing their dim light access to the world once more for a brief time. It made for an ideal night for what was planned.

Hidden in the shadows of their meeting place, Auska waited for the others to arrive. She fought back the shiver that rippled through her. She wished she had dressed warmer, but tonight she expected stealth and agility would be more practical then comforting warmth. Once she started moving, she knew she would warm up, but until then she would be uncomfortable. She was used to that, though, and had trained herself over the years to embrace it, to let it strengthen her. Often Auska would underdress in the colder months, forcing herself to work through the discomfort, to ignore it, to not let it demoralize and weaken her. Now she was used to the biting cold of the winter months, or at least as used to it as she could be.

She rubbed her hands up and down her arms; used to it, but that didn't mean she would ever like it.

After a few long moments, Jennifer rounded a corner and swiftly merged into the shadows beside Auska. "I almost half expected you weren't going to show," she whispered, blowing warmth into her fingers. She was dressed far warmer than Auska, but at least they were dark colors and weren't noisy with movement.

"Why would you think that?" Auska replied, watching Nick's shadow drift across the ground from above as he made his rounds.

"Not sure. You just don't seem like the kind of person who enjoys working as a group or who would willingly put themselves in danger for others."

Auska's smile was cold. "I have no intention of putting myself in danger for others. I'll go along with this because if it works out I'll come out ahead, but if, when we get there, I think it's too risky, I'll tell you and then I'm gone. What you choose after that is up to you."

The taller girl was nodding. "If you say it's too risky, we will abort the plan. Won't be doing my brother any good if I am dead and I'll just have to find another way to get him extra treatment. Guess I could always let the doctor have his way with me. The bastards wouldn't even let me see him today, said he was doing worse and they couldn't risk the sickness spreading!" She kicked at the ground. "Damn it all, I hate feeling useless!"

A pang of guilt washed over Auska for a moment; it was likely her brother was already dead. Her mouth opened to speak but she quickly shut it again. Telling her that wouldn't help anyway; if he was dead already there was nothing to be done to stop that. And if he managed to hold on until the morning, Jen might very well have what she needed to help him. If not, she would have enough supplies to bring her some comfort in the future.

"I'm sure you wouldn't be the first to offer your body to the good doctor."

Jennifer chuckled solemnly. "I'm not sure if that makes me feel better or worse." Her tone became suddenly more serious. "So, tell me Auska, why aren't we friends? I'm only two years older than you. I'm smart, witty, know how to have fun. There are only a few girls in our age range. Hell, why don't you have any friends? You seem likeable enough. A little sour and bitchy around the edges but one can work around that with time."

Auska rolled her eyes; she was afraid this was going to happen. Anytime she interacted with someone for more than a few minutes, they decided it was time to become friends. She understood options in Sanctuary were limited, but still, why couldn't people just leave her alone in that regard? "Ever stop to consider I don't want to be your friend? Nor anyone else's, for that matter?"

"That's nonsense, who doesn't want friends? Shit, life would be boring here if we didn't have friends. I think after tonight we should hang out more. Who knows? Maybe you'll even grow to like it. Think of all the shit we could get into!"

Now it was Auska's turn to be serious. "I don't want friends. I figured after eight years people would have come to understand that."

Jen looked almost hurt. "But why would you want to live like that?"

"Because friends die or get you killed," she replied without hesitation. Words Archer had repeated often and, in the end, held true. He was dead because he chose to get close to Vincent and Kelli… and worst of all, to her.

Jennifer cleared her throat to mask her discomfort. "Well, I guess after tonight I'll just leave you alone then. Wouldn't want to be a burden on your life by dying or getting you killed. Though if you ever change your mind you know where to find me."

"Good," Auska said pointing across the pathway. "Here come the others. Let's get going."

With a quick signal whistle, Nick turned his back and walked the other way along the wall. A rope was tied to a strut in the wall that wouldn't be easily noticed if someone else came around. The four quickly made their way down to the ground thirty feet below. A quick check showed their pathway was clear from the view of the other sentries and they sprinted the hundred-foot clearing into the safety of the trees.

Their pace was quick as they jogged east for nearly two miles before Auska finally stopped them.

"Why are we stopping?" Ross huffed, though he was clearly relieved for the break. Being a perimeter patroller, he was unused to running such distances.

Auska turned on them all, her face dangerously serious. "We are near my stash place." She could see everyone's eyes light up as they glanced around trying to determine where it was. She had several places she stashed things; this one was just where her weapons were because it was close to home. But after tonight she would have to move everything to a new location. "Before I grab anything, I need you all to swear you know nothing about this place nor will you ever try and steal from me." She gave them all a threatening glance. "Because I'll know it was one of you and I won't be nice about rectifying it."

"Wouldn't dream of stealing from another member of the Eighth, Auska," Matt stated proudly. "Besides, after tonight we'll all need stash spots." Jennifer nodded her head in agreement.

"And you?" Her eyes roamed over Ross, looking

for any hint he was a snake in the grass.

He laughed nervously. "Me? Not likely. I wouldn't go this far out by myself to steal from you. Plus, you terrify the shit out of me."

"Good." She almost smiled at the response. It was good that they feared her; fear was a good ally to have and to use with people.

Auska moved off to a stand of thick dead bushes and lifted them aside. With a quick sweep of her foot, she revealed a plank of wood with a handle. Lifting it she pulled out her rifle and slung it across her back and pocketed the nine extra bullets she had for it. With the five rounds in the clip, she had fourteen in total, which she hoped would be more than enough for tonight.

"I don't have weapons for everyone." She looked at Jennifer. "Did you get that revolver?"

Jen pulled out the gun from inside her jacket. "I sure did, just hope the three rounds in it actually work."

Auska took the weapon and inspected it. It was old and not well maintained, but it still looked like it would fire. Opening the cylinder, she examined the three rounds; they were worse for wear then she had hoped. She loaded them back in and handed the weapon back with a grimace. "Your guess is as good as mine. Hopefully, we won't have to use them but if we do, remember to have another plan just in case."

Pulling out an old crossbow, she handed it to Matt with four bolts. It was in no better shape than Jen's revolver. The string was fraying badly and the left limb was warping. She had tried to find newer parts for it but over the last two years had had no luck. "It pulls to the left two inches for roughly every fifteen feet."

Matt lifted the weapon and inspected it thoroughly. "I think I can remember that."

"Don't think, do." She scowled him. "And try not to lose any of my bolts, they're hard to come by."

He grinned and shook his head at her. "Not my first day in the apocalypse, but I'll remember."

"What about me?" Ross asked stepping forward trying to peer into the underground crate. "What do I get?"

"Sadly, not much," Auska muttered pulling out a five-foot spear, tipped with a serrated knife blade.

"A spear?" he said in disappointment. "What the hell am I going to do with that?"

"Throw or stab with it," Jennifer cut in sarcastically before anyone else could. "With the pointy end, hopefully."

Ross took the weapon with sagging shoulders, clearly disappointed.

Auska took the weapon from him and took aim at a thick pine tree twenty paces away. With a grunt she let the spear fly, it hit the tree with a thud, burying near three inches of the blade into the hardwood. "Now you try."

Ross, along with everyone else, seemed confused but he complied; retrieving the weapon, he took aim and threw. The blade sunk deep into the wood nearly five inches.

"I know it's not an ideal weapon," Auska began, "but when we had that flood last year, I saw you throwing sandbags for hours on end onto the carts. You've got a strong back and shoulders and a good center of balance. I threw as hard as I could and you nearly doubled it." It was a lie, but she needed him confident. "Plus, your aim was true with the first throw of a weapon you've never even held before. Out of all of us and the weapons available, you're best suited for it. It's either that or nothing."

Ross grunted loudly as he pried the weapon free, a grin creeping across his face. "I guess that makes sense. I'd still prefer a gun, but I get it now." He swung the spear a few times. "I'll make it work."

"Good. Now let's move out. Jen, lead the way to the end of the rainbow," Auska commanded, already regretting this.

The night was still and quiet; only the chilling breeze that ruffled the treetops could be heard as the four crept closer to the small camp. The trees were thick in this part of the forest, their canopies blocking out most of the night sky, making it near pitch black. Each step had to be carefully placed in hopes to not snap a fallen branch or crunch a pinecone.

Auska motioned them all to crouch further down as they neared the perimeter and its soft glow of torches around the long-forgotten pump house. She had been here only a handful of times in passing and knew the layout only vaguely from memory.

It had a large open room where the main pump had been, now all that remained were some rusted pipes and a wooden grate covering the floor where the hole to an underground water supply had been. On the far back wall, there were two smaller rooms; one had been the electrical room and the other the generator, both stripped clean and left empty. There were only two openings: the door, which surprisingly still worked, and a large half boarded up window on the side of the large room.

Voices around the backside of the building alerted them that there were at least two guards outside. From the sounds of their conversation, they were playing a game of cards or dice. A moment later a shadow passed by the window going towards the back.

"See, only three guards," Jen boasted proudly, relief clear on her face even in the darkness.

Auska scanned everywhere she could see, hoping noise, movement or a shadow would pinpoint anyone else that might be there. But no matter how long she looked there was nothing; only the three.

"Three that we know of," she whispered back after nearly twenty minutes of watching. Unease made the hairs on her neck stand tall. "There could be more than just one inside."

"So, what now?" Jen asked; they were all looking to Auska for direction. "Do we just keep waiting around freezing our asses off, or do we attack?

The role of leader bothered Auska; she didn't like overseeing people. She could plan and adapt well on her own, but others were wild cards that she didn't care for. But if they played their hand right, they could do this with ease and keep the element of surprise in their favor, so long as three was all there really was, but she somehow doubted that.

Auska took a deep breath, the urge to back out and leave nagged at her and yet there was no reason for it. Three, even four guards wouldn't be an issue, at least not for her and so she pushed the thought aside. "Matt and I will circle around back to where the two are playing cards. We will try and take them out without alerting whoever is inside. If we can do that then we can hopefully convince whoever is in there to give up without a fight. If not, well, we kill them, too."

"What are we to do then?" Ross cut in, almost hurt that he was to be left out.

Auska did her best to keep her annoyance from her tone. "You and Jen wait here and keep a lookout to make sure no one else shows up and watch that fucking door. If anyone comes out of that door, take them out quickly. If not, wait for us to be done and we will signal you over."

Jennifer moved in closer. "I should come with you. I've seen combat before, Matt hasn't."

That was something she hadn't considered, but she held firm in her decision. "Matt has the crossbow. Stealth kills are what we need right now."

"That rifle isn't going to be very silent," muttered

Ross holding up the spear as if to make a point.

Auska pulled her throwing axe and grinned angrily. "One more complaint and I leave with my things. Are we clear?"

Realizing their error, they all quickly nodded.

"Good. Matt let's go."

<hr>

"I want you to know, Auska, I won't let you down," Matt whispered, as he followed behind her, trying to make her movements his own. "I may not have killed anyone or even an infected yet, but I am solid. I won't freeze up or choke, you have my word on that."

Fighting for calm she turned to face him and growled, "The only ones going to get killed tonight will be us if you don't fucking shut up."

His face paled at the realization and he nearly apologized out loud but was able to contain it with a nod of his head before continuing behind her. She was right; silent nights like this carried the sound far and clearly. It was something they had learned very early on in basic training. He cursed himself for getting caught up in the excitement of being chosen for this task.

Skirting around a thick willow bush, Auska's mind berated her. What was she doing with this group? She worked alone, had always worked alone, well always after *he* had... she forced the memory from her mind before it could take hold. This was foolish; she should have told Jennifer no and left it at that. But the promise of new weapons and more importantly ammunition had been too much for her to refuse. If this night paid off, she would have enough supplies that come spring she would finally leave and go off on her own.

The thought made her smile inwardly. Leaving Sanctuary had been a goal of hers for years. But always she wasn't strong enough, old enough, experienced enough, but most importantly, equipped enough. She was all those things now, she was sure of it, and after tonight she would have everything she needed to venture off on her own. Where she would go, she hadn't a clue; what she would do didn't even matter. Freedom is all she required. After tonight she would gladly play through the months of winter within Sanctuary until the first taste of spring arrived; then she would slip away and never look back. So, this had to work… she would make it work!

They neared the rear of the building where the two men were playing cards. Auska was thankful the area was well grown in, giving them plenty of places to remain hidden from sight. The glow of their torch only pushed the gloom of night so far from their area that they were able to get within twenty paces of their targets.

Auska leaned in close to Matt's ear and whispered, "We need to do this perfectly."

He nodded, not sure if he could talk and not wanting to anger her further than he already had.

"I want you to aim for the one on the right." She pointed to the largest of the two; it would give him the biggest target for she wasn't sure how good he would be with the bow. "Do you think you can pull off a head shot?"

Fear gripped him now and he swallowed back the lump in his throat. "Never having shot this bow before, I wouldn't count on it, but I could give it a try." He was uneasy and didn't like the idea, but she was already shaking her head.

"No, we won't risk it. From this vantage point, you have a near-perfect clear shot on his chest. At twenty feet you should be able to hit him cleanly, and hopefully in the heart."

Again, Matt's unease prodded him, but he needed to remain calm and in control, so he nodded instead of informing her he was skeptical of his ability. He placed an arrow into the bow and steadied his breathing as best he could. He could do this... he would do this. The bow was off about two inches every fifteen feet to the left... he could make it work. He had to make it work.

"I will move around to the side of the building. When I signal you, you fire, and I will attack a second later. With any luck, they will both go down without a sound."

Before he could say anything, she had slipped away. Licking his lips, he returned his attention to his target. A barrel-chested man with a week-old beard and what looked like a black eye. The way he was sitting made it an easy target. Only an idiot could miss. "I won't fail," Matt whispered to himself, setting the crossbow up against his shoulder.

Auska moved swiftly, thankful for the light breeze rustling the treetops, masking any noise she made on the dark ground. Within moments she was at the side of the pump house. Pressing her ear to the rotting wood, she listened for voices or movement from within but could hear nothing. Satisfied that it was likely only the one man inside, she crept to the corner.

Matt was ready, his bow was up, the string locked into place. Auska adjusted her grip on the throwing axe, ensuring it was in the right placement for an ideal throw that she had practiced a thousand times before.

It was now or never. She took a deep breath and waved to Matt.

The arrow cut through the air as she stepped around the corner launching the axe at her target's back. The arrow found its mark perfectly, the man stared down in confusion before he slipped from his stool and hit the cold earth, dead. Her axe hit the other man with such force that it threw him forward onto the makeshift card table with a garbled cry, spilling the table over loudly.

Auska cursed as she sprinted forward, a knife already in hand as she quickly ran it across the man's throat silencing him before he could make any more noise. But the sound of the crashing table would surely have alerted whoever was inside.

Matt was already beside her, a new arrow notched as she snatched up her axe.

"That went well," he whispered to her with a boyish grin.

"No, it didn't. I didn't account for the force hitting him into the table!" she chided herself. It was a rookie mistake, one that would never happen again.

Just then, they heard quick movements from inside and knew the element of surprise was forgone.

———————◦———————

"God, she's a bitter, mean little thing," Ross muttered, blowing warmth into his hands. "It's no wonder she hasn't any goddamn friends."

Jennifer tried to keep her attention on the door and the back of the building where the other two from their party had ventured to make the first strike, but Ross's words annoyed her. "Do you even know anything about her? What she went through before she came to Sanctuary?"

"Just the odd story and rumors." He shrugged as if it didn't matter. "Something about thinking she had the cure when she and the cooks showed up. But of course, they didn't, but could stay due to proving themselves useful."

She shook her head, trying to hide her disgust at the simplistic reply. "We've been lucky. We've spent our whole lives at Sanctuary, protected, safe and sheltered. She was a child and spent her entire life out here, surviving, watching those around her be killed or ripped apart by infected as they tried to keep her alive. That's a heavy fucking burden to shoulder," she shot back. "Harder still finding out it was all for nothing, wouldn't you say?"

Ross felt uncomfortable at the retort and lifted the spear again. "Yeah, well, she could still try and be more friendly. Not our fault any of that happened to her."

Just then they heard something crash to the ground from the back of the pump house.

"Shit! Time to move!" Jen moved forward out of the trees towards the door, gun poised and ready to fire, knowing full well the noise would have alerted the man inside. She whispered a silent prayer that it really was only one other guard inside.

They just about made it to the door when it suddenly flew open and a large, potbellied man exited, a shotgun held in nervous hands.

Jen and Ross skidded to a stammering halt, staring in disbelief. "Andy, what the hell are you doing here?" Ross exclaimed at seeing one of the wall guards from Sanctuary standing before them.

"Ross? Jen?" He gripped the gun tighter, not lowering it from their direction. "What the fuck are you two doing out here? No one told me you two were taking part in the trade tonight. I'm always the last to know anything! Shit's going to start falling off the rails if everyone isn't kept in the bloody loop!"

"Trade?" Jen asked confused. "What are you talking about?"

"The people the doc makes sick so we can say they died and..." he stopped midsentence, seeing the horror on their faces and knowing they were not part of the operation. "Oh, sweet fuck, you're not here to help with the trade! Why the fuck are you here?"

Jen stared at him aghast. "What are you talking about Andy? My brother is one of the ones who are sick. What the hell are you saying?"

He ignored her, licking his lips clearly conflicted with some inner turmoil as he stared at the ground. "Goddamn it! Goddamn it! Why tonight out of all nights?" He brought his gaze back to them. "Damn it, why? Why'd you have to come around here tonight? Do you know what this means I got to do? Fucking all to hell!"

"What's this about the sick people, Andy?" Jen asked, the gun shaking in her hand. "What the fuck is going on out here? What trade? Why are you with these people?"

Andy stamped his foot hard in frustration. "You idiots! Stupid, stupid damn kids! This is going to complicate everything! The council is going to be pissed right the hell off, and since I'm the one that found you, I'm the one that's gonna catch the most shit for it!"

"Andy, you are scaring me," Jen said, getting a very bad feeling as she tried to process everything she had heard. But none of it made sense.

"Scaring you? Ha!" he bellowed back. "You should be, but not for long! I'm the one that's got to live with this." He leveled the shotgun at them again.

"It's hard enough living with the shit that's happening out here, and now I got to live with this, too! There better be a bottle of something strong at the end of this night."

"Jesus Christ, Andy!" Ross bellowed out, dropping his spear and throwing his hands up to protect his face like it would somehow help. "What are you doing, we are your friends!"

The gun lowered a little. "I don't want this anymore then you kid! But you are the ones that had to stumble onto this!" he cried out, clearly conflicted. "And no one that doesn't already know can know! If this got out to the others..." he trailed off, "well, it won't, I'll have to see to that now, thanks to you."

Voices and movement from the woods pulled all their attention briefly. It sounded like a large group of people were making their way towards them in a hurry.

A crestfallen look fell across his features. "I'm sorry, I really am, but this is better than what would happen to you if I let you live, you'll have to believe me in that." The gun came up and took aim at Ross.

Auska sprang from her hiding spot. She was too close to throw the axe and hoped she could strike him with it before he got a shot off, but her shadow betrayed her. Andy spun around. Seeing the danger, he fired hastily, buckshot exploded through the air, several pellets grazed her shoulder but the blunt of it went passed her, punching Matt from his feet square in the chest in a spray of blood.

Growling through the sudden pain, Auska

71

swung the axe wide, embedding it into the side of Andy's head. As his body crumpled to the ground, the axe was pulled from her weakened grasp as her shoulder screamed in fiery agony.

"Matt!" Jennifer cried, rushing over to her friend to help him. But as she neared the body and looked upon the ten-inch hole in his torso she knew he was already dead. No one could have survived that.

"What the fuck did he mean trade?" Ross cried out, statue still, afraid to move as he stared down at the two dead bodies, bodies of people he had known well over the course of his whole life. Now they were simply corpses in the matter of three heartbeats.

The voices from the forest were getting closer, the sound of a gunshot tipping them off that something wasn't right, and by the angry shouts now it certainly wasn't a rescue party.

Auska put her boot to Andy's head and wrenched her axe free, returning it to her belt and picking up the shotgun, throwing it to Jennifer. She thought about giving it to Ross but in his present state, she guessed he would be useless with it. "We need to get out of here right now!"

"What about Matt?" Ross stuttered. "We can't just leave him here. Not like this."

Jen grabbed his arm and shook him. "He's dead, there's nothing we can do for him now. We have to go or we will be joining him."

"But... but what the hell is happening here?" Ross mumbled his feet still planted firmly. "This has got to be a misunderstanding or... or... I don't know.

This can't be happening. Something is fucked up and this is all wrong."

Auska had had enough of this and sprinted into the tree line. If they didn't follow, they were on their own. Dying here was not in her plans for tonight. Before she had made it more than a few feet within the tree line something arced out from behind a thick tree and slammed into her midsection. She stumbled back and doubled over, hitting the hard earth, trying desperately to draw a breath, but all she could manage was ragged gasps.

"Well, well, what do we have here?" A deep, resounding voice cut through the night. "Isn't it passed your bedtime, little girl?"

Auska's vision swam dangerously to blacking out. She fought bitterly to push herself to her knees and look up at her attacker. He was large, easily a foot taller than her, and powerfully built. Shoulder length brown hair framed his high cheek boned face and the bright white teeth that grinned down at her condescendingly.

Knowing every second wasted drew the rest of the group closer she had to act quickly, or escape would be impossible. "Got to hide behind a tree to fight a girl," she sputtered out between coughing fits, wondering if he had broken any ribs. "You must be so proud of yourself." She needed him angry, and his guard down.

Screams and yelling from behind her alerted to her that Jen and Ross were no longer potentially helpful and would likely be dead soon; so would she if she didn't act quickly.

"I didn't want to fight you, just stop you, and I did," he replied coolly, placing the bat across his shoulder boastfully. "There's no profit in dead girls."

"You wish!" she growled shrugging the rifle from across her back. As she had expected her attacker moved quickly to intercept. As he grabbed for the gun her left fist shot up, connecting with his groin as hard as she could muster. A bellow of pain erupted from him as he staggered backward, her rifle the only thing keeping him on his knees as he fought back the pain.

Movement behind her informed her time was up. If she was going to escape it was now or never. Twisting around with a snap of her wrist a knife cut through the air nailing a woman high in the shoulder; not fatal but it was enough to slow her down and draw caution from the others in pursuit.

Scrambling to her feet, she made a run for it. As she passed by the man that had hit her, she connected her knee to his chin flipping him over on his back. She wished she'd had time to retrieve her rifle, but it just wasn't possible. She ran, forcing her wobbly legs to work, ignoring the bitter burning of her lungs and the grating feeling of her ribs. She needed to put distance between them, and then she could either avoid them or try picking them off one at a time.

"Don't let her get away!" someone yelled far behind her. Several gunshots echoed through the night after her, the sounds of hungry bullets chewing into trees around her added fuel to her steps. She felt no new pain and knew they had missed.

Weaving in and out of trees to shake her hunters, she lost them in the dark woods that she knew well within several minutes. But she had to slow her pace; her lungs burned and she did her best to muffle the coughing fits that rattled her whole body. She could still hear them behind her, looking for any sign of where she might have gone. They knew her destination, and they needed to stop her before she got there, meaning they would likely have sent others on a more direct path to Sanctuary to intercept her before she could reach the safety beyond the walls and get help.

The thought almost made her laugh; what was safe there now? People were being traded as slaves for supplies by the very people who were supposed to be keeping them safe. It was a grave realization. Who was she to trust within the walls? Who was she to tell? There was only two that she knew she could trust. Vincent and Kelli. If she got to them and told them they would know what to do. They were respected enough that others might listen. At least that's what she hoped, and hope was all she had to work with right now.

Auska picked up her pace again, her lungs having coughed themselves out for the time being. As she ran, she lifted her axe clear. It was the only weapon she had now, and she knew before this night was done, she would need it again.

Nearing Sanctuary, she slowed to a careful walk, she was still half a mile from the walls and needed to catch her breath. There had been no sign of anyone else, and this bothered her. Surely, they would have sent out others ahead to intercept her. Or, maybe they just gathered their things and fled as quickly as possible, fearing the repercussions of what was to come when she reached the walls. Both were possible.

Through her labored breaths, she nearly missed the quickened pace of pounding boots on the forest floor getting closer. She swung around just in time to duck beneath a wild swing from a machete, barely managing to get her axe up in time to block the next savage cut. She stumbled under the impact and her assailant's shoulder checked her hard into a tree, causing her wounded shoulder to send out waves of fresh agony that numbed her fingers.

Slashing her axe upwards forced her opponent back a step, but they followed up with a righthanded punch that connected with her jaw, the back of her head hit the tree again. Auska's vision doubled and her attacker moved in for the kill, slashing his blade for her neck.

Without thought, Auska pushed herself off the tree as hard as she could right into her attacker. He hadn't expected the move and was ploughed to the ground, his machete slipping from his grip as he tried to break his fall.

Auska forced the handle of her axe under his chin and pushed down, choking him. But he quickly got his hands on either side of the weapon and slowly pushed it back up. She threw her full weight down, but no matter how hard she tried he was slowly overcoming her. Her wounded shoulder screamed at her and slowly was losing strength, second after second.

Her knee slammed up into his groin and his eyes bulged from his head. But still, he struggled to keep his throat from being crushed, knowing if he faltered, he was dead. Relentlessly Auska repeated the move again and again and again, screaming in his face ferociously. Soon the man's strength and resolve failed him; the axe handle crunched back down onto his neck, slowly stealing the last of his existence.

Once she knew he was dead, she rolled off and wished she could just lay down and rest awhile; but more voices could be heard in the distance, getting closer with every wasted second. In her condition, she likely wouldn't be so lucky as to fight off another attacker and hope to win.

With a grunt of discomfort, she forced herself back to her feet and ran as fast as her legs could go to the edge of the wall.

Quickly, she located the rope and breathed a sigh of relief that it was still there. She grabbed hold and tried to climb, but her wounded shoulder refused to support her full weight.

"No, no, NO!" she screamed in frustration. So close and yet without help, she was stuck on the outside where her enemies would find and kill her before long. She tried one last time, forcing her shoulder to obey her and she fought through the pain, but still, she got nowhere, and time was running short.

"Nick!" she called up in desperation. "Nick, hurry I need you, damn it!"

A few moments passed and she was about to call up again when finally, Nick peered over the wall. "Shut up!" he hissed down. "You're going to get us all caught! What the hell's going on? Why are you yelling?"

"No time for that." She tied the rope around her. "Pull me up, quickly!"

Nick grabbed the rope and began hauling her up.

"Faster, damn it!" she growled up at him, glancing over her shoulder expecting to be shot at any moment. "They are coming!"

Cursing, Nick redoubled his effort, knowing the panic in her voice was real as fear for his own safety grew.

Once she was over the wall, he looked back down ready to drop the rope again. "Where are the others?" He looked back to Auska, but she was already sprinting down the stairway. "Fuck, what the hell is happening?"

———●○———

Auska wasted no time for anyone in the way; if she couldn't get around them in time, she pushed through them. She didn't know who was trustworthy and who wasn't and couldn't risk telling anyone until the two people she knew she could trust had been told. As she forced herself around another person, she began to wonder why there were so many people awake and about at this hour. It was the middle of the night, only a handful of guards and night workers should have been about.

"There she is! There is Auska!" someone cried out from behind her. "Stop her! She is a murderer!"

Stealing a glance behind her, she saw four guards rushing across the courtyard. All eyes were on her now, some in shock and horror at what they had just heard, others began moving to intercept her. It dawned on her then, the reason she hadn't met more resistance outside was that someone had already made it inside to alter the story against her!

She angled right, cutting away from the growing crowd and in-between two storage sheds. Speed was necessary above all else now. The whole compound would soon hear the lies, and none would believe her. No, in fact, she doubted those behind this would let her live long enough to blow the whistle on their 'trading'. But if she reached Vincent and Kelli, she could at least tell them. They would know what to do; others would listen to them and then Conwell and the other council members would be exposed. Hopefully, the people would stand up as one and force the council out of power and new leaders could be chosen… or something… anything.

Taking the quickest route she could without encountering anyone, it was not long before she had reached the living quarters. She skidded between the towering box units, her goal in sight finally.

A hand lashed out grabbing her arm and pulling

her from her feet to crash to the ground. "Gotcha now, you murdering bitch!" Jonas, the head plumbing engineer barked out, hefting a large pipe wrench up to strike her if she moved. "She's over here! I got her!" he screamed for others to hear.

Without thinking, Auska snatched her axe from the ground and buried it deep into Jonas's shin; causing the older man to scream out in agony and drop to the dusty ground, all thought about detaining her gone from his mind as he grabbed at his ruined leg.

Auska had no time to retrieve her axe; already others were coming into view. Pulling herself to her feet, she ran as fast as she could the last two hundred steps and slammed into the steel door screaming. "Open up! Hurry!" She pounded her fists desperately. "Vincent! Kelli! Open up, I need you!"

The metal locking bar shifted, Auska wasted no time and ripped the door open, throwing herself inside, angry voices close enough behind her to grab her. She tried to slam the door shut but a metal bar shot through the opening, making closing it shut impossible.

"What the hell is going on?" Vincent muttered, rubbing his eyes and staring at the blood and dirt covering Auska before realizing something major was happening; something bad.

"Give yourself up Auska! You have nowhere to go!" a commanding voice barked from the door as they tried to force their way in. "There's nothing you can do, murderer!"

Auska's grip was failing, and as more people came the door would be pried from her grip. She had seconds to get the information out. "They are trading the sick as slaves for supplies!" she cried out feeling the door handle slowly slipping from her fingers. "They're not dead!"

"Auska, what have you done?" Kelli asked confusion and worry etched across her face. "What are you talking about?"

"Listen to me!" Auska pleaded, the door finally wrenched from her grip. "They're not dead...!"

Before she could say more meaty fists and boots rained down on her, crumbling her small frame to the floor. She tried to defend herself, but there was nothing she could do. A hard boot kicked the side of her head and it slammed off the metal wall, her vision blurred then went dark...

"We got you now!"

As if waking up from a dream, Vincent leapt into action. "Get off her! What is the meaning of this! You're going to kill her!" He pulled the five guards off the unconscious girl.

"Stand back, cook!" a bitter voice growled. A handgun leveled at Vincent's chest.

Vincent lifted his hands in surrender. "Hold on, no need for that, Marshal! There has got to be a misunderstanding here!"

"Do not interfere," Marshal ordered, no remorse in his tone. "Drag her out of here and get her to lock up!"

"What did she do?" Kelli asked, worried, as she

watched two men drag the bloodied form from their home.

"She is a murderer," Marshal replied, gun still at the ready, clearly on edge about what might happen.

"Impossible!" Vincent gasped out. "Who did she kill? Auska is many things, but a murderer she is not."

"Tell that to Andy Sims, Matt Locke, Jennifer Romwell and Ross Anderson." He watched as the others left with the prisoner, then turned an unwavering eye towards them. "What did she say to you?"

"What do you mean?" Vincent asked, growing even more nervous now as he tried to piece together what Auska had cried out to them in her last moments.

Marshal stepped in closer, his gun still gripped tightly as if the intent of use was unsure. "I asked, what did she say to you?" He eyed them coldly. "And don't lie to me, I heard her yelling something to you when we pried the door open. Now, what was it? It could be important information."

Kelli stepped forward and wrapped an arm around Vincent; she too realized something wasn't right about the situation. "Just barged in here yelling for us to help her, that she needed a place to hide," she lied. "Before we were even awake enough to respond, the door was being pulled open and here we are."

Marshal eyed them both suspiciously. "What else did she said? She was crying something out as we pulled the door open."

"I... I don't know," Vincent replied. "So much was happening all at once, I wasn't really paying any attention to what was being said."

Seemingly satisfied, Marshal holstered his gun and nodded. "Very well. If I have any more questions I know where to find you." He made his way out.

Vincent stepped out with him. "What is going to happen to her?"

"She killed four of our own. She will likely hang for this or worse. I am sorry, I know this must be a shock for you, but it would be best if you accept it and talked little about it. I wouldn't want her actions to negatively affect either of you in the eyes of others here." With that he walked away into the night, shouting orders to all the onlookers to go back to their beds.

Stepping back into their small living quarters, Vincent closed and locked the door, while Kelli lit two candles.

"What the fuck has she gotten herself into," he began to pace the small space. "What the fuck happened tonight?"

"If she killed four people, there isn't even anything we can do for her this time." Tears glistened down Kelli's cheeks at the reality of what was going to happen.

"She wouldn't just kill people, not from here, not even if she hated them," he said out loud, "at least not without a real reason to. If this is true and she did kill them, something had to have happened, something bad. But what? Why?"

Kelli sat down on their cot. "She was hanging around the Jennifer girl this morning, which was odd. I have never seen them talk before and they seemed close this morning."

"I don't know... I just don't understand it, any of this," he replied, running his hand through his hair. "But we will go to the council tomorrow morning first thing and do what we can for her. Find out what we can..." he sighed. "What she tried to say though, that really bothers me, but it's all a jumble in my head right now. The sick are being traded for supplies?"

Kelli hugged him tightly. "What Marshal said rings true, my love. If we press this and make a spectacle, it will only make us stand out and then who knows what blame will fall our way."

Vincent pushed her back at arm's length, his eyes aghast. "What are you saying? Do you think we should just accept this? They'll kill her, Kelli! We deserve answers. You can't tell me you are just okay with this?"

"Of course, I'm not okay with this! I love her, even if she doesn't believe it. But if they know she did this, she is as good as dead, Vincent. There is nothing we can do for her now, and to pull attention to ourselves is likely to spell disaster for our own lives here. I don't like it but what is there really for us to do?"

"The truth, that's what there is to do." Vincent scowled. "I will find it, one way or another. I don't believe for a second she killed anyone without cause or anyone for that matter. And I want to hear from her what she was trying to tell us."

———————◦———————

A soft, persistent squeaking of an ungreased wheel slowly pulled Auska back to the present. The rough swaying and jarring of rolling over bumps sent fresh agony through her bruised and battered form. She couldn't remember a time when she had felt this sore and beat up before.

Her eyes shot open as the last images she could remember came back to her. Trying to move, she soon realized she was bound securely, hands and feet, with no give in them. She was on her back, looking up at a low hanging roof, that looked like the inside of a mine shaft, except bigger.

Dim torchlight flickered around her as she came to understand she was being pulled down a tunnel in a cart by a group of five heavily armed men. She was sure she recognized three of them; the other two she knew she had never seen before, but they had the look of dangerous men. Men like those she had seen at the pumphouse.

"Looks like sleeping beauty had finally woken up," one of the men she knew said as he looked down at her. "You fucked up badly this time, girl, which is a real shame. You had real potential." Rogan, from the council's very own First Division, told her with a look of sadness that appeared to be genuine. "A few more years and you'd have really made a name for yourself in Sanctuary. Could have done a lot of good, had a really good life here."

A short but heavily built man stepped over and glared down at her, his right side of his face pockmarked and red. "Oh, don't worry, she still has plenty of exploitable potential for what she'll be doing now." He ran a rough hand up the inside of her thigh, grinning wider as she struggled against his unwanted touch. "I wonder how long it will take before the fire leaves those pretty little green eyes of yours?"

"Won't matter," Auska spat, "you won't be alive long enough to see it, you fucking pig!"

"We shall see, little bird, we shall see," was all he said before moving back to the front of the group.

Rogan shook his head in pity. "Would have been better for you to get killed by them when you attacked their camp. I fear what awaits you is going to be very unpleasant."

Auska struggled against her bindings again, though she knew it was in vain. "Then let me go, Rogan, so I can die fighting! Not like some prisoner bound together! Let me fight and die like a fucking soldier!"

"I wish I could, really I do, Auska," he told her in a whisper. "But your fate is sealed now, same as Ross, Jen, and the others. What the fuck were you doing out there anyway?"

Glaring at him with hatred, she spoke with venom-soaked words. "How could you do this? How could you allow this to happen? This is sick, even for the council! I used to think you were a man of at least a little honor, but this just proves you are nothing but shit. Selling your own people like cattle, people who look up to you to protect them! You are worse than the raiders beyond the walls."

"It's a dirty business to be sure," Tavish, another of the elite First Division, cut in, "but survival always is. Had you not been where you shouldn't have been tonight all this wouldn't even be happening, and you'd be sound asleep none the wiser to the way things have to be."

"You won't get away with this!" she hissed back, pulling once more on her restraints. "People will find out and then you'll all be as good as dead!"

A humorless laugh left Tavish's lips. "Have been for the last decade or more, but you should be more concerned about yourself now."

"You two will regret this, I swear it on my life."

Again, Tavish laughed. "Knowing what awaits you and your attitude, you're as good as dead within a month." He shook his head and moved away again.

"For what it's worth, I am sorry you got messed up in this, Auska," Rogan told her.

"Fuck you, Rogan."

The butt end of his rifle connected with her skull and all went dark again...

———◦———

Vincent and Kelli moved their way through the crowd of people. Nearly every single inhabitant of

Sanctuary's population was there in the crowded courtyard awaiting the news of what had happened the night before. Guards had gone around that morning bearing news of this mandatory assembly. It took little convincing for people to gather; rumors and stories were already on nearly everyone's lips.

After the council had spoken, Vincent and Kelli planned to meet with them, to discuss what would happen to Auska, and what could be done to prevent the execution. If all else failed, they hoped to buy some time and try to help her escape. Better for her to be wandering out in the world then dangling from a rope, or worse. And if it came to it, they would all take banishment.

Vincent's heart pounded against his chest as he watched Conwell and the other three council members stroll out onto the causeway. He silently whispered a prayer that what happened last night was all a mistake, that Auska would be freed and what she had said to them had been terrified rambling. That somehow, someway, whoever was responsible for those deaths had been found and caught, clearing her name. But inside, he knew that wouldn't be the case. He knew this was bound to get a lot worse before anything got better.

"My good people of Sanctuary," Conwell began, with his powerful voice, "it is with a deeply heavy heart that I stand before you this gloomy morning. For, as I am sure you have all heard, last night tragedy struck our little community, not once but multiple times in many horrible forms."

Dozens of voices murmured out through the crowd but with a raised hand Conwell took full focus again.

"Sadly Dr. Brown has informed us that all those who had last week been quarantined due to a strange and fierce illness have passed away in the night. No matter what treatments the doctor and his staff seemed to give, the illness simply would not relent. Medical supplies and medicines are in short supply and so proper treatment couldn't be done and for that, I am truly sorry. But those are the times we live in now."

Once more the crowd erupted into the conversation; several mournful wails of family members of lost loved ones cut through the air like a knife. The mood among the crowd grew darker, the air almost thickening with their anger and grief.

"Know that the council mourns with all of you who have lost beloved members of your family," he paused, "of our family. Cremation has already taken place, as we couldn't risk the spread of such a vile illness, but the remains will be reunited with those of closest family within the week once all is done."

Conwell paused letting the news sink in, letting the people digest the tragic news before he continued.

"I wish that horrible, tragic news was the worst of the news I must bear to you all this morning, but sadly it is not, and it would be hard to judge which of these things are worse. Further catastrophe struck out last night in the form of one of our very own residents, who it seems for some time was plotting devious deeds to cause devastation to us. We all knew her and now, considering recent events, it seems obvious due to her very nature and attitude towards life here, but sadly, we didn't see it until it was far too late and several more loved ones were taken from us. It burdens me that I must inform you, Andy Sims, Matt Locke, Jennifer White, and Ross Cooper have fallen prey to the murderer Auska Morgan."

He waved his hand to the side door that they had entered from minutes ago and four armed guards pushed out a dirty and bloodied form of a girl, a bag wrapped tightly around her head. The crowd erupted into an angry frenzy. Violent shouts and jeers were screamed out, even the odd rock was thrown in hopes to hit the murderer. Quickly the mood went from mournful to violent and baying for blood. The air around the compound burned with vehemence and it grew dangerously by the second. The people of Sanctuary were peaceful and casual in nature, but the bitterness of human nature still showed its head now.

The prisoner was stopped before an opening on the suspended causeway, looking down twenty feet to those in the crowd below. A thick, short rope was looped over her head and pulled tight. The figure struggled and fought to pull away, but the four men held her firmly in place.

Vincent tried to push himself forward. "Sweet heavens, no!" he cried out, but the crowd around him showed him no mercy and held him back. Remorse shone in some of their eyes, hate in others as they pushed him back.

"This can't be happening, not like this!" Kelli gasped. "We need more time!" But her words were drowned out by a hundred others demanding death.

"It is hereby within the councils ruling right to sentence this traitor, this murderer and fiend, betrayer of hope and cause, to hang from a rope until dead. May God show her no mercy!" Without another word, he nodded to the guards surrounding her. With a violent push, the figure was dropped from the causeway, where the rope snapped tautly. Her legs kicked and jerked for mere moments before all going still.

"No!" both Vincent and Kelli cried, knowing it was over before a chance could even be taken.

The crowd went wild, cheering and screaming, throwing rocks and whatever else they could find. Soon several guards had to make their way into the crowd to ensure things didn't turn riotous.

Conwell and the other council members stood and watched as the prisoner dangled lifelessly for several minutes, allowing the rage within the crowd to playout a little. They needed to vent, or else it would turn dangerous and more people would die, and that just wouldn't do.

"Good people of Sanctuary!" Conwell yelled out several times, slowly gathering their attention again. "Justice is served, though the wound is still raw, do not let this anger and bitterness consume you! It will take time, but the wounds will heal, and life will return to normal. Now go! Life must go on for those of us among the living!"

The dispersing crowd gave Vincent and Kelli a wide birth; some whispered their condolences, other's uttered things of a cruel and malicious nature. Within minutes it was only them left in the courtyard, staring up at the lifeless form of their adopted daughter.

"How could we let this happen?" Vincent muttered. "How could we have failed her so badly. How…"

Kelli wrapped her arms around him and forced him to look at her. "We cannot fall into self-blaming. She was an adult now. If what they say is true, then these are choices she made on her own," she swallowed back the bile in her throat, "and consequences she was aware of."

"We need to talk to Conwell and the other council members."

"But why?" Kelli asked confused. "There is nothing that can be done now. To put ourselves in their line of sight in only asking for further trouble our way. What's done is done, Vincent; there is no bringing her back, no saving her. Now we have to learn to move on. Let us grieve, cry, curse, whatever we must do, but it is over, she's dead."

He knew she spoke the truth and nodded, though he did not agree. His mind raced feverishly for answers he did not have. "I will get to the bottom of this," he swore under his breath as the moved away. "One way or another."

———————◗◦◖———————

Auska woke with a jolt, hitting the ground hard, and was dragged across the cold, bumpy ground for several dozen feet. She struggled in vain against her rough caretaker, but she was dazed and far too weak to even make it inconvenient for him. Her vision swirled around her, unable to focus on any one thing except that she was moving. Her head throbbed as if she was being hit with a hammer repetitively every few seconds.

Finally, the dragging stopped and a chain was looped tightly around her throat and locked into place, the other end secured around the base of a tall pine tree. With a satisfied grunt, the short bald slaver walked away to join the others around one of the four campfires who were already eating and drinking. Three others casually patrolled the campsite just outside the tree line, occasionally stopping to threaten one of the dozen people similarly chained to trees around the camp perimeter.

"I was beginning to think you would never wake up. Thought they might have broken your brain or something, given the lump on the side of your head. Fuck, but do you look like you took a shit-kicking."

The voice was familiar, but Auska couldn't place it just yet as she fought back nausea that threatened her. Finally, after several moments her vision settled, her insides calmed enough that she didn't feel like she was dangerously drunk or ill. She still felt like she had been run over but a truck, but at least she was confident she was no longer going to vomit or blackout again.

Then the voice returned, though this time it was clearer and pained emotions could be detected. "I had really hoped you had made the escape and made it back to Sanctuary to warn the others and get us help. Seen what you did to that man that attacked you in the tree line. Damn, that was awesome! Figured for sure after that nothing would be able to stop you."

Pushing herself up to sit against the tree, Auska took in her true surroundings for the first time. The forest around them was lessening, meaning they were travelling south-east, leaving the denseness of the protective forest for less rural areas. Dangerous areas she had travelled once before long ago in similar unfavorable circumstances.

Glancing around she saw a dozen others similarly chained to the trees surrounding the camp. All of them she recognized; faces of those quarantined with a deliberate illness for this very vile purpose. Even in her condition, it didn't take her long to realize they were chained up like this around the camp as a defense. If a group of infected attacked the camp in the night, whoever was unfortunate enough to be chained up in that area would slow any attack, buying the slavers time to arm themselves. It was genius but twisted all the same.

She noticed Jennifer leaning up against the tree

next to her, looking at her pleadingly and guessed that was who had spoken to her, though she could hardly remember what had been said.

"So?" Jen whispered again eagerly.

"What?" Auska wheezed, her throat swollen from thirst.

"Did you make it back before they caught you?" Jen's eyes screamed for some form of good news; some taste that help was coming. "Did you manage to tell anyone? Is anyone coming for us? Does anyone even know what's happened to us?"

Auska's hazy memory tried to remember her final moments in Sanctuary... Holding onto the door handle with all her might, trying to buy herself enough to time tell Vincent and Kelli what had happened... She remembered crying out the words as she fought, but there had been so much noise, so much confusion, had they even heard her? No, if they had, surely things would be different right now. Their captors were too relaxed, too carefree, to be worried about repercussions. "No." She told the taller girl. "They were already waiting for me by the time I got over the wall. I tried to get to Vincent and Kelli but was caught before I could make them understand."

"So, that's it then," Jennifer sagged against her tree, seeming to shrink in size "No one is coming for us, no one even knows we are still alive. They likely made up some bullshit story that everyone will believe." Her voice cracked into a sob. "We truly are slaves then."

The word burned into Auska's resolve as she slowly shifted her body, forcing her bound hands under and in front of her. Almost instantly her shoulders and back thanked her as the tightness and spasms began to fade. She undid the rope around her feet, but her hands were bound to tightly to undo.

Before she even thought of escaping, she would need to watch and to learn. There were far too many slavers to expect she could just free herself and make a run for it. Not to mention these were hard men who knew what they were doing out here. A runaway slave wouldn't be anything new to them. They would know how to track and give chase and all the advantages were in their favor. She would have to be smarter, ruthless, and time it perfectly.

"Have they fed us yet?" Auska asked, her stomach growling in protest, but more than that she was thirsty. She had to guess she had been unconscious for nearly a whole day.

"Not yet," Jen replied. "Maybe they don't plan on feeding us at all. Why waste food on people you plan to sell off and make someone else's problem?"

"Slaves that starve to death don't bring in trade," Auska countered logically. "No, my guess is they will feed us very little to keep us weak, making us less likely to try anything 'stupid'."

"I guess you'd know, you've been out in this shit before. Seen it all firsthand, not like the rest of us chained to these trees. Ignorance has sheltered us."

Auska ignored the sarcastic bitterness in the girl's words and decided to change the topic. "What happened to Ross and your brother?" Not that Auska really cared, but any information could be useful in navigating her escape.

"They were put in the other travel trailer on the way here, but I saw them get locked up on the other side of the camp. So, they are alive, but no better off than the rest of us," Jennifer sobbed. "How could our own people do this to us? I mean, there had to be better options for dealing with overpopulation. Tighter rations, longer and further expeditions. We could have expanded a field out beyond the wall so we could have grown more. Hell, we could have found a new place at one of the other old sites around the area. But no, they choose on trading us for supplies like we were livestock."

"To them, we are livestock, but it could have been worse."

"How do you figure that?" she snapped back.

Auska shrugged at her tone. "They could have just killed people."

"Might have been kindness in disguise. I'm not really looking forward to being sold to some pig fucker and raped every day until he gets bored of me and strangles me to death."

"Being alive means there is still a chance at escaping and being free once more," Auska reminded her, surprised at how quickly despair was taking hold of the usually fierce girl. But then again Jennifer had been born within Sanctuary and had never had to live the reality that was beyond the only world she had known. Being told what happens out here and seeing it, and worse living it were very different things.

Nearly an hour slipped by before two men made their rounds to the prisoners. Each was given a small piece of dried meat, a stale chunk of bread, and a large ladle full of water.

The water was warm and tasted like spit, but it eased the tightness and burning in Auska's throat. The bread was like eating sawdust and the meat she was sure was a rat or some other rodent. She ate it all without complaint; she would need every ounce of strength she could muster if she were to get out of this. *I will get out of this*, she told herself forcefully, refusing to allow the taller girls' gloom to seep into her own thoughts.

Giving in to depression and despair would destroy any chance at a realistic escape being made. She would stay sharp, clear and focused on every detail she could see. Then when the time came, she would get out of this. Until then she had to remain calm and forgetful in the eyes of her captors... easier said than done after what she had already done to them.

"Hey, guys, look at what I found earlier," one of the guards chimed in, climbing from the back of one of the trucks.

Auska's eyes widen with fear and rage seeing the skull in his hands. It couldn't be the same, and yet even from here, she knew it had to be. Within seconds she could feel the warm, sticky flow of fresh blood oozing down her arms as she violently twisted her hands about trying to pull them free of the rope.

"Auska, what the hell is wrong with you?" Jen barked over, seeing her seething with an unknown fury, pulling aggressively on her confines all the while a low growl escaped her. "Stop it before you draw attention to yourself and get kicked around even more then you have been!" she pleaded, but if Auska was listening it didn't show. "We aren't allowed to stand up, damn it!"

The neck chain tightened as she stood up, glaring over at the man as he used the skull as a hand puppet; what he said she didn't know but it got a hearty laugh from the five others around him. If she had been free, she would have slaughtered them all like the vermin they were for this alone.

"Hey, get back on the ground, bitch!" a rough, irritated voice barked out, a voice she vaguely recognized. Within moment's the man that had touched her in the tunnel stood face to face with her, a small club in hand. "I fucking said back on the ground, cunt!" He stared hard at her with a crooked grin. "Give me a fucking reason to teach you a lesson, I fucking dare you!"

The thought of his hand upon her sent a fresh ripple of hatred through her. Before she could think to reason, before she could stop herself, she lashed out; her head connected with his nose, shattering it against his broad face.

"Stupid bitch!" he screamed, lunging forward swinging his club. As he stepped in, she jumped up, kicking out with both feet, connecting solidly with his gut, throwing him back and to the ground hard.

Before Auska could ever hope to regain herself, two other slavers were on her, aggressive hands held her down before she could do any more damage to anyone. They cheered and taunted her as she tried to struggle against them, but there was nothing she could do with her hands tied and neck chained.

Her opponent got to his feet, his face contorted with a bitterness that was terrifying. "Oh, you're gonna wish you hadn't done that." He spat blood onto the ground as he advanced on her, his body heaving with every violent breath, blood leaking down his face and lips.

The first few hits Auska's adrenaline and defiance allowed her to ignore, but soon each blow could be felt with its full intent, breaking through her defenses. As much as she had tried to fight it, she was soon crying out and curling herself up trying to tighten herself into a ball.

"Brock," a powerful and all commanding voice rang out in the night air, silencing the cheering slavers instantly, "I think that is more than enough."

"Fuck me mate," Brock yelled back, his fury far from spent, "look what the little bitch did to my nose!"

The powerfully built, long, brown-haired man moved closer. "It seems to me you have repaid that thrice over." He patted Brock thick shoulder. "She is a pretty little thing and will be worth a lot, but only if she remains pretty. Besides, she isn't an extra, but a replacement for the one they needed to cover up the mess."

Brock spat a glob of blood at the whimpering form. "True enough, Everett, true enough. I might just buy her myself, so I can finish what I started."

Everett laughed rich and loudly, "I hope you don't, for I'd hate to have to give you a deal and lose out on what we could get for her." This drew a laugh from everyone nearby. "Now I would suggest everyone get some rest, I want to be moving before first light. We still got a long way to go before we get to our first stop." He looked down at Auska. "And the sooner we are there, the sooner we can unload some cargo before it gets damaged."

Soon the men shuffled away, some to the fires or their sleeping bags; others to stand watch over the prisoners and for stray infected that might attack the camp in the night. The game with the skull was quickly forgotten.

Everett moved closer to the battered form on the ground. "It would serve you well to let this be the last time you attempt such a stupid thing. Brock isn't known for letting things go, and I'm not known for allowing insubordination to go unchecked."

Auska glanced up and instantly knew the face. It was the man who had attacked her the night before at the pump house. "Looks like I didn't hit you hard enough to markup that face of yours," she whimpered out, trying to sound harder than she was now. "A pity. I'll have to try harder next time."

He suppressed a chuckle. "Takes a harder hit than a little thing like yourself could give to mark me up."

Auska glared up at him, her eyes radiating defiance. "The wobble in your step tells me I hit hard enough the first time."

This time Everett did chuckle. "Oh girl, you are just full of fire! I do not envy what that's going to cause you in time, but I do pity the man that will break you. For sure, you will make him hate me for selling you to him."

"I'd be more concerned with what I am going to do to you and your men before I am done here."

His eyes flashed dangerously at the threat, but he maintained his grin over her. "You'd best learn your place and quickly. You've amused me tonight so I will let this slide. Tomorrow is a different day and with it, different consequences." With that, he walked back to the center of the camp to his men.

"Are you out of your fucking mind?" Jennifer gasped, not having realized she had been holding her breath for the whole exchange. "That hit to your head must have knocked you stupid!"

"Something like that."

Crawling back to the tree was pure torment. Auska's legs refused to follow instruction and she was truly surprised they weren't broken. But with the way her sides hurt, her ribs might not have been as lucky.

Jennifer moved as close as she could without choking herself with her chain. "Care to tell me how getting beaten to a pulp fits in with your escape plan? Because if you have a sound argument, I might give it a go, too, if it means escaping."

"I don't have a plan," Auska admitted through gritted teeth, "nor do I think trying to make one would help."

"Well, that's not very uplifting coming from you."

"To escape these men will require acting when the perfect moment arises, taking the chance and letting nothing stop you." The effort of talking took far more energy and effort then it should have and Auska closed her eyes.

"Okay, so we keep our wits about us to find that moment to free everyone and escape. I can try and work with that, just make sure I know what the signal is."

"There will be no freeing everyone. It will be a save yourself moment."

There was silence for several moments.

"I won't just leave my brother behind. The rest if I have to, fine... my brother, no." Jennifer's voice had lost its edge and was fearful.

"Then you won't make it, and neither will he." Auska had barely gotten the words out before exhaustion took her in its embrace. The chill of the night all but ignored.

———◦◦———

Without opening her eyes, Auska knew where she was again. The cool, clammy caress upon her skin that made the hairs on her neck stand up was more than enough to affirm it. But she kept her eyes held tightly shut. Ignoring the queer sensations across her body, the flutters in her stomach, the lightness of her thoughts. Ignoring it would make it go away without having to deal with it; it was a dream, nothing more. She could wait it out.

No, I'm not doing this again, I'll not watch that happen again, I won't! It was too hard losing him the first time; I'll not watch it again and again! She told herself firmly fighting her urge to open her eyes and find Archer standing there.

If I just stay still, keep my eyes closed and ignore this all, I will wake up sooner or later. I am in control, I am the master of my dreams, I don't have to do this!

"Or you could just open your damn eyes and get this over with and stop fighting something you have manifested yourself," came a sharp but friendly reply. "Besides, you need to get me out of this thing again. It's too cramped for my tastes."

Auska sighed in defeat. "Goddamn it, fine!"

With her eyes open she found she was laying on her back staring up at an uneven rock ceiling. The faint flicker of torch lights giving the room a sinister feeling, well-keeping the grey fog of her dream world at a distance. This wasn't what she had expected at all; this was different from last time, entirely different.

"Where the hell are we this time?"

"A place I certainly don't have many fond memories of I can assure you of that," Archer said. "And one you'll find yourself in, or worse, if you keep letting your sentiment get in the way of logic."

"I couldn't help it."

"You could have, should have, but instead you let

your feelings get in the way of your fucking brain," he scolded. "Now you are laying on the cold ground, bruised, battered and nearly defeated. Your chance at escape might have been right now and you'll miss it because you are a stupid child still. All for a piece of bone."

"It's more than that to me," she chimed in, trying to keep the whimper from her voice. "It's... so much more than just bone."

"And yet the facts remain the same. Now get off the ground and help me already."

Auska pulled herself to her feet and saw Archer was locked in a small cell beside several others, with faint but blurred figures within them. The harder she seemed to look, the more blurred and distorted they became. Even the one that she knew had housed Vincent had nothing more than a blurred human-looking figure moving within.

"You never knew any of them, never took full note of who they were, what they were," Archer explained to her, seeing her confusion. "That's why they are nothing more than blurs to you."

"Then why is Vincent a blur?" Auska asked. "We saved him that day, too, and I've known him ever since, very begrudgingly sometimes, too."

Archer laughed. "You know anything I tell you is just what you already know deep down inside. Now get me out of here already, I hate being caged up."

She rolled her eyes and went to the cell. As soon as she touched the door it clicked open. "Humor me anyway. I'm a stupid child, remember."

Archer stepped out of the cell and stretched to his full height with a groan. "Clearly you blame him for your current predicament."

"That's absurd. No, I don't."

"Is it really?"

Auska looked into his cold grey eyes and found even in her dream they held such strength. "What could he have done for me?"

Her mentor kicked the cell that should have held Vincent, but the gloomy creature didn't even notice. "You tell me."

"Nothing," Auska spat back annoyed by the cryptic reply, "nothing at all. I already know that this is all my fault for being stupid to agree to go with Jennifer and the others."

"You'll get no argument about that from me, girl, but deep down you know what you had wanted, needed from him even at that moment."

She rolled her eyes again. "Being cryptic isn't really helpful."

"Then stop being cryptic and use fucking logic. Stop hiding behind a wall from yourself."

Auska took a deep breath. He was right, damn it; even here he was always right. She was trying to hide her real feelings from herself, no less; what a stupid notion that was. "Well, he could have tried to help me. Should have known I wouldn't have run to them like that if it wasn't important."

Archer kicked the cell again but this time the creature did stir with a cry of fear, its form not so hazy now. "What else?"

"He should have followed them when they took me, even if it was in secret." Her tone was angry now. "They could have seen what they were doing with me and know without a doubt something wrong was going on and that

I was telling the truth! But no! He let them take me without so much as a fight! Kelli was no better!"

Now the cell held the vision of Vincent trapped within like he had been so many years ago; frightened and dirty.

"I'd say you figured out what the problem was, kid."

Auska turned her attention to the dirty man she had known for nearly half her life now. He looked scared, weak and broken within the cage. Nothing like the man she knew he was now.

"You are holding on to resentment against him."

"Only because he did nothing to help me!"

Archer shrugged. "Didn't you say there was nothing he could have done?"

"He could have tried at least," she countered. "You would have."

"Only because you made me, stupid kid."

"So, what does all this mean then?"

Again, he shrugged. "Only you can know that kid. But now the question is left, will you leave him in there, or let him out?"

"It's only a dream what difference does it make?"

"Everything and yet nothing."

Archer's voice sounded far away and when Auska turned to look at him, he was gone...

A thick-soled boot ripped Auska from the vividness of her dream world as it kicked her legs cruelly. The dim light of dawn stung her tear-encrusted eyes as she pulled herself to her knees, only to have a ladle full of water thrust in her bruised face.

She drank greedily, half of it spilling on her, hating how she must have looked to her captors. Desperate, dependent, weak and trapped. The thoughts almost made her spit the brackish water back out, but her strength and survival for escape demanded she take the humiliation. Ego was a killer when survival was on the line.

Every inch of Auska hurt and she could barely keep her feet beneath her as she was forced towards the trailers. Collapsing now would likely only attain her another beating, one she could ill afford. Already she berated herself for last night's stupidity. Dream Archer had been right. How could she possibly hope to escape when she could now barely stand? Not to mention now she was even more of a wild card to her captors. If they weren't already keeping a close eye on her for what had been doing at the pump house, they certainly would be now. But seeing someone else handle his skull in such a disrespectful manner had overwhelmed her common sense; it was all she had left of him. He had been right about that, too; it was just a piece of bone.

She stole a glance at the open door of the truck before she was shoved within the cage and noted the skull on the dashboard and sighed inwardly with relief. It was just a piece of bone, but it was hers! And she would find a way to get it back... one way or another.

Within minutes the camp was packed, the slaves loaded and the slavers climbing into the three trucks. The trucks roared to life and they set off again. They followed a long-forgotten dirt road that was grown in and rugged, making progress slow even for the trucks. Each bump, root or washout they drove over jarred and rattled the trailers horribly, making it impossible for those inside to get comfortable for long. Had it not been for the ability to contain the prisoners and move them together, on foot would have only been a little slower.

It took all Auska's remaining willpower to not cry out each time the trailer hit something. Each bump was like another kick to her battered body, yet she did her best to accept them. Using the pain and discomfort to make her stronger and fortify her resolve for the escape she would sooner or later make. This wasn't permanent, just a hiccup.

The talk within their confines was what anyone would have expected. 'Why is this happening?' 'There must be some mistake.' 'How could they do this to us?' 'What are we going to do?' 'What are they planning to do to us?'

The despair and betrayal in their voices were understandable. All of their lives, they had believed themselves safe and protected from a world just like this. Most of them had been born in the safety of Sanctuary or were there early enough at the beginning that the reality of outside was just bad stories. It had to be a knife to the guts to find out those whom they had allowed to give them that

109

comfort had only betrayed them in the end.

Auska ignored them, adding nothing to their sorrowful discussions, even the few that played with the idea of escaping. Jennifer and herself were the only two that had any combat training and experience. Ross had some training but nothing in way of experience, and likely nothing that would help against the hardened slavers that guarded them. Unless, of course, he was used as a distraction or sacrifice. The only chance they had was if they got lucky and something happened and they scattered, but even then, they would likely die within a few days on their own out in this world. Or when they were sold, if they found a way to escape their buyer.

Looking over to Jennifer, she cursed to herself. If only her brother wasn't among them, maybe then she would be a useful tool and ally in escaping. But with her mindset on freeing her brother at least, and the others if she could, she would be useless in any planning and likely get Auska killed.

Auska understood Jennifer's dilemma; it was her brother after all, and she had to wonder if she had such a person here, her own mind might be set the same. The thought only assured her that years of keeping everyone at a distance was well-founded. She would escape; if in the process she could free others, she would but only if she could still guarantee her own freedom. Survival was the key, not becoming a hero or martyr for the sake of people she didn't know or care for.

Jennifer noticed Auska looking at her and

frowned, slowly moving closer. "Did you really mean what you said last night?"

"I make it a point not to say anything I don't mean."

"So that's just it for you, everyone is just to fend for themselves? No joint effort to try to overcome our captures and escape?" Jen's voice was dripping with bitterness.

Auska tried to make herself more comfortable but found it impossible within the small confines that bounced aimlessly at any moment. "What more is there to do?"

"Are you talking about escaping?" a young man named Parry asked, licking his lips with obvious fear and excitement. He had been one of the field hands for the gardens that grew most of Sanctuary's food supply. "Do you have a plan? Or at least the start of one?"

Soon the others were moving closer to listen and Auska cursed; this was the last thing she needed. People were sheep, and their minds would listen and wander to whatever talk fit what they wanted.

"Auska here thinks we just fend for ourselves and anyone who can escape should and the rest of us just get left behind to whatever fate has in store for us," Jennifer replied, knowing full well she was throwing Auska under the bus. She didn't care, maybe this would prompt her to feel guilty and finally agree to help them.

"How could you say that?" several people cried in dismay over the rumble of the truck.

"That's horrible, we are all from the same group, we can't just abandon anyone!" another called from the back.

"We are like a family!"

"…no one can get left behind…"

All eyes were upon her now and a tingle of guilt touched her with all their fearful and accusing stares, but not enough to change her mind. The facts remained the same: these people were weak, clueless and unprepared for what was going to need to be done. "Those men out there are killers, murderers, rapist, and highly-skilled in all of those things. What are any of you?" She pointed to the man who had first spoken. "A gardener, and you, you cart water for the livestock, and you," she pointed to one the of women near the back, "you mend clothing. The others in the other trailer are hardly more than children, no older than fifteen."

"What are you trying to say?" the women she had address cut in sharply.

"Want it spelled out? Fine," Auska growled, pushing herself up. "You try and fight these men, you'll die. It'd be better if you let them sell you and try to escape from whoever becomes your owner. Fake acceptance, pretend to submit, play the game, block out whatever happens, until the moment where guard is let down, then escape from wherever you end up. It won't be pretty, and you will never have the life you had in Sanctuary, but that is the world we live in."

There were murmurs of shock and disbelief for

several moments. Others seemed to understand the reply and almost accept it for the truth it was as they slumped back against the floor and hung their heads.

"And what about you?" Ben, the water cart driver asked. "You're a fighter, one of the best Sanctuary had if what I have heard is to be true. With you and Jennifer beside us, we can do something. Strength in numbers and all. Just tell us what to do, and we'll do it! If we are all fucked anyway, we might as well make a go for it!"

"I don't want to die!" someone muttered from the back, and another person moved from view, accepting her words.

"Not even with Jen and myself do we stand a chance of overwhelming these men in any hopes to free everyone," Auska replied coldly. Why couldn't they just grasp the situation and leave her alone? "My advice to all of you, if you get a chance to escape, do it and don't look back at any of us. If not, play the long game and escape if or when you can. The life you once knew is over. The sooner you accept it the better you'll feel." With that said she turned away, ending the conversation before anything more could be said.

More conversation continued, about how she was right, or how she was wrong; how there had to be a way to escape, or how it would be better to just die now. She ignored it, tuned it out as best she could. Before this was over, most of these people would be dead or broken mentally beyond fixing.

Vincent paced in front of the worn, double oak doors where the council ran business, waiting to be allowed admittance. It had been three days since they had hung Auska, and every day before and after work duties he was there seeking an audience with them. And every day they had been "too busy" with other matters to see him and he had been sent away.

But today he would be seen and heard, even if he had to kick the door in and corner them to do so. They had ignored his requests and pleas long enough. He had been patient, he had been understanding, he had even continued working regardless of the emotional trauma suffered. Today he would have his answers. Demand them, if he must!

If he had slept more than four hours since the hanging, he'd have been surprised. He was exhausted, but every time he closed his eyes, he saw her falling from the causeway, and then the voice of Archer echoed within his head... *"You failed her!"* He needed to talk to the council, to find out what happened that night. Once he had the answers, he hoped he'd be able to move on. But right now, it was all a mess and he was nowhere near closure.

"Come and sit," Kelli told him from the bench in the hallway. "Pacing around like a cornered dog isn't going to make time go any faster."

"I can't sit. I need to keep moving until this is over." He stopped and looked at her. This had taken its toll on her as well; he could see it in her eyes and the deepened lines around her face, though he wondered how much of it was from what had happened to Auska and how much of it was worrying about him. "How can you be so calm about this?"

Kelli smiled wearily at him. "I may be calm on the outside, but inside I am screaming in rage and mourning the same as you, my love. But no matter what happens when we talk to them, nothing changes. She is still gone." Shrugging, she sighed. "I guess I've just been able to come to terms with that part."

"I just can't get over what she said," he paused, looking around to ensure no one was around, "before they took her."

Kelli shot him a warning glance as fear glazed her features. "We were half asleep, and she was running for her life, we don't really know what she said." She knew that was a lie; they had both heard her clearly, but now was not the time for this conversation to be rehashed.

"It just can't be true, it just can't and yet..." he started, "Auska was a lot of things, but a liar and a cold-blooded murderer were not among them..." he paused, "at least not like this."

"Auska was a lot of things we have no idea about." Kelli reminded him. "She was a woman now, not a child, and she did a lot of things no one knows about. They found all sorts of hidden and stolen items in her home. Not to mention all the things others are coming forward saying about her, and what she did and said. Even others from the Eight are coming forward with how she used to disappear for hours at a time or bring back supplies that she used to bribe them with for their silence."

Vincent scoffed at her. "I'll never believe she was what they are accusing her of, never! The rest of it is just rumors with little truth involved. People are cruel and fearless when there will be no repercussions."

Finally, the doors opened and an armed guard from the First accompanied the council's assistant, Mr. Greenfield. A short and portly man with an ever-growing bald spot on the top of his head, he nodded to them both with a forced smile. "Thank you both for your patience. The council has a few moments to spare today and will see you now if you wish. But remember they are very busy, so please try to keep it as brief as you can."

"About bloody time," Vincent muttered louder than he intended to. The sound of a shifting gun made him instantly regret his words.

Mr. Greenfield turned a stern eye on him. "I would advise you not to allow such ill mannerisms to become you once inside. Such insolence wouldn't bode well for you after what has happened of late. The fact that the council has made time for you is a large step in their trust and admiration for what you do for Sanctuary, nothing more. But to provoke or prove that trust otherwise," he glanced at the guard, "would be foolish."

"Yes, yes," Vincent told him with a wave of his hand. "It has been a trying couple of days. I'm sorry. I forgot myself for a moment, it shall not happen again."

Mr. Greenfield looked over to his armed companion and for a moment it looked as if he would refuse them, but after a long pause, he dipped his head again. "Very well, I believe I can understand your position. Please follow me and please do not touch anything."

"What is with the armed escort?" Kelli asked, never having seen such a thing before as she spotted two other guards in the hallway beyond.

"These are trying times and one can never be too careful." The balding man replied. "Sadly, we know not if Auska was acting alone or not, so precautions had to be taken."

Vincent rolled his eyes. "Just say it, we are suspects, too."

Mr. Greenfield looked hard at him. "Everyone outside these doors is suspect at the moment." He turned back to the doorway. "But yes, your relationship with the murderer does not help your cause, nor would you really expect it to. Now if you would, this way."

Vincent and Kelli followed the portly man along the long, decorated hallway. The sight was truly breathtaking and a wonder. The dark red carpet took in the eyes right away. It was impossible to tell that twenty-plus years had passed into the apocalypse, for the carpet seemed as bright and lavish as if it had just been installed. Even the painted walls were bright and vivid, showing their age and wear not at all. A handful of paintings and artwork adorned the walls; they, too, were in near perfect condition, making the whole of the hallway look like they were entering a successful businessman's office from the pre-apocalypse era.

"This room doesn't look like the world outside has touched it for a moment." Kelli gasped, running her finger along the framework of one of the paintings. She doubted they were expensive originals, but their beauty in a world so dark made that matter not at all.

"Why, thank you." Mr. Greenfield replied, though he didn't turn around to look at them; he appeared to have grown taller and his steps seemed prouder. "I do my best to keep the upper quarters and conference rooms clean and tidy. But please, I ask you not to touch anything! Oils and grime from the skin will slowly ruin them!"

"Must be a lot of work," Vincent muttered back, pulling Kelli back to the center of the hall. The sudden thought of how these people lived over those down below was making him angrier than he had been when this had started.

"A clean and color-rich environment helps the mind work," Mr. Greenfield replied, not noticing his tone, "and the clear, peaceful minds of our councilors are paramount to their success of keeping Sanctuary running smoothly and efficiently, wouldn't you say?"

"Absolutely." Kelli cut in, seeing Vincent's mouth

twist, about to reply something that likely wouldn't have ended well for them. "We wouldn't want them making mistakes with our safety."

They turned a corner, and another set of double, polished oak doors with shiny brass fittings stood before them, ominous and proud. Another armed guard stood beside it. It was another of the First Division. Vincent knew the face and thought the name 'Rogan' sounded familiar, but he wasn't confident enough to address the man with that.

"Right this way." He opened the doors and ushered them in before quickly retreating and closing the doors behind him with a soft click.

Vincent and Kelli did their best to suppress a gasp at the room that would have been more fitting for a fancy cruise ship then the upper rooms of an old work yards apartment complex. The hallway had been impressive, but the room was awe-inspiring, almost melting the hard, bitter and violent decades lived outside these walls away.

"Ah, our guests have arrived. What is it we can do for you two?" Patricia Thornhill asked, barely taking the time to look up at them from a folder she was reading.

Vincent pulled his eyes away from the white window drapes; it was by far the whitest thing he had ever seen in his life. He cleared his throat. "We are here to discuss what happened with Auska."

"Oh yes," Bruce Harlow mumbled as he packed what appeared to be fresh tobacco into an elegant hornpipe, "a nasty bit of business, that was." He lit the tobacco with a match. "A shame really. She could have had great potential, from what I was told by Captain Barry of the Eighth."

"Yes, a sad day that was, indeed. So much tragedy to befall our beloved little settlement," John Conwell surmised. "What is it you'd like to discuss about that day? I must inform you though, we have already closed the matter as far as any further investigating and such. It was an open and shut case with the witnesses and the evidence that was collected."

Vincent could hardly believe how casually they were referring to that day as if it were no more than a bad storm that had passed over and not a life that had been taken. "You hanged Auska."

"Yes, we most certainly did." Mr. Harlow cut in. "That is the punishment for murderers within our walls, lest you forget. Might be we have another announcement of the laws and rules here for the people to be reminded just what awaits them if they go against them."

"We are well aware of that, but is there not still supposed to be a trial period?" Kelli jumped in. "So that all the facts are gathered and presented before such a judgment is passed?"

"We had all the facts darling." Ms. Thornhill countered with contempt in her tone. "She murdered them in cold blood and so she got what was coming to her. It was not a decision we wanted to make or that we made lightly, but it was the right one to make."

"Surely you can't believe that." Vincent shot back, keeping his tone in check, but just barely. "In the few hours that it happened, there is no way the whole situation could have been uncovered."

"Do you doubt the efficiency of the council?" Mr. Harlow cut in, his voice bordering irritation.

"No, of course not," Vincent lied. "Just seems to me maybe not everything that could have been done was done."

"Now look here," Mr. Conwell said dangerously. "We decided to entertain your request for what we assumed was for the sake of closure to a terrible and regrettable tragedy. And only have done so because you two have, for a few years now, been extremely proficient in your duties, helping stretch our resources out longer, helping keep the bellies full of all that live here." His eyes hardened. "But I will not tolerate our judgment being questioned by the likes of you."

"You must accept our apologies," Kelli stepped forward, knowing if she didn't act now Vincent was likely to do or say something that they would both regret. "It has been a long and trying few days, surely you can understand."

"Yes, well, I suppose we can understand that." Patricia nodded in acceptance, as did the others, slowly if not begrudgingly.

"But you are right, we are here for closure. But to have closure we need to know what really happened, how and why." Kelli hoped this line of reasoning would loosen tongues and give Vincent what he needed to move forward.

"What happened is your stepdaughter, or whatever she was to you, lost her damn mind!" Mr. Harlow grumbled, puffing vigorously on his pipe now, filling the room with a sweet, musky aroma.

"But why?" Vincent begged, putting his hands on the large table they were around. Ignoring their stares, he went on. "That's doesn't make sense. She was different, yes, but she wasn't a killer! She didn't like conformity, but she wouldn't just kill someone without reason."

"Well, from several eyewitness reports, and the four-innocent dead in her wake, I think it's safe to say that she was." Patricia Thornhill replied, matter of factly and without the slightest hint of remorse.

"Who?" Vincent asked far more forcefully than he should have.

"Excuse me!" Mr. Conwell barked back, standing up from his chair. "You forget yourself, Vincent, and are heading towards a very thin ledge that there will be no coming back from!"

Vincent knew he was pushing his luck, but he had to, he had to know. "Please, just tell me who the witnesses were. I can talk to them and maybe piece..."

"I've had about enough of this!" Harlow's sharp tone left nothing to debate. "We have answered enough of your questions and wasted more than enough time with this dastardly matter. Auska was a traitor to our lives here and a murderer, and for that, she was hung by the neck until dead! She is dead and gone, and that is that!"

Vincent was about to snap back a retort, but Kelli was quick to silence him by squeezing his arm painfully. If he continued now, they would both be punished.

"Now if I am not mistaken it is but an hour or so until lunch." Patricia Thornhill stared at them coolly. "I would have to assume our two main cooks would be needed in the kitchens rather quickly to ensure lunch is not late today."

"Yes... of course, you are right." Vincent gritted his teeth. It was over. They had achieved nothing, learned nothing; they had failed her once again. They turned to leave, shoulders slumped and eyes moist.

"But there is no reason to end this little meeting with a bad taste in anyone mouths." Mr. Conwell called to them, leafing through a pile of papers until he found what he wanted. "Ah, here it is." He stepped over and handed it to Vincent.

"What is this?" Vincent eyed the document and his eyes widened in surprise and wonder.

"I thought this might help ease the rift of this unfortunate conversation. The First Division intercepted a raider gang from the west. A small group was moving a rather large stockpile of goods to their settlement of Hollow Rock. Fortunate for us they were under-guarded and ill-prepared."

"There's... there's months' worth of food on this list!" he gasped.

Conwell smiled. "Yes, and I am sure with you two it can be made to last until spring. But to celebrate this good fortune and to help ease the pain of the tragedy of a few days ago, I want you to increase portion sizes on breakfast and dinners for the next two weeks and then alternate between them afterward for two weeks." He sat back down and looked pleased with himself. "With the last of the crops harvested this week, we should have more than enough to sustain ourselves through the long, cold winter."

"Plus, it's always good to add a few pounds on before the cold winter months come," Patricia added. "Helps keep you warm while you work."

"The food will be delivered to the kitchen's storage locker within the next day or so. I shall leave it to you to make proper use of it over the next month to help uplift the populace. With all that has happened, the people need something good right now and extra food always helps ease the troubled mind." With a nod of his head, Conwell dismissed them, but before they reached the doors, he called back to them. "Vincent," he waited until there was eye contact, "I consider this matter to be closed now and want no further interruptions regarding it. I hope you can appreciate the situation and understand that the sooner the people put it behind them the better... for everyone."

"Understood." Vincent could barely choke the word out as he left.

The next two days and nights blurred together.

They made slow progress through the rough terrain most of the day; stopped in the evening, where they were chained to trees, fed, watered and watched until morning, only to do it all over again. The further they moved out of the mountains, the more depression and despair gripped all those who were prisoners.

Resting her head against the rough bark of the tree, Auska breathed in the fresh, cool night air. They had been lucky so far; the nights hadn't gotten bitterly cold yet. Nights were still uncomfortable and spent shivering, but it wasn't unbearable yet. The further south they moved, the longer winter's bite would take to get them.

They were almost out of the forest now. Another day and they would hit more open space, rolling hills that had once been grassy and full of life, but now were barren rocky dust swells. The trucks would make faster time if they didn't run out of fuel. She had overheard a few of the guards talking about how low they were and that the gas canisters were nearly empty. That would mean soon they would have to search for some.

She decided that would be her time to try and escape. Already her body was nearly back to normal; very little soreness remained from the beating she had received. She would be able to fight, to kill, if necessary; but most importantly, to run and fight another day.

One major problem remained and that was the chain around her neck. She needed to find something soon that would work for picking the lock or breaking it. She wasn't the greatest at picking locks, though given enough time she could open most, but do so when the lock was dangling from her neck and she couldn't see what she was doing? That was going to be tricky.

Laughing brought her attention to the firepit. Once again the skinny, spiked haired guard was using Archer's skull as a prop in some derogatory display at his poor attempt at ventriloquism. Every night, he brought the skull out to get some cheap laughs from his comrades, and every night Auska killed him a hundred times in her mind; tonight, was no different as she pictured cutting his hands off and burning his eyes out with a hot poker.

"I'm going to kill you before this is over, you fucking worm," Auska muttered.

"Well, that is quite the bold and dangerous statement for a slave to make towards one of her captors," a deep voice said from behind her.

Auska spun around to see the leader of the slavers standing next to her tree, his arms folded over his broad chest and an all-knowing smirk on his thin lips. He was a powerfully built man; how had he moved so silently that she hadn't been alerted?

"A slave in your mind, maybe, but a free and dangerous woman on this end."

He flashed her a grin. "Dangerous I have seen and even felt a taste. But you must understand that chain around your neck makes the free part not so believable anymore, or ever again for that matter.

You are nothing more than a dog now, at the end of a leash. Dogs that try to bite get punished until they learn, or until they need to be put down."

She knew she should shut up, just bite her tongue, look away and shut the hell up; but she couldn't. The way he was looking at her with his steel-grey eyes, the way he grinned, the arrogant manner he stood there so casually as if he hadn't a care in the world, made her blood boil. "Guess we will just see how long this 'leash' remains there and how badly this 'dog' bites back."

"Until morning for sure, but then you'll be in a cage again and if you try anything, I will have you hobbled. But that's all trivial," he pointed to the small, wiry man still putting on a show to the others with the sun-bleached skull, "what do you have against Dirk? Besides him being an ugly son of a bitch. To my knowledge, he hasn't even spoken to you, let alone give you any more reason to want him dead then all the rest have."

"That's my business and his problem."

With startling speed, he grabbed the chain around the tree and pulled down hard, throwing Auska forward and to the ground before him. "Anything and everything that happens here is my fucking business." He stomped his foot down on the chain forcing her to lay flat on the ground next to his boots like a worm. "The sooner you realize that, the better. Now answer my fucking question... please."

Auska tried to control herself from struggling, it would achieve her nothing and only set her back in her plans. "I will tell you this, once and only once, after that what happens is forever on you." She replied deathly calm. "Release me, let me walk away right now to disappear or before I draw my last breath in this life, I will make sure you die before me."

Everett's deep, booming laughter cut through the crisp evening air, drawing the attention from everyone within the camp. "You are something else, aren't you?" He took his foot off the chain and stepped back, allowing her to pull herself up onto her knees. "So, if I let you go right now, you'd just leave all your friends behind, abandon them to their fate? Not a care in the world, not a shred of guilt?"

"I don't have friends."

"What a horrible way to live. We all need friends."

"Friends are a weakness I have no time for."

"Interesting philosophy…" he paused, "What is your name?"

"Auska," she told him proudly, "and it will be your death."

He started to walk away. "Well, Auska, I will find out what the deal with Dirk is, with or without your help. In the meantime, 'dog', sleep well."

After he had gone and the others within the camp had settled their attention back to what they were doing before, she rubbed her neck. It stung painfully where the chain had dug in.

Curling up by the tree, she pulled her knees up near her. The night was already chilled and growing uncomfortable; the longer she could hold off shivering the more energy she could conserve for escaping.

"You just can't help yourself from making a scene, can you?" Jennifer said dispassionately with a sideways glance at her. It was the first thing she had said to her in nearly two days. Hopelessness had sunken its fangs into her and many of the others, and now they seemed to be little more than husks of their former selves. "Going to get yourself killed if you keep it up."

"I'll die with my chin in the air before I die cowering in fear," she shot back.

"So, tell me, Auska, when you finally escape and leave us all behind, will you even feel bad?"

Before Auska could reply a commotion began in the camp again.

"We got fresh stock, boys!" one of the slavers called out as he and four others returned to camp; in tow was a younger man and woman, and an older woman well into her fifties. Their hands were bound tightly behind their backs as they were led staggering into the camp.

Everett walked over to the group and began inspecting the newcomers with great interest. His imposing frame making the three prisoners shrink back as he paced around them, eyeing them like you would cattle you were going to buy.

"We found them huddled up in a small cave about a mile and a half from here," Brock told him. "Idiots had a fire going, could see it from a long way off. Not a weapon to be found, made it for easy pickings."

"Good work my friend." Everett clapped him on the back. "But we are overweight as-is. I fear to add three more bodies will slow us down more than we already are."

Without a word Brock pulled his hunting knife out and ran it across the older woman's throat, surprising everyone within eyesight. "How about just adding two more young able bodies?"

The woman's eyes bulged as she tried to cry out, only to sputter and choke as blood filled her lungs. Her legs finally gave out and she crashed to her knees staring up at her killer with contempt. She tried to mumble something but all that came out was a sputtered groan before she crumbled to the ground.

The young woman screamed out in distress trying to drop down to the woman, but the man holding her wouldn't allow it. "No, no, no! How could you do this! You are fucking assholes, she did nothing to you! She was innocent..."

"Might have done that out of the camp to not attract infected with the scent of fresh blood," Everett replied with a bit of irritation, "but yes, I think we can manage two more." He turned to the younger woman. "No one that has lived as long as she would still be able to claim innocence. But it all fairness that was likely the kindest way she could have hoped to die. Better a throat cut than to be torn apart by the infected or starving to death in the cold."

"You are monsters," the man said, staring down

at the dying old woman, his emotions detached.

"What was that," one of the guards that had brought the group in growled, "no jokes this time, funny man? No little quip and jab?"

"My wit would be wasted on the likes of you."

"What's that supposed to mean, funny man?"

Other slavers began to chuckle. "Mean's he's calling you dumb, Pike."

Pike turned a dangerous eye on the restrained man. "Is that so?" He unleashed a blow to the man's guts, doubling him over. "Maybe stupid, but I'm not the one tied up like a little bitch." He spat and walked away.

"Let us go, you filthy bastards!" the younger women screamed, pulling at her restraints only to have the man holding them yank her off her feet and push her to the ground.

"Got ourselves a lively one here," he jeered, smelling her blonde hair. "Lively normally means fun."

"You four did good work tonight, these two will bring in a decent price," Everett told them, looking the two survivors up and down. "Secure the 'funny man' and get this body far enough away from camp before it attracts any unwanted visitors." He stopped and looked over at the young woman. "Then you four may have some fun with our new guest as a reward. Don't damage her face and nothing that will cause scarring."

"You got it, boss!" they all chimed with devilish glee, their eyes burning with cruel lust.

"No!" the girl cried, trying to fight tooth and nail as two of the men dragged her across the camp to the far side, knowing what awaited her. "You can't do this to me! Let me go! Stop! Please don't do this!"

Auska turned her eyes from the scene; she knew what would happen next. Her blood grew dangerously cold and she almost wished she could help the woman. But deep down she knew if she had stumbled across this scene that she would have left it alone knowing the odds of helping were slim. The woman's fate was sealed, as were most of the people here.

"Get over there, idiot!" Pike grumbled pushing the man down to the ground near Auska's own tree as a new chain tether was put in place.

"You'll all pay for this," the man said with a chilling calm as the chain was secured around his neck and a heart-wrenching cry ripped through the night. "I'll make sure of it."

"Shut up, funny man," Pike tapped the knife at his side, "lest I feel the need to cut that smart tongue out. We can still make as good a profit off a mute as we can a comedian!" With a kick to the man's guts, Pike walked away towards the muffled screams on the other side of the camp, already loosening his belt.

"Remind me to kill that guy, slowly, when I get the chance." The young man groaned, pulling himself into a sitting position against the tree, clearly in pain. It didn't take him long before his bound hands were in front of him and free of the length of cord, which he stuffed in his pants.

Auska looked the newcomer over and nearly laughed out loud. He was no taller than herself and firm but skinny; if he weighed twenty pounds more than her, she would have been surprised. His face radiated a boyish softness in the growing darkness, with patchy facial hair that looked more suited for a seventeen-year-old boy. It made her wonder how he'd survived this long. She winced as the poor woman cried out again across camp and cheers from the slavers followed. That was how this man had survived... off the backs, misery, and death of others.

"The name's Wren."

The smooth voice cut through her thoughts and she realized she was still staring at him. "What did you say?"

"I said my name is Wren, what's yours?"

"I didn't ask."

He shrugged. "No, but I figured if we are to be tree neighbors we might as well know each other's names. Seems a better way of communicating than, "Hey you", don't you think?"

Auska rolled her eyes at his attempt at witty charm. "'Hey, you', suits me just fine."

A blood piercing wail that lasted for nearly a minute tore through the still evening and chilled everyone's blood to the bone instantly. All those chained to trees huddled closer to them, turning their eyes away and trying to shut out the sounds.

Jen edged her way closer. "God, what are they doing to her?"

"Destroying her," Wren replied, his voice

"I would have thought you'd be more concerned about your friend's predicament then you appear to be," Auska said, watching Wren closely. There was something different about this man, something she was unsure about.

He sighed remorsefully. "Truth be told, I've only known them for four days. The group I was travelling with for the past four months got overrun by a pack of infected. We were low on ammo and so we all bolted, hoping to find each other once we scattered the monsters." He rested his head up against the tree, clearly distraught. "I found a few of their bodies, even saw a few of them walking around with the infected that attacked us. The rest, I assume, just kept on running. So, I was on my own, again. I worked my way through the mountain passes for a few days solo, until one evening I smelt a campfire. I approached with caution and saw Caitlyn and Ellen huddled in the small overhang in a rock face. They looked like they hadn't eaten in a few days and I still had some food in my pack, so I approached them with my hands in the air. Thankfully they didn't have any bullets in the rifle they had, or I am sure they would have shot me dead before I had had a chance to speak. Turns out they were part of a similar-minded group travelling out this way before the turn of winter to find someplace called Sanctuary. Apparently, they are hidden out here in the mountains and take on able-bodied survivors. Or at least those are the rumors going around." He shrugged. "I doubt there is such a place, but the idea of hope is powerful."

Auska and Jen shared a glance, and before Auska could mouth the words "don't" Jen piped in. "We are from Sanctuary!"

Wren's interested showed easily in his eyes. "So, it's not just a myth, it is real. Well, at least I don't feel like such an idiot for joining the group to come searching for it. A shame they aren't going to see it, though."

"Neither will you," Auska cut in.

He looked almost hurt. "Surely you have no intention of telling your people to leave us to die out here when they come to save you from these heathens?"

"Our people are the reason these heathens have us," Auska explained, still annoyed that Jen gave such information out so easily. Not that it mattered now anyway.

"They sold us like cattle for winter supplies!" Jen spat bitterly, staring dangerously at one of the slavers as they walked by.

Wren cursed under his breath. "Well, that's very disheartening news. The rumors made it sound like it was different from the rest of the 'rulers' of the wastelands. A place that might care about the common folk for more than just slave workers. Guess even fantasy is twisted and cruel behind the covers."

Tears streaked Jennifer's face. "Yeah, everyone here thought that, too, even the ones that were born there. Raised plump and healthy to be sold off to the highest bidder."

Wrens eyes grew wide at that news. "That must have been a bitter pill to swallow. For what it's worth, I'm sorry."

They all grew quiet as a guard came around with their meager dinner and water. The slaver's urges at what he was missing out on kept his mind and eyes wandering over to the other end of camp where they had taken the girl, whose screams were lesser now as she tired and gave in. As soon as he moved onto the next group, Wren moved closer once again.

"So, when do we make a move to escape?"

Auska rolled her eyes. Of course, this man would try to latch onto a new group as quickly as possible; leeching onto others was the only way someone like him could hope to stay alive. "Escape whenever you feel you can," she muttered curling herself upon the ground.

"Well, that doesn't seem like a very good plan," he countered. "Strength in numbers and all seems better suited for this kind of thing."

"Auska doesn't believe in all for one, one for all," Jen replied with contempt. "More of a save yourself, kind of girl."

Before Auska could fire back a response, an all too familiar and terrifying sound filled her ears. The awkward, stumbling charge of flesh-hungry fiends from behind them. "Fuck, we got company!"

In one smooth motion, Wren was on his feet and back from the tree as far as his chain would allow, a fist-sized rock clutched tightly in his hand as he prepared himself for the attack.

"Coming in-between you two!" Jennifer called out; her fists balled up as her only weapon.

"Auska, go in low!" Wren called out.

Auska was taken back by the sudden command but knew their best bet was to work together. If he had even a faint plan, it would serve them well for her to play her part as needed, but she would be ready to act further.

The deranged, rotting fiend tore through the underground just behind their trees, locking its milky white eyes on Wren. It charged with a blood stopping screech, covering the distance quickly.

Auska dived forward and kicked out, her foot snapping through the knee of the ghoul. It pitched forward hitting the ground hard in a snarling rage, turning its attention to Auska, who was now closer prey in its eyes.

Even with a crippled leg, the fiend moved with frightening speed, launching itself at Auska, its chipped, blackened teeth snapping in eagerness at the meal to come. She tried to scamper back, but her metal tether had reached its length as it threw itself upon her. She got her legs up just in time to catch it in the chest with her feet. Its raw strength proved nearly too much for her as its putrid mouth snapped impossible close to her throat and she struggled to push it back.

Auska knew she would one day die horribly, shot down in a gunfight or ripped apart by a fiend just like this, but tethered to a tree by slavers was just excessively insulting.

A loud crack sounded in front of her and the weight of the creature gave way, slumping to the side. Over the top of her stood Wren, gore-splattered rock in hand.

"It's not over yet, up now!" Wren reached down and hauled her to her feet.

Auska turned just as another infected broke through the tree line. With a scream she charged, grabbing the chain tether in both hands as she banked as far as it would let her to the side, catching the fiend in the chest with the chain. She kept her momentum as she circled the tree pulling as hard as she could, slamming the creature into the trunk, pinning it with the chain.

Her arms and shoulders bulged as she pulled back, using the tree for support. The chain cut deep into the rotting flesh of the creature and through its pained howls, she could hear bones snapping.

The ground beneath her feet was quickly chewed up as she fought to kill the thing before it could overpower her efforts.

"Another one!" Jen yelled out. "Coming right for you!"

A gunshot rent through the chaos and all resistance left the chain, then another and the new threat dropped a dozen paces away in a gurgling sputter.

Auska fell back and gasped for air; the muscles in her arms and legs burned far more than she had noticed.

"Well, well, that was quite the show." Brock sneered, holstering his sidearm. "Though I have to admit I was rooting for the infected for a while." He gave all three bodies a solid kick before tearing the rock from Wren's hand with a disapproving glare.

The camp was alive now. Slavers were arming themselves quickly, their eyes feverishly on the lookout for any movement from beyond the dull reach of the light from the camp.

"What are you standing around for!" Brock growled at a few of them that were just standing around. "Perimeter check! No more damn surprises tonight!"

"That was quite the display." Everett clapped exiting his large canvas tent. "I, for one, was on the edge of my seat the entire time. But unlike Brock here, I was rooting for you two the entire time. I wouldn't be much of a businessman if I got excited over possibly losing talented merchandise."

"A man has got to have priorities," Wren spat in disgust.

Everett eyed them both with growing interest. "That he does, and this man's priorities have just grown in a different direction. Brock, get this mess cleaned up and get patrols out half-mile around camp. I want no more fucking surprises tonight! Tomorrow we change course for the Abyss!"

Auska didn't need to know more about what place Everett was talking about; the terrified or eager looks on the faces of his men told her enough. The growing pit in her guts told her it was a place she might have known once, and deep down she hoped she was wrong.

———————◦———————

"We got a runner!" was screamed at the top of someone's lungs just as the first rays of morning broke through the canopy of trees, tearing everyone from slumber.

Instantly, the camp was in motion. A group of five set off in pursuit of whoever was lucky enough to make a run for it. Other guards swarmed around the prisoners checking the chains and locks, ensuring no further escape attempts were being made.

"Who was it?" someone asked from two trees over.

"I don't know, I can't see," another called over.

"Shut up!" Dirk barked, cradling this rifle eagerly. "No talking."

"It was Parry!" a woman's voice beamed from across the camp. "He's going to get help! We're going to be saved!"

"I said shut the fuck up!" the guard growled, stepping closer to the woman, threatening.

A man a few trees down stood up proudly. "We will be free soon, help will come!" he proclaimed.

One of the guards laid him low with the butt end of his rifle. "Stay down and shut the fuck up!"

Auska grinned to herself; so, he had taken what she had said to heart and made a run for it to save himself. She made no illusion that he would make it back to Sanctuary alive; on foot, it would take a week. Parry had no food or weapons, nor the skills needed to fight off the infected he would surely come across. Even the slim chance that he did make it back, what would happen to him? He would no more have a welcoming return to warn them as she did. No, he was as good as dead, by one means or another. Still, she respected him for taking the chance.

Auska laid down. When her time came to escape, she knew she would be more than capable of surviving on her own. The only issue with Parry escaping first was now the guards would be even more alert than they already were, more so with her no less.

"Lucky bastard," whispered Wren. "Though whenever you are ready, just say the word and we, too, can make a run for it."

"If only it were that easy."

"Have a little faith in me, and you might find that it is."

"I've seen what happens to people you group up with," she countered coldly. "You just need someone to help you stay alive."

"I am wounded, but you aren't completely wrong," he said with no hint of offense taken. "But we all need others to stay alive, as we all have our strong points and uses. One of mine happens to be very useful in the situation we are now," he tapped the chain around his neck.

"I stay alive just fine by myself, it's only when working with others," she glanced at Jennifer who was clearly hurt by the words, "that I end up in situations like this."

Wren looked between the two women and could see the tension and growing animosity. "Don't forget my offer, Auska, it might not last forever."

———○———

The sound of angry jeering and cries of pain shifted the camp into nervous alertness once more. It had been nearly three hours since Parry had made his escape, and everyone was beginning to believe he had truly gotten away.

"Everett, we caught the little bastard!" one of the men who had given chase announced proudly, strutting into view with a cocky grin on his dirty face, a very bloody and haggard Parry in tow.

Auska was on her feet, trying to get a better look as they came in through the tree line. She could hear the murmurs and whispers of those around her. The disappointment and realization that help would not be coming were clear in all their crestfallen expressions.

The slaver's leader made his way from his tent to where Parry knelt on the ground, blubbering like a child, his cheeks stained with countless tears already. "Good work, gentlemen." Everett nodded to the group that had brought the slave back. He started to pace around the kneeling man. "Did you have a fun little run in the woods? Was it exhilarating thinking you had escaped from the vile clutches of the bad men?" The big man moved around to face Parry. "Well, come on now, was it? You can tell me."

Parry's lips quivered in fear as he tried to lift his eyes to the giant of a man in front of him, but terror prevented him from reaching his eyes. "F...uck... youuuu...," he stuttered out.

Everett stood up, a look of mock surprise upon his face. "Such bitter vulgarity! When all I did was ask a few simple little questions." His demeanor turned hard as he grabbed a fist full of Parry's hair, jarring his head back forcing him to look up into the violent, steel grey eyes. "I hope your little outing was worth it because you've wasted my time now!" He spat and stood up. "Hobble him and let's move out! Another day and we will be at the Abyss, where there's money to be made!" This brought a round of cheers from the slavers, though some still were clearly not eager to go there. But the promise of wealth always pushed back fear.

Before Parry realized what was happening, a blade sliced through the back of his right achilleas tendon. A scream of anguish tore through the late morning air, sinking the prisoner's morale even lower.

Auska stood firmly as Everett walked closer to her, his eyes burning with excitement. "Let what you just have seen sink in deep, because keep up the shit and you'll be next." Without another word, he walked off.

Watching Parry struggle as they wrapped a cloth around his wound and threw him into one of the trailers sent the first true shiver of fear through her. To be hobbled would be to forfeit any hope of escaping or long-term survival out here. It would be worse than death; it would be suppression. She would die before she allowed that to happen.

The last of the dried, canned food supplies were carted into the storage room. The three men from the First Division that had been bringing it in over the last three days wiped sweat from their faces as they accepted glasses of water from Kelli.

"Well, that's all of it, finally," Owen, a middle-aged man who had been in Sanctuary for twelve years, said.

"So much more than I expected," Vincent told them as he eyed it all. This was only about seventy percent of what had come in, the rest had needed to go into the freezers or cold storage.

"Yeah, it was a good haul," another of the men replied with a sly grin. "Got a good deal this time."

"A good deal?" Vincent asked confused.

"A good deal from those raiders," Owen spoke again, his eyes glaring at the man who had spoken, "had we not found them and killed them, this would have only made them stronger, more of a threat."

"Right," Vincent replied, "of course. A great find for Sanctuary, indeed. You boys did well, plus fewer raiders in the world can only be a good thing for everyone."

"You know it," the third man finally spoke, though he shuffled nervously. "Hope now that everything is here there will be a big dinner tonight."

Vincent nodded. "I got something good planned, might even toss in a little extra for you three since you had to do so much work the last few days."

Owen clapped him on the back. "That would be mighty fine of you, Vincent, we'll be looking forward to it."

Finishing their water, they took their leave and left the kitchen with haste.

"Well, that was weird," Kelli said, cleaning up the mess they had made on the floor. "The men from the first always make me nervous."

"That's because they are dangerous, and they know it," he explained. "The worst part is they know people know it, and they flaunt it around like a badge of fucking honor."

"I can't believe how much food they got. Far more than what we first expected and what was on that list. With what we grew this year, and this, we will have plenty of food for the winter and well into spring." She was smiling warmly at the stockpile.

Vincent was thinking the same thing. The list the council had given him had been large enough, but what was brought in was clearly more. He stared at the full storage room, suspicion running wild in him once more. "What if she was right?"

Kelli looked around cautiously. "Don't start again Vincent. I just got you to calm down about it, things are just starting to go back to normal. People we called friends are finally coming around and talking to us again. Don't start again… please!"

"But what if she was telling the truth? Look at it all, Kelli. You can't tell me a band of raiders could have gathered all that in a few days of raiding around here." He walked into the room and touched several of the boxes and crates where various canned good and boxed food was now stored. "Think about it! What Auska said makes more sense than raiders, way more sense and the more I think about it, it would start to piece other things together as well."

"They wouldn't do that. They built this place up for the safety of the people here. They may be assholes and full of themselves and live far better than we do, but they still shaped this place for the purpose of protecting the people within. And we are safe here, far safer than we ever were out there."

"Or maybe they shaped it for the protection of themselves?" He caught her eye and knew she wished he would stop thinking about it, but he couldn't, or more to the point, wouldn't. "To them, what are a few lives for a winter supply of food? A few lives to keep the walls safe, to keep them safe. They don't risk anything but ask and take everything from every other soul here."

"Listen to yourself!"

"I'd rather you listened to me!" he snapped back, with more venom then he had truly intended. "Think about it, Kelli! Every year, we struggle to find and grow enough food, and yet every year we get by. Also every year, people get sick and die, or go missing out on patrol to never be seen or found again."

"People go missing and die out there, you know that." She scorned him. "It's a dangerous place, or have we been here too long that you've forgotten what it is like? Maybe you should go out with one of the Divisions and see what it's like again for a few days."

"I have forgotten nothing of the world out there. But maybe you've forgotten the horrible nature some people can turn to for survival... for power."

She packed away the broom now that the floor was clean. He needed to let it go; what was done was done, nothing would change that now. But he was holding on for dear life to something that pushing would bring nothing but problems.

"Think about it, how long could any one of them survive out there on their own?" he questioned her. "You've seen them. They are soft, fat, old, nothing in their features show the hardships of what this world has done to those who have had to live in it! They have stationed themselves in a place of power, found this place at the beginning, rallied stronger men and women to it, promised them safety, food, shelter and as close to a 'normal' life as one can have. All without ever having to put themselves at risk."

"That doesn't make them monsters, Vincent. Just means they used what they had to stay alive. We survived because we were tough and had sense; they survived because they got lucky and had a vision and knew how to rally people."

"But how long do they stay alive if we all run out of food? When do the people start looking to them to fix it? I've talked to others before we arrived; they had some hard years, people starved to death, riots that needed putting down. What better way to stay on top and keep the population down enough to keep in check then to sell a few off each year? A sickness here, an accident there, a patrol that was ambushed, runaways? Tell me it doesn't make sense to you!"

Kelli hated this. "Vincent, you are reaching too far."

"But what if it is?"

"What would it change Vincent? What difference would it really make? We are alive, the people within the walls are alive, we are safe, we have food, we aren't fighting every second of every day just to see the sunrise once more!"

Her words cut him deeply. "How can you say that? How can you justify it like that?"

"What else is there?" she countered. "If it's happening, it's horrible, but WE, Vincent, are alive and well. WE have a place to call home. WE no longer have to fight every waking moment." She sighed. "Ever since the virus hit and I had to kill my first infected, then my first person, all I have wanted was somewhere safe, somewhere that I could feel some form of normal again. Before I met you, the hospital base was great, life there was good. Dangerous, still, but manageable. Once that got destroyed, I never expected to find a place I could truly feel safe again.

These last years here have been the closest we are ever going to get, and I accept that and don't want to risk losing it."

In all his years he had known her, loved her, he had never expected this side of her, never dreamed she could be so cold. "I need to get some air."

"Vincent, please!" she begged as he left the kitchen without another word.

———◦○◦———

Vincent threw open the door and stepped out into the chill of the afternoon. The sun was shining brightly, but the promise of winter's first snowfall was days away.

He stalked off, with no particular place in mind, he just needed to be moving, his mind was his worst enemy right now, and he needed to get it right before he could face Kelli again. Her words had wounded him greatly, angered him, confused him, made him sick to his stomach and worse, almost made justifiable sense. And that thought made him hate himself even more.

Something wasn't right in Sanctuary. Something sinister was happening right in front of everyone and he needed to find out what, not only so Auska's name could know peace but so the people of Sanctuary could know the truth. Then and only then could Sanctuary become what it should have always been.

Before he realized it, he was standing outside

Preston's shelter. It was an old structure, once the work camp's small mailing house; now turned into the small home of one of the oldest people living in Sanctuary.

Preston had been one of the first settlers, had come within the first few months that Sanctuary was first being established. He knew the whole history; every nail hammered, every bullet fired, every person that lived and died there.

"What are you doing here now?" a gruff voice barked out. "It's not time yet you fucking idiot! Were you followed?"

Vincent was stirred from his thoughts and saw the older man moving around from the back of the shack; the sixty-three-year-old looked none too impressed to see him. "I'm... I'm not sure. I was just going for a walk and ended up here I guess."

"You guess?" he questioned, his eyes searching all around them for any hint of movement.

Cocking an eyebrow, Vincent began looking around, confused and suddenly worried. "I'm not sure... I wasn't trying to hide my movements. As I said I was just walking. Needed to clear my head."

"Well, get your ass inside already before anyone sees you, damn it!" he growled, stomping off into his house. "And close the damn door!"

Unsure of what was happening, Vincent quickly followed the old man and closed the door as he had said. "Look, Preston, I'm not sure what this is about or anything. I really was just going for a walk."

"Don't play stupid with me. You're here, which

means you found my note," he said, putting a kettle on a small propane burner to boil water.

Now Vincent truly was confused. "Note? What note?"

Preston turned a dangerous eye on him. "The note I left inside your boot," he looked down and cursed. "Those aren't the boots I put the note in!"

"Note? Note about what? Jesus, what the hell are you talking about man?"

"About meeting me tonight! Not in the middle of the fucking afternoon!"

Vincent sat down on a chair by a small table. "Okay, now I truly am confused."

"I am guessing the other set of boots were Kelli's?" he asked with all seriousness.

"Well, yes they had to be."

"I am assuming since she didn't give you the note that she must have not seen it and it is still in the boot. When she takes them off, be sure to remove the note and destroy it or we all might regret it."

"Okay, what the fuck is going on?" Vincent burst out.

Preston moved to the window and looked out from the crack in the thick curtains. "Keep your fucking voice down idiot! Look, the more time we waste the more likely we will get caught talking and then we both will have more problems than we will know what to do with."

Vincent threw up her arms in defeat. "I am all ears for whatever it is you feel you need to tell me."

"Your suspicions are likely correct." He poured

two cups with steaming water and added a random teabag to each and handed one to his unexpected visitor.

"My suspicions?" Vincent knew what he was talking about, but this topic was a dangerous one, and letting it slip out to just anyone would be stupid.

"I said enough with the dance. You know what I mean. The council, the missing or 'sick' folk." He sighed. "I have lived here a long time, and I have witnessed a lot, and slowly pieced together all the small but subtle changes that have occurred. And when I heard you talking to Kelli after what happened with Auska, it was like a key piece that I had been missing clicked."

"So, you believe the council is trading its own people for supplies then?" Vincent asked, excited to finally be talking about it to someone who believed in the possibility.

The older man sipped his tea. "After what your girl told you before they took her away and killed her, there isn't a doubt in my mind anymore."

The reminder made him wince. "So, she caught them in the act, and they lied to justify killing her to keep the secret?"

"It would seem most likely."

"Holy fuck. We need to tell everyone," Vincent stammered. "People need to know this. Then we can storm the council's little castle and put an end to this!"

"That would just get us killed, and likely not as nice as Auska died, granted."

Vincent was confused. "Not once the secret is out! Once we blow the whistle, everyone will know. Then any move made against us would only prove it!"

"And we'd still be dead and I'll not be made a martyr, not like that anyway," Preston told him without give. "Besides, not a single soul out there is going to believe a word we say, at least not without solid proof. They are cattle, Vincent. They will do and believe what they are told because a carrot of safety and a full belly dangle in front of them."

Vincent was about to argue the fact, but the man was correct. The people here had come to rely on the council and all it did for them. They trusted them, revered them in a way. The council gave them all the safety of Sanctuary. If he tried to blow the whistle without solid proof, all they would hear is fabrications from a man whose adopted daughter betrayed them and murdered several of their own. No, Preston was correct, they needed real hard evidence.

"How do we get that proof?"

Preston looked out the window again. "Million fucking dollar question right there. But I may have some clues that might lead to some solid evidence. About twelve maybe thirteen years ago, near the same time the first major 'accident' happened and people went missing, a friend of mine told me the council was digging a secret tunnel out of Sanctuary, in the event we were overrun and needed to get out. Claimed he was one of the workers on the job and was sworn to secrecy with the promise of extra rations for the next five years. Now, he was a drunkard and wasn't sober when he told me, so I passed it off as bollocks, but he was one of the first to have an 'accident' and go missing. Along with several others who often were gone long weeks at a time, 'scouting' the area. People who, as I recall now, were awful quiet and strangely secretive."

Vincent was listening intently. "So, you believe there is a tunnel, and that would be how they transferred the 'sick' outside without anyone seeing? Claim they died and the bodies had to be burned before anything could spread!" He slapped his leg. "Fuck, it makes so much sense."

"It does, now the only problem is finding the fucking thing to prove it. I have a few ideas but nothing for sure, though if I were a betting man, I would suspect it was somewhere close to the infirmary. And I'll tell you this right now, son: you'll be doing this on your own. If you can find it and find enough proof, I'll stand by you, but I'll not get myself killed for anything. I've survived too long to go out like that."

"Well, if I can find this tunnel and where it leads, maybe I'll be able to find all the proof we need. Then we can turn the tides and expose the council for what they are!"

Preston waved him silent, as he perked up. "Someone is outside!" he whispered and went to a picture on the wall, which moved aside, and he peered out a small hole. "Two of them. It's Tavish from the First Division and another fellow." He replaced the picture and cursed. "Damn it, they know you are here! Or they are looking for you!"

Vincent's heart began beating faster. With everything they had just talked about, then it was likely they were indeed keeping tabs on him. "Shit, is there anywhere in here I can hide?"

Preston rolled his eyes. "Don't be fucking stupid! That'll never work if they come to the door, idiot."

"Fine, just play along then!" Vincent grumbled, pulling a plan from his ass, knowing he needed to leave before any more suspicion could be cast.

"What the fuck are you doing!" Preston went to grab for him, but Vincent was already opening the door and stepping out.

"Look, Preston, I like you, I really do old man, and I thank you for the cup of tea," Vincent began, "but any tea or coffee that was brought it this week is to be rationed out during mealtimes. I can't trade food supplies under the table like that. You out of all people should know this."

Preston caught on quickly. "I know, I know, I wasn't trying to make it sound like that, but if you could ask the council on my behalf, maybe they'd listen to you. Winter is coming around, and something warm on those bitter cold nights help this old body sleep just a little bit better."

Vincent threw up his hands in defeat. "Fine, I will ask them when next I get the chance, but I make no promises. Now I have to get back to the kitchens and start getting dinner ready or I am going to have a lot of pissed-off hungry people."

With that said Vincent turned and walked away, catching from the corner of his eyes the two men hiding in the shadows of several small trees. Good, he thought, that would curb any suspicions they might think… at least he hoped so. Suddenly this was becoming all too real and all too dangerous. But the danger he could manage if it meant finding out the truth and exposing the lies, for all of them… and Auska.

———————◦◦———————

"Thank you for meeting with me on such short notice."

"Yes, yes, of course. What news do you have that is so important to bother us?"

"Someone knows the truth or is close to the truth."

"Vincent?"

"No, but they tried to contact him. A note was found, they were to meet up tonight, by the old water tower."

"Who?"

"The note gave no name, just said it was important and to meet them there tonight just before midnight."

"I see, and what about Vincent. What have you been able to find out?"

"He is still confused it seems, but I believe he isn't a threat, at least not yet."

"Are you sure about this?"

"Yes."

"Good. Keep up the good work and don't get caught. You are proving most useful. We would hate to see that end."

———◦———

Auska stared out the bared window slot in the rolling prison that housed them as the trucks slowly bounced their way through the densely wooded area. She could see the large rock cliff face jutting up in the distance in the direction they were going.

Already flashes were coming back to her of a time that almost felt like forever ago; when Archer and a young girl had been ambushed in this very spot by wire across the path. Flipping the motorcycle, they had stolen from men who only hours before almost killed them. Cannibals had attacked them moments after the crash. Archer had been badly wounded and unable to defend himself, and she had run, killing two in the process.

She shook her head, hardly believing that she had once been so young and naïve, so foolish to the ways of the world. Her parents had damned her by keeping her ignorant; had it not been for Archer she would have been dead a long time ago. If it hadn't been for her parents a lot of people might not have died from the grand lie they were living. But at the same time, she never would have met Archer either, and that was time and memories she would never regret.

"Jesus Christ!" Someone mutter behind her. "Are those... human remains?"

"Where the fuck are they taking us?"

"Those... those are human bones! So many of them!" A woman cried out.

It was true. There were far more now than there had been when she had last been here, hundreds more. They dangled from the trees like sick ornaments, swaying in the breeze like some morbid wind chimes. Others were nailed to the trunks, splayed out in warnings of the fate to come to those who wondered to close to the den of beasts.

"It's called the Abyss. It's the realm of cannibals," Auska told them, her tone dead flat.

The word 'cannibal' was muttered around her in fearful tones.

"How do you know this?" asked Wren.

She turned and her face was hollow. "I've been here before... a long time ago."

"We're all going to die, aren't we?" another man asked.

Auska turned back to the small window. The smell of death was growing thicker as they drew closer to the cliff face where the entrance was. Flashes of bringing the axe down on the man stuck in the mud... the sleeping guard on the cliff face trail... the fear... the panic... back then had nearly destroyed her.

"You've really been here before, haven't you?" Wren asked, seeing the darkness in her eyes.

"It was half a lifetime ago."

"You couldn't have been more than a kid?"

"I was twelve."

He leaned back against the metal wall as the trucks slowed and a large group of people could be seen gathering ahead. "So, what can we expect?"

"They are going to make us fight to the death against other slaves. Those who die become food."

"Oh, that's all?" Wren muttered. "Here I thought it was going to be something horrible and morbid."

The trucks stopped a hundred feet from the massive mine entrance. Nearly fifty cannibals were already crowded outside, more slowly filtering out. Their clothing was tattered and pieced together with bones, metal and human skin. They all carried weapons; many had rifles or handguns, a few had crudely made bows, others carried sadistically constructed melee weapons of all varieties.

Everett climbed down from the truck, keeping his weapons holstered and making sure his men kept theirs in check. Dealing with the Abyss dwellers was always a challenge, one that could very easily result in death on a large scale for either side.

"Greetings," Everett called out, "I wish to speak to Tonka."

A tall, lean man stepped out, wearing nothing more than a loincloth made of human skin. Blood was smeared in designs all over her face and body. "What makes you think Tonka is even still alive?"

"That's true," Everett replied, "it has been a while since I was last here, much could have changed. But I somehow doubt it."

"What makes you doubt?"

"Well, his markers are still up. If he was no longer chief, then new ones would have replaced them," he told the cannibal. "But mostly because he would never have let a single one of you stupid pricks overtake him."

A booming laugh came from the entrance as a large, brute of a man stepped out, trumping all those around him. Tonka was nearly seven feet tall and well over four-hundred pounds of both muscle and fat. "You always were too stupid for your own good."

The two men clasped hands, Everett feeling like a child next to the massive man. "I was almost worried someone else was in charge."

Tonka grinned rubbing his belly. "Many have tried."

The thought made Everett uneasy. He knew Tonka very little and had sold him slaves before, but what the man was and what his followers were, scared the shit out of him, though he'd never show it.

"So, Everett, what brings you to my realm?" The massive man looked over to the trucks.

"Why else would I come? I have wares to sell, though most of them are spoken for, but a few I can part with."

"Any worth anything to me?"

Everett motioned for his men to bring the slaves out and line them up. "Might be a fight or two in some of them. At least they will taste good, they have lived a soft, comfortable life."

"Come, we will talk trade inside; your men can stay out here... where it's safe." Tonka turned to leave.

"Well, there is something else I wouldn't mind talking to you about."

"What is it?"

"I have a fighter I want to bet on in the pit."

"Ha!" Tonka laughed. "You bring a fighter, but want to keep them for yourself?"

Everett shrugged. "A man can't give everything good away. Besides they might not prove to be that good against hardened fighters like yours."

Tonka eyed the group of slaves that were lined up. "Doesn't look like a fighter in the lot to me. Everyone looks soft and pathetic."

Everett turned to one of his men. "Bring her out."

"Her?" Tonka was grinning now.

Auska was pushed out in front and forced to stand in front of the two large men. At first, she thought to act weak and pathetic, hoping the cannibal leader would turn down the offer, but she couldn't bring herself to do so. She stared defiantly up at them both, her shoulders burning with the effort of trying to break free from her restraints.

"The fire in this one's eyes shows strength," Tonka said. "But that doesn't mean she can fight."

Everett rubbed his jaw. "I know for a fact she can."

"I will be the judge of that. Come, we will talk,

barter, and maybe tonight we will see what your fighter can do."

———————◦———————

Everett sat on the surprisingly comfortable and well-maintained couch within a large, nearly smoothed walled room of the underground city. This was likely the nicest room in the whole underground world the cannibals had created. It was the leader's dwelling, likely had always been the leader's dwelling.

He wondered how many different leaders had ruled here since the infection had destroyed the world. Ten? Twenty? Thirty? How many people had died here? How many people eaten? Thousands, he imagined and fought back a shiver that ran up his spine.

The massive cannibal leader poured two glasses of an amber liquid from a faded bottle. "Pure rye whiskey not watered down. Won't find much of that out in the world anymore." He placed the glass in front of Everett who picked it up and inhaled the aroma deeply, savoring it fully before taking a sip.

"Been a long time since I have tasted pure anything."

Tonka grinned. "We may be savages, but some of us still enjoy the finer things that life still has to offer. So," he placed his drink down on the wooden table between them as he sat his massive frame down on the seat across, "tell me about these slaves you have. They do not look like your typical bunch. They appear healthier, cleaner… the hardness of life hasn't aged them nearly as bad."

Everett sipped the drink again relishing in the warm burn that slid down his throat to rest in his uneasy stomach. "That is because they haven't. I have acquired a new source of slaves, all like the ones you see in my possession now. Though it only comes once a year and is costly to me, the profits of such slaves prove worth it. My buyers enjoy soft, clean, healthy girls and women that have never felt a cruel hand far more than the roughly broken tramps you can catch out here on the daily. The men, well, they also sell well for entertainment purposes."

"You evade my question well."

"No question was asked."

Tonka's face turned sour. "Are we going to continue to play games with one another? Fine, I will ask plainly. Where did these slaves come from?"

The slaver put his hands up in defense. "That I will not tell you. Surely you know a good source of 'wares' is to be guarded in this day and age. Besides, I wouldn't want you going there and eating all my future profits. The deal I have once a year pays well, leaving enough to 'repopulate'."

Tonka boomed with laughter, his thick neck bouncing with each breath. "Fair play." Then he turned serious. "You know I could just torture it out of you. You and your little band of slavers would be easily overrun by my hordes."

Everett knew he was on dangerous ground, but

still, he held firm. "No need for threats; you are my first stop, I thought of you first of all. I know cannibals enjoy the 'finer' tastes of life. Surely a few well 'raised' cattle would be worth bartering for each year." The thought of this conversation made him sick, but he held his conviction; if he didn't, he doubted he would leave this room alive.

Tonka took a large gulp of his drink, his eyes never leaving the man in front of him. "You're are not wrong in this. We would be willing to pay a decent price for such delicacies. But do not play me for a fool. You did not 'think' of me first. You thought of that woman you have with you, that fighter you think she is."

He nodded. "That is the truth, she cost me dearly to get her. She wasn't part of the original deal. But because she happened to mess up the transaction, her people were kind enough to give her to me as compensation for the men she killed. Also to keep her quiet about their dirty little secret."

"Let us talk fights, then."

"Gladly." Everett smiled, happy this conversation was going better than he had expected.

"Your fighter will fight three fights. She may pick the first, you may pick the second and I shall pick the third. If she can survive them all, I will pay you what you would get for all your slaves. But should she lose, then I get all your slaves."

It was a huge offer. If he won, he would be set for the rest of the year; if he lost, he would have to work far harder to recoup his losses than he wanted to.

Was this girl worth the risk, he wondered? Worst off now is he doubted he could back out of this without dying. "I can agree to those terms. But she should be permitted a few hours rest between fights, to have wounds looked at and to regain her strength."

"Fine. But as a token of this deal, that slave of yours, the one who can hardly stand, I'd like to have him for dinner tonight." Tonka said, putting out his meaty hand.

It took everything within Everett to keep from retching in front of the man. "Deal." He took the cannibals hand in his own and they shook.

"Excellent, I will send a man out to collect him. I want him prepared just right for my meal during the fights tonight. Hopefully, he tastes as good as he looks."

Everett quickly left the leader behind, feeling dizzy and nauseous. He stopped in the tunnel just outside the door to gather himself. "What the fuck am I doing?" he muttered to himself. He should never have come here, but there was no leaving this unfinished now. But he promised himself he would never return. This was cruelty beyond even him.

Auska sat crouched on the balls of her feet in the small cell. It wasn't the same one she had found Archer in all those years ago. She wasn't even sure if it was the same room, but none of that mattered. The smell of human waste and death hung in the air like paste, burning the eyes and coating the tongue with a bitter film of despair.

Looking around, she was relieved to see the guards had finally moved on. She edged herself to the lock, being sure to avoid the barbed wire that encased her cell. The dried blood covering dozens of the razors showing many passed visitors and their clumsiness or failed attempts to break free.

Searching her cell, she looked for anything, anything at all, that she might be able to use to pick the lock, but there was nothing. Of course, there was nothing, they wouldn't be so foolish. Not like she was overly skilled in such a talent, but it was better than doing nothing.

"Only one way out of here girl." A battered form three cells across from her called over. There were several others, but most were sleeping, or maybe even dead in their cells.

"Had to try, right?" She slumped back down.

His chuckle was void of emotion. "Yeah, we all do, but even if you got out, you'd never make it out of here alive."

"I did once before."

This time his chuckle had mirth in it. "Of course, you did, girl, of course, you did."

"I wonder if someone will come to save me," she sighed. No one was coming for her, she was on her own. She would find a way; she had to.

"If they do, can I tag along?" he asked.

"Sure, why not?"

Everett and three cannibal guards walked into

the large carved rock room where prisoners were being housed. The smell nearly overwhelmed him, but the three guards hardly seemed to notice. He eyed all the cages until they locked on the one he was looking for.

"Hope they are treating you well," he teased, with little mirth behind it.

Auska glared at him with disgust. "Better this than your company."

"You wound me," he tapped his chest, "but enough of the formalities. I have a deal for you, one that might interest you greatly."

"Only thing that would interest me right is you stepping into the pit with me and let me show you how pathetic you really are in front of a crowd!"

"That would be quite the feat, but I think I can do you one better. How would you like your freedom?"

She rolled her eyes. "Because I am going to believe you would be so generous."

"Regardless of what you choose to believe, I am telling the truth. I have arranged a 'contest' if you will. One that, if you win, will see me with far more then you could bring me. I am a businessman first; a cruel, heartless slaver second."

"You tell me this as if I have a choice."

His grin was wicked. "You do... well, kind of. You could just die in spite of it, then I will lose a great deal. See, if you lose, all the slaves I have in my possession right now will, well, become food. So, your friends from Sanctuary will all suffer for your loss. Now I know you claim to not care, and I almost believe you, so I sweetened the deal by giving you your freedom. You win and you walk away from here, with weapons and supplies to see you on your way for a good while. You have my word."

Auska wanted to throw herself at the cage wall, to lash out at him, grab him and slam him into the barbed wire, but she knew he was too far away and it would only injure her more.

"Since I don't have a choice, I might as well know what this 'contest' is."

"That's what I wanted to hear." He clapped his hands excitedly. "You will have to win three fights. Don't worry, I am kind enough to ensure you will get breaks in-between."

"Who will I be fighting?" She was not keen on the prospect of fighting three different times, but there was nothing she could do about it... except win!

He shrugged his massive shoulders. "You get to pick your first fight from his warriors, I will pick the second, and he will pick the final, should you make it that far." He reached into his jacket and handed her a bottle of water and a large cut of dried meat. "I need you to have your strength up for this."

She eyed the food suspiciously.

"Don't worry, it's deer, not human. I'm not sick like them," he told her, knowing what she had to be thinking. He stared hard at her, feeling her hatred towards him, which he understood. How could he not? "Look, girl, do this, and live until the end and you will have what you want." He stepped back, eyed her again. "Do not disappoint me." With that, he left.

Auska grabbed the water and food and ate it quickly. There was no choice here; she would have to fight soon and to survive she needed any advantage she could get. Even if it had been human meat, she would have eaten it.

Glaring at the doorway where she had watched him leave, she spat. "I will fight and I will win, but I already promised you death and I will make sure that happens before this is over."

Auska was forced down the torch-lit tunnels. Ahead of her, she could hear what sounded like rushing water, but knew it was the roaring of a hundred cannibals baying for blood; her blood… her flesh. *They will have blood, but it won't be mine, at least not the last of it,* she told herself firmly as fear crept into her with each step. Survival in the wastelands was one thing. This… this was something else entirely. This was demonic and base in the worst way humanly possible.

As she was pushed along, she remembered vague memories of these very tunnels and knew one of them led to the secret entrance at the top of the cliff face they had used to escape over a decade before. She couldn't for the life of her remember which turn off it had been, but then again, she had left a small mark on the walls near the floor; she looked for those marks now but saw nothing. The years had likely worn them away long ago.

Each one she was forced passed… her imagination tried to create the markings, her senses told her she could smell fresh air coming for that one, or the next one. But she knew it was all bullshit. She was scared; for once in her life she was terrified of what was about to happen. The likelihood she could make it out of this alive was slim, the odds too stacked against her.

"How the fuck did you manage this?" she whispered to herself, remembering Archer having to fight for his very life in this same place. She knew how, though; he had been so much stronger than she could ever hope to be. He had been cold, calculated, hard, and deadly… all the things she had tried to become, all the things she told herself she was, but now doubt was ripping through her fabric, exposing her to herself.

The hairs on her arms and neck stood on end at the raw energy pouring through the tunnel exit, where a locked gate stood before her. The noise coming from within was deafening and turned her blood cold as ice. This was the path to hell, where death was the only absolute.

"Time to die, slave," one of the guards grunted, pushing her through the opening before slamming it closed again.

Auska felt her stomach tighten as the crowd roared even louder. Some cheered, others booed, while others seemed not to care so long as there was blood. Every single set of eyes was upon her, and they all were cruel, glistening with malice.

The pit was roughly twenty feet by twenty feet and as close to a circle as they had cared to carve it. The floor was bumpy and jagged in areas and was slick and crusted with decades of spilt blood and gore.

"Welcome to the pit!" the massive cannibal leader called down to her as he waved his hands, calming the hordes to a minimum level so he could be heard.

Auska saw he had what looked like a cooked arm in his hand that he had been chewing on. Resting in front of him was a sight that nearly made her knees buckle: Parry's severed head, his eyes staring blanking down at her. This was really happening. Dying was one thing; being eaten was something completely different. The thought of being eaten sent a wave of violence rippling through her as she had never known before. *I will not fucking die here!*

"Your owner has put great faith in you and your abilities as a fighter," Tonka called down to her, grease from his *meat* dripping from his chin.

The word 'owner' stirred her blood even more and she felt the fear leaving her, replacing it with a cold, calculated rage. She had to survive this, if nothing more than so she could kill that bastard!

"He informed you already of the terms of your challenge. The fight, I hear, is for your very freedom. How exciting for you! Though I don't wish you any luck, your flesh will be sweet as candy and I can't wait to taste it!" Tonka yelled down to her and the crowd roared up again louder than before. "Now, pick your opponent!"

"Everett!" she cried out, pointing her finger straight at the slaver. "I want him!" Her eyes burned into his in her death stare.

Tonka grinned but shook his head. "I admire your spirit, girl, but those were not part of the terms. You must pick from my fighters."

Cursing, she stole once last glare at the slaver, who was clearly not enjoying himself. *He's scared, too,* she thought. *His life rides on this likely as much as mine does.* "Fine, him." She pointed to the biggest man she could see in the front row. If she had to pick, she would show them all she was not afraid of them, that one by fucking one she would kill each and every one of them if she had to.

"Blackfist, you have been chosen!" Tonka announced, and once more the room shook and Auska was sure they would cause a cave in.

Grinning, Blackfist jumped from the stands and landed on the other side of the pit. Waving his arms in the air, causing the crowd to chant his name. "I will crush this little bitch's skull and feast on her brains!" he roared.

Tonka turned to Everett. "She has chosen very poorly. He will tear her apart limb from limb in seconds. But let's make this even more interesting." He turned back to the crowd. "Knives!"

Blanching, Everett turned to the cannibal leader. "Seriously? Knives? Could you put her anymore at a disadvantage with a man that size?"

"I thought you said she was a fighter. A fighter can use anything at their disposal to win and not always it is something that is in their favor."

Everett felt his guts twist. This had been a stupid idea; he should have known Tonka would find a way to cheat him. Looking over his shoulder, he wondered if he could get passed the crowd fast enough to escape when this all went poorly. He wasn't about to be cheated out of his slaves like this. If he could get passed the crowd quickly enough, he could get out to his men and, if they were lucky, get away before too many of them were killed.

A worn and rusty blade bounced down in front of Auska and another in front of her opponent. She watched Blackfist pick up the blade and swing it through the air as if it were a sword. He was slow, clumsy with it; he was clearly used to wielding much larger, heavier weapons. More so he was overconfident, thinking his size was to his advantage.

Auska bent down and retrieved her knife. It was heavy, but there was a balance to it and it looked sharp.

"Time to bleed, little girl!" Blackfist roared stepping towards her.

Fuck it!

She sprinted towards him, cocking her arm back and let fly the blade. It flipped through the air, and her opponent saw it coming but could not move out of the way in time. The blade smashed into his thick chest, hilt first, but made him stumble back as though he had been impaled.

Before he could recover and realize he was fine, Auska's boot sailed up between his legs as hard as she could, connecting fully with his groin. His eyes bulged and he dropped to his knees. In one fluid motion, she grabbed his arm, twisted and thrust it up, driving his own knife into his throat before he had a chance to comprehend what was happening.

Auska stepped back, watching as Blackfist struggled to stem the flow of blood from his severed jugular, until he collapsed to the rock, drowning in his own blood in gurgled fits.

All around her was stunned silence, as the crowd of a hundred cannibals stared down in utter shock. Almost as if on cue they roared to life again, more excited than mad, which surprised her.

"Holy shit..." Everett muttered, not believing what he had just witnessed. He had thought she was as good as dead.

Tonka slapped him on the back with a giant grin. "So, you have brought a fighter to my pits!"

"I told you I did," he replied, still in wonder and awe.

"Good, now pick her next opponent!"

"She is to be allowed rests in-between each fight."

Tonka glared, his humor gone. "She killed the last one in less time than it takes me to fart. She needs no rest, now pick!"

"Fine, that bitch right there." He picked a wild-looking dirty blonde ten feet away. She was smaller than Auska but not by much, and already looked as if she had had too much to drink.

"Tara!" Tonka bellowed out gleefully. "You have been chosen!"

The woman's smile was the stuff of nightmares that would haunt you for the rest of your life and Everett was positive that she was possessed. "My pleasure!" She pushed through the crowd and dropped into the pit, her eyes eagerly searching Auska's as she paced back and forth like a caged lion.

Instantly Auska knew this wouldn't be an easy fight; this woman knew how to kill. Her movements were graceful and fluid, but it was her eyes that worried Auska the most. They were ice blue and showed nothing but a hunger for violence... a need for it.

An ice axe dropped down beside her and a curved sickle dropped down by her opponent and instantly the crowd erupted into a frenzy, calling down words of hate and hostility.

Snatching the blade up, Tara smiled. Her teeth were filed to broken, jagged points, making her look even more deranged. "You better pray to whatever gods you talk to, bitch," she began pacing, "because you are going to meet them soon!"

Auska began to circle, keeping her enemy in front of her, wondering at what point she would attack. The body of her last opponent still lay within the pit; it would cause a hindrance when things got heated, either in her favor or against her.

Watching her movements, Auska could tell an attack was coming any moment. Tara's muscles were twitching and her arms tensed as she adjusted her grip on the sickle.

Being on the defensive worked well, unless you could attack in that perfect instant when an enemy broke from defensive to offensive.

Springing forward, Auska caught that perfect moment. The ice axe sliced through the air back and forth, forcing the stunned cannibal back until she hit the pit wall. That was what Auska had been waiting for. Changing the arc of her axe she swept it up, hoping to embed it into the woman's guts and end this before it turned against her.

The tip of the axe punched into the rock, spraying rock chips into Auska's face, stinging her eyes. Her enemy had moved impossibly fast to avoid the hit. And a flash from the corner of her eyes proved her opponent had recovered just as fast.

Auska dropped down to her knees as the blade slammed into the rock, a finger's width above her head. Before she could react further a booted foot found her ribs and sent her reeling backward. She couldn't keep her feet under her and crashed to the jagged floor, the rock tearing into the skin of her back.

The sickle blade slashed down and Auska was just in time to block it with her axe. The strength of the cannibal's blow was devastating causing her arms to buckle, the only thing that saved her was her elbows hitting the rock below her, not allowing her arms to drop further.

Another kick to her side nearly sapped all strength from her arms, but the next one she saw coming and trapped the leg with her arm and threw her body into a roll. All power in the blade left as her opponent was toppled over backward.

Scrambling on top of Tara, Auska was fraught with keeping control of the arm holding the blade as the woman beneath her struggled to throw her off and regain the advantage.

With victory in sight, Auska raised her ice axe ready to drive it down into the cannibal's skull when she caught sight of her enemy's fingers lacing around the hilt of one of the forgotten daggers. She dropped her arm, praying she could deflect the strike in time, but feeling the blade slammed into her side proved she was too slow.

Auska knew this was a losing struggle to maintain and rolled herself backward, disengaging from the fight. Coming up into a crouch she leapt forward, bringing her ice axe down into Tara's knee as she struggled to raise. The tip punched deep.

With a savage twist, Auska yanked her weapon free and stepped back. Crippled now, her enemy would be easier to deal with, but she was surprised to see the woman grin with frenzied eyes, as she slowly gathered herself up. Not a whimper or groan of pain left her twisted lips.

"I'm going to enjoy eating your face!" she hissed, limping forward, her damaged leg not being able to handle much weight. "Come to me, bitch, and die!

We have played long enough!"

Auska watched the blood pour freely from the cannibal's wounded leg. The fight was over; the artery had been nicked and she would bleed out in a short time. All Auska had to do now was stay away from her.

Tara looked down at her leg and grimaced seeing the truth of it. "You think you've won? Not before I've tasted your fucking flesh!" She threw the sickle and sprang forward.

Auska battered the blade aside easily but was hit by the woman and they crashed to the rock again, the ice axe clattering away. Before she could realize what was happening pain erupted in her shoulder as the cannibal bit deeply into her flesh.

Panicking, Auska punched the side of the woman's head, again and again, trying to get her to release. Slowly, she felt the body sag against her, and the agonizing chewing sensation stopped.

With more effort than it should have, she pushed the corpse off and tried to stand. Her shoulder and side screamed in protest; thick blood oozed from both. Gritting her teeth and fighting past the waves of dizziness, she forced herself to her feet, glaring up at the two men who had made this all happen.

"Well done, girl!" the giant cannibal leader announced, raising a glass of something to her before taking a deep draught. "You have earned a small reprieve! Tomorrow night we will see if you can win your freedom!"

The armed guards escorted her back out; the

deafening sound of the crowd slowly faded behind her. She was barely aware of what was happening, the harsh words and shoves all that kept her moving, one foot in front of the other.

***

...Auska stared up at the grey sky, watching the depressing clouds idly make their way by, only to be followed by more. How long she stared up, she didn't know... she didn't care. She knew where she was again, could feel it; the same tingle throughout her body, the same smell in the air, taste on her tongue.

"...help... me..." a desperate voice croaked out, nearing death.

Her eyes widened; it was a voice that she knew, had known. A voice that had, for years, brought her comfort. "Father?" She rolled onto her side and her heart sank at the sight before her. She was at the truck stop... where her life had forever changed.

She watched Archer walk towards her father and stop to regard him. She got to her feet and rushed over. "Enough of this shit!" she growled. "I am tired of seeing this fucking shit! Why do you torture me?" But this wasn't the Archer who had been with her in all the rest of her vivid dreams. No, this Archer was part of the dream itself. The Archer she had met at that moment; the Archer who had changed her very life.

Archer leaned down, his eyes showing indifference, "You're going to die."

Aaron looked up at him with pleading eyes. "Hope... it... it's all... she has now... don't let her... lose it...

179

please..." His final words were barely auditable as his body went still.

"Papa!"

Auska's heart froze in her chest at the sound of her younger self. That voice... so young, so pure, so naïve and innocent. This was the moment that everything changed; the exact moment where reality crashed down on her, where life began to choke that naïveté out of her.

The figure ran by her. "No, Papa, no, please don't leave me," the young girl pleaded, holding the dead man's hand to her dirt-stained face.

Tears trickled down Auska's cheeks as she watched the bitter scene unfold. "I could protect you now... but not back then." She glanced around at all the bodies... her mother, James, Mathew... and others.

"This wasn't just the moment everything changed for you, kid," Archer said as he stepped in beside her. "My world changed the second this happened. I fought it. Oh, how I tried! But in the end, it happened as it needed to, I guess."

"They didn't need to die..." she whispered back, not caring that tears still ran freely, "...you, didn't need to die... shouldn't have died."

He rested his arm across her shoulders and pulled her closer to him. "I didn't die, kid. I gave my life for something I believe in."

She pulled back and looked up at him. "You never believed in anything except surviving and because of me, you couldn't even do that."

Archer grinned and lightly slapped her face. "I gave my life because I believed in you, kid. You were the worst and greatest thing to ever happen to my miserable, *wretched life. But I failed you, it would seem. Failed your father's dying wish and for that I am sorry."*

Auska was taken aback by this. "You never failed me. You made me stronger, better. You kept me alive! Made me who I am now!"

"Yes, I did," he smiled, "but you've lost hope."

Her face twisted in defense. "Hope? Hope doesn't help you survive!"

Archer pointed to the little girl weeping over her father's body. "That little girl right there once told me she didn't want to just survive..."

"...she wanted to live..." Auska finished for him, a strange feeling of dread and guilt flooded over her. "What have I been doing?" She looked up, but Archer was gone, and the scene around her was already fading...

———————◦◦◦◦———————

"...she's lost a lot of blood. It'll take a miracle for her to be in any form to fight tomorrow night." A deep voice said.

"Do you have nothing that can help?" a familiar voice growled. "Anything at all? At this point, I care not for the cost! I need her to be able to fight tomorrow, damn it!"

The man shuffled around in his bag. "I have some mild pain killers that will at least make the pain bearable, but I am afraid time and rest are what she needs."

Everett slammed his fists down into the small

table, cracking the wood. "We don't have the luxury of time! She has to fight tomorrow night, or we are all as good as dead."

The man shrugged, "I don't know what you want from me."

Everett snatched the pills from the table. "Get the fuck out of here! Useless cur!" He turned his attention back to the battered and bloody form on the moldy mat within the cage. Her eyes were open staring up at him. "You're awake!"

"So glad someone cares so much for my well-being," she grumbled, shifting to sit up against the cold stone. She felt down at her side, feeling through the linen wrapped around it to the many stitches beneath.

"The knife grazed off your ribs and got stuck between them, going no further than a couple of inches," he explained. "Another inch and you wouldn't have woken up." He tossed her the small pill bottle and pointed to the cup of water in her cell. "Pain killers. You'll want to take them to help you recover as much as possible. Your next fight is going to be your last... one way or another."

Auska stared down at the pill bottle. "So much more rides on this then what you told me," her eyes met his. "Your life hangs in the balance of this too doesn't it?"

"You are perceptive," he chuckled. "Depending on the outcome of the next fight, my life could indeed be forfeit."

"Good. Then I won't mind if I lose so much."

"Think of everything else on the line!" he growled. "Forget your hatred for me! Think about yourself! About your freedom! About the lives of all those taken from Sanctuary with you! Do you want them to end up doing this? Suffering through this as you are? Friends or not, are you really so cold and heartless as to allow those people to become food?"

"Coming from a slaver, that's rich," she hissed back. "You could sneak out of here right now, jump in your trucks and run far, far away. If you cared so much for the lives of those you've traded for, you could easily just let them go! So, don't try and make me look like the fucking bad guy here."

"The life they will live after I sell them won't be kind and won't be pretty," he confirmed, "but it won't be anywhere as cruel as will happen to them here."

"Fine, you want me to fight and try to win?" she questioned.

"Yes, of course!"

"Then do me one small kindness."

He looked hard at her. "And what is that?"

"Bring Wren to me for a few hours."

Everett raised a brow. "Why?"

"I'd rather not chance leaving this world a virgin."

The words struck the slaver and he nearly laughed out loud. "Truly?"

"Did I fucking stutter?"

He looked her up and down; what a strange, and yet realistic request. Though he would never have thought she would have been a virgin... "And if I refuse?"

"Then I guess you'll see just how cold-hearted I can be when I let myself be killed."

Too much rode on this fight to be petty now. "Fine, I will bring him to you. You'll have two hours, I suggest you make them last. But first get some sleep, I'll have food and water brought to you. I expect you to eat it all!"

"Fine, whatever." She closed her eyes and drifted off to sleep again.

Preston watched from his hiding spot as the three men searched the area around the water tower. The same area he would have been meeting up with Vincent, had the man gotten his note, right now. Meaning someone had found the note and told the council.

"We are on to the truth aren't we!" he whispered to himself.

"You were!" a voice said from behind him.

Before he could react, something hard smashed into his head and his world went black...

Auska stirred awake again, hearing her cell being opened. Everett stood with two guards flanking him, as he pushed a confused and worried

Wren inside.

"You will have an hour," Everett told them, locking the cell again, "I suggest you use it wisely."

Auska pushed herself up. "I thought you said we'd have two."

"I doubt you'll have the energy for two, not to mention I don't want you to waste that much energy fucking." He glared at Wren, a hint of jealousy in his eyes. "Please her well and I'll make sure you get double rations tonight. Disappoint her and you will be cannibal rations!"

"Umm, ya... of course," Wren stumbled. "I'll do my best?"

Auska grabbed his hand and pulled him towards her. She pressed her mouth against his and kissed him hard, her tongue dancing with his as she guided his hand up under her shirt to her breasts. His hands were gentle as they caressed her smooth skin and she found herself kissing him with more passion, something stirring within her that she hadn't expected.

The sound of the door closing in the background echoed off the walls and made her curse as she stopped and laid back. Part of her wanted to continue and she didn't know why. Sex had never been something she had cared about. She wasn't a virgin, but neither was she at all experienced.

Wren stopped also and looked around. "I assumed that was for show, but a guy can always dream, right?"

"Depends. You said you wanted to escape and

were willing to help me." She looked up at him; he wasn't ugly by any means... boyish, but cute. "You still willing to help?"

"Say no, get to have sex and be sold as a slave... Say yes, escape, and likely be killed in the process..." He sighed, "These are hard decisions for a man to make."

She grinned and shook her head, slowly pulling his hand from under her shirt and, sitting up with a wince, she looked him in the eyes and kissed him again. "Yes, but you forgot, we get out of this alive, maybe we can finish this under better circumstances."

"When you put it that way, yes, yes I will help you escape." He paused, suddenly remembering where they were. "Not sure how, though. Would have been easier before we were locked in a mountain full of cannibals."

"Can you get us out of this cell?"

Grinning, he pulled two pins from his shaggy hair. "Locks are never a problem. It's the mile and a half of armed human eaters that worry me."

"Just open the door and we will worry about the rest when we need to. I am sure I remember the way out of here." She quickly swallowed six of the pain killers. She had already taken four but knew she would need to be numb for what was likely to come.

"Yeah but outside the front will be crawling with guards and slavers. I just came from that way. It would be suicide."

Auska rolled her eyes as she watched his nimble

fingers work the lock. "I told you, I have been here before. When I was twelve, I was travelling with a man who was helping me stay alive and bringing me to Sanctuary. There is another way out of here. There is a tunnel that leads up the cliff to an exit near the top."

The soft click of the lock popping open was music to their ears.

"So, I did my part," he pushed the cell open and helped her out. "Now how are you going to keep us alive and see us out of here? Not going to lie, you are looking in rough shape."

Auska almost felt like laughing. "Good thing I'm not used to being the damsel in distress. You'd make a piss poor knight in shining armor."

Wren held up his hands in his defense. "I told you, we all have our talents in this world."

She felt the pull of her crudely stitched side. Wren was right, she was in bad shape. Any physical fighting and she would be badly pressed, more so without a weapon. Pressing her ear up against the door she listened, she could hear breathing outside, but couldn't tell if it was just one guard or two.

"What's the plan?"

"You're not going to like it," she told him with a grimace. "Open the door and see who's out there, then high tail it back in here."

"You're right," he muttered, "I don't like it."

"We don't have the time or the resources to come up with anything fancy. Straight and bold is all we have, and the timer is ticking."

"Yeah, yeah," he grabbed the door handle. "Fuck me this is going to suck."

Wren opened the door quickly and stepped out. The guard turned in surprise. "What are you doing out!"

"Just thought I'd go for a walk," Wren joked, stepping back into the room as the guard leveled an axe at him.

Auska watched Wren step passed her. She was pressed up as hard as she could against the door wall, making herself as invisible as possible. The axe head came next, hand, arms, then the middle-sized man himself. He didn't notice her; his attention was locked firmly on Wren.

Using her leg, she pushed off the tunnel wall, shoulder checking the guard with her good shoulder as hard as she could. The attack worked well; she hit the guard squarely, toppling him into one of the barbed wire cells.

Auska gave him no reprieve, knowing if he regained his senses, he would likely be able to overwhelm her. Ignoring the searing pain in her side and the throb in her shoulder, she grabbed fists full of his matted hair and forced his face down. He fought against her, trying to push himself off the razor wire. Not being able to do it one-handed, he quickly discarded the axe and put both arms into pushing off. Auska kneed him as hard as she could in the ribs, again and again, driving the air from his lungs and the strength from his arms.

Slowly she lowered his head down, mere inches

away from the thick tangle of tiny blades. Another knee to his side and she heard ribs splinter and his arms give out. Savagely she pulled his head back and forth across the wire, leaving a bloody, pulpy mess, until final the blades worked through his throat and gouts of blood poured free, his body sagged, and the fight was over.

"Look out!" Wren cried.

Auska turned just in time to see a second guard bearing down on her, a weighted club in hand. She dropped herself down, bring the body of the dead guard with her. The impact of the club smashed into the bloody corpse and was like a punch to her chest. But still, it was better than the full force the blow would have caused.

She heard a crash as she struggled to pull herself from beneath the dead guard. Within moments Wren was there, blood was splattered across his arms and face.

"Here, let me help you up." He offered his hand and pulled her to her feet.

Auska glanced down at the second guard. An axe wound had opened his midsection, while another had cleaved halfway through his neck. "Aren't you full of surprises?"

Wren shrugged. "You distracted him. I just took advantage."

Pulling the axe from the dead guard, she went to the doorway to make sure the noise hadn't been heard. "We've overstayed our welcome."

They moved out of the room and down the left

side of the tunnel. She knew she had gone left after freeing Archer and Vincent. Quickly they ran, she ignored the pain plaguing her whole body.

"What are you looking for?" Wren asked nervously after they stopped for the third time and Auska bent down to inspect something. "I thought you knew the way out of here!"

"When I was here as a child, I marked the way, with little arrows, so I wouldn't get lost!" She growled, annoyed at finding nothing again. "I was hoping some faint trace remained."

"And if we can't find one?"

Auska pushed herself back up; Wren helped to steady her. "Then we take a guess."

"Life has always got to be suspenseful," Wren muttered.

"Come on, our hour is ticking by."

They continued down the tunnel and had to turn off to a side tunnel as several men were coming. Both knew now it was only a matter of minutes before the dead guards were found.

"Wait!" Wren whispered grabbing her arm. "I smell something."

"Other than blood and death, I'm surprised," she hissed pulling her arm free and moving back down the way they had come, they needed to get back on track and fast.

"No, its… its fresh air!"

She needed no more than that. "Can you follow it?" She sniffed the air and could smell nothing but death that clung onto her.

"I... I think so. This way!"

Auska followed behind him, as he sniffed his way down the tunnel, turning at several intersections. Twice more they had to detour and hide from several cannibals that moved by.

Before long Auska could finally smell the fresh air, too, and glanced down at the wall and saw a faint arrow mark she had made over a decade ago. Her heart nearly leaped from her chest. "This is the way!"

Together they ran, the slope of the cliff leading up; slowly, then as they round bend after bend, it steepened, until they caught the faint dimness of sunlight.

Auska grabbed Wren's arm and stopped him, putting her finger to her lips. "Last time I was here there was a guard outside the door."

He tightened his grip on the club he carried. It was a heavy and awkward weapon, one that he would be next to useless at using effectively, but it was better than nothing. Slowly he followed her, keeping to the side of the tunnel.

Creeping to the entrance, Auska peered out. A table and two chairs were set up twenty feet away, empty. But two rifles were leaned up against rockface beside it. They wouldn't have just left guns up here. There were two guards, maybe more, somewhere... but where?

"We should just make a run for it," Wren whispered. "If we can make it passed the first hundred feet, we can slip through the trees and lose them."

"Or get shot in the process." Had she thought she would be able to sprint for more than a few seconds she might have agreed with him, but there was a plan there. "You want to run, run, make sure you grab a rifle on your way and be ready to use it."

"What the hell are you going to do?" There was concern in his voice.

"I'm going to make sure they don't shoot you in the back, now go!" she urged.

Cursing, Wren ran for the small table, his eyes taking in everything he could, but he could see nothing; there was no one. He slowed as he got to the table and snatched up one of the rifles. Still, it was silent. "It's clear," he called quietly to her.

Would it really be so easy? Auska made her way out, scanning everything until she made it to the table and grabbed the other rifle. At that moment they made out soft grunts and muttered voices.

"What the hell is that?" Wren whispered, leveling the gun in the direction of the noise.

Auska knew what it was: someone was fucking. "None of our business, let's get out of here!"

They made their way down the slope of the cliff to the tree line; no shouts or calls of alarm could be heard, though they knew it would come sooner or later. Their hour was up; someone would be checking on them, find the dead guards and then all hell would be after them. They needed to be as far away from here as possible.

"Come on. If we are quick, we can make it through the forest, there use to be a small city on the other side. Might be somewhere we can hide for a few days until everything settles down."

Wren slowed and looked back. "We can't just leave them to that fate."

"What?" Auska asked, turning to regard him.

"Jen, Caitlyn and the others back there," he said. "We can't just abandon them."

Auska wanted to yell at him. "And the two of us can just somehow change that? If we go back there, it's over for us, too, and we just escaped! We won't be so lucky a second time!"

"So, you would just leave them?" he asked, his expression boarding mortified. "I know you are cold, Auska, and hard but even you can't be so cruel to people you've lived around for years. You know what will happen to them if we don't help them."

Auska was about to growl a rebuttal at him about how she was when the image of her standing defiantly in front of Archer assaulted her. *'I don't want to just survive! I want to live!'* "Fuck!" she barked out at him. "Fine, we will go down and see what we can do, but nothing stupid. If we can free a few, great. If not, at least we looked."

Wren knew that was the best he was going to get from her and nodded. "That's all we can do."

Everything in Auska's instinct told her not to be so stupid, not to take this risk, and yet she moved closer to the cannibal's lair that she had just escaped from. It wouldn't be long before an alarm sounded and everyone was alerted to the fact that they had escaped. When that happened, things would get ugly, really ugly, really quickly.

Creeping through the thickly wooded area around the cliffs, they neared the slaver's camp. Glad that they were wary enough to keep well away from the cannibal entrance, but it could be seen they were nervous, on edge, and their guard was up. Thankfully, it was mostly projected towards the cannibals' lair, as if they were expecting an attack at any minute.

The slaves were grouped closer together, most of their leashes running from the same four trees, forcing them more into a huddled group.

"This is good," Wren whispered. "I can try to blend in and pick their locks close together, and hopefully I won't be noticed as out of place among them."

Auska counted four guards nearby, three were sitting around a small fire, talking in hushed tones; the fourth was patrolling back and forth, his attention more focused on the others than what might be out in the trees. "I will take out the one walking around. That will give you time to work faster without having to worry about being noticed. Downside you'll have only a minute or two before his presence is missed." She looked towards the cliff face. "Chances are that's all the time we will have before shit gets loud. If this goes bad, I'll draw their attention and will lead them away. You get as many of those locks off as you can, then scatter!"

"Will do, boss lady." He winked and dropped to the ground and began his slow course towards the group of prisoners.

Auska watched him go with a shake of her head with a small grin. "Don't get yourself killed either… idiot… I still want to finish what we started before." The words and feelings truly surprised her; she had to push them away. She needed to focus… to be hard, cold… a killer.

Following around the edge of the trees, she placed herself between the furthest place she had seen the guard walk by that was also out of direct eyesight of the three men around the fire. She would have to be quick and clean with this; any noise and she knew those other guards would be on her. They were already on edge. Anything out of place would trigger trouble and in her current condition, she doubted it would end well for her.

Waiting, she gripped the small spear-like branch. It would work so long as she was fast and her aim was true. "Fuck me," she muttered to herself, "what the fuck am I doing out here… was this what it was like for you, when I was around?" she joked, almost expected his dream voice to answer.

Seconds felt like minutes as she waited in the undergrowth, her eyes flipping between Wren and the guard. It looked like he was well on his way, with more than a handful already freed, but from here she couldn't be sure. The guard was moving slowly, distracted, his attention elsewhere, his footsteps lingering after each step.

Finally, he got closer but stopped just out of her range. He looked around idly and placed his gun against a tree, pulled his cock out and began to relief himself.

Close enough. Auska lifted herself out and stepped forward. Her hand clamped around his mouth and she kicked the back of his legs, dropping him to his knees before he had a chance to realize what was happening. The broken branch sunk deep into his eye, and she forced it to go as far as she could. His thrashing slowed and jerked to a stop as she felt his last breath leave him. Simple.

Moving back into place she watched Wren with the others, she had no idea how many be had freed but was happy to see none of them had tried to make a run for it yet. They were remaining calm, natural, something she was truly surprised at.

A deep resounding horn bellowed from the cliff face. Their time was up. Things were about to get dangerous and pass the point of no return.

Instantly the three guards were on their feet looking towards the noise, all thought of anything else long gone from them. That was Wren's moment; the group picked up and ran, fanning out into the woods as quickly and quietly as they could. But Wren wasn't among them.

Auska caught sight of Jennifer and Wren struggling over the last two prisoners. She cursed loudly; one of them was Jen's brother. Keeping low she ran closer, keeping out of sight in case the element of surprise was needed still. "What the fuck?"

"The damn locks are jammed!" Wren told her as

he tried another attempt on the chain around Kalvin.

Jen looked panicked as she tried to unlock the other woman's chain. "This one has dirt and shit in the hole, there's no getting it out! Not without more time!"

"We don't have more time, we have to go, or we will all be dead!" Auska hissed back, keeping a watch on the guards. It was only a matter of time before their luck was going to end. Then her eyes landed on something by one of the seats between the three distracted slavers.

"I'll not leave without my brother, Auska," Jen barked, "I told you this already!"

"I know!" Auska replied, unshouldering the rifle. "I'll buy you some time, but when you see me running, your time is up. What happens after is on you!"

Wren looked up from what he was doing, "What the fuck are you doing?"

"I made a promise, I need to keep it," she called over, as she sprinted across the open ground towards the three guards.

As she ran, she aimed the gun and fired. A bullet punched through the left man's neck and he pitched forward. The other two turned around to see what had happened when Auska slammed the rifle stock into the middle one's jaw spinning him wildly around to crash into the fire pit. She tried to reverse the swing in time to catch the other, but her wounded side and shoulder couldn't react in time and her target was able to swing out of reach.

"You, stupid bitch!" Dirk growled, his fist connecting with her face, spinning her around.

Auska almost lost her footing but managed to stay upright. Her vision was dazed; bright lights exploded all around her and nausea threatened to consume her. She berated herself for thinking it would be that easy. These men were hard men, killers, fighters... survivors, like her.

Lifting the rifle back she tried to aim, but his arm shot out and slapped the barrel aside and her shot tore through the side of the truck. The screams of the man who had fallen in the fire and the gunshots had drawn attention as others who moved cautiously closer.

Another fist thundered into her side and she nearly blacked out from the agony that ripped through her as stitches and cracked ribs broke.

"Don't know where you came from, but the boss will be glad we found you again!" Dirk grinned, ready to throw another punch.

A gun went off and Auska watched as he was bucked back to crash into the truck, his eyes wide as blood pumped from the hole in his chest. Stealing a glance, she saw Jennifer standing a dozen feet away reloading.

"Time to go!"

Auska gritted forward and snatched the skull up into her arms and took off behind Jennifer into the trees. A look to where they had been showed Jen's brother had been freed but the older woman remained. One left behind was better luck then they had any right to.

Gunshots went off, but they couldn't tell if they were coming their way or the other. Confusion had taken over between the two camps, and that was good for them. Hopefully, the two groups would kill each other and be too distracted to do anything else for a while.

They ran for several hard minutes, slowly making their way back to where the cliff trail brought them to the forest, where Wren and Kalvin were waiting with watchful eyes. A path Auska had travelled over a decade ago with night looming in on them and men and infected clawing at their backs. Looking up at the darkening sky, it was going to be a similar experience now, too.

"Why the fuck did you come back for me?" Auska gasped, needing to slow down before she collapsed.

"I could ask you the same thing," Jen countered. "I could also ask why you risked your life like that to buy us more time." She looked at the skull Auska had clenched in her hands. "But I am sure the answer would disappoint me greatly."

Auska stopped beside Wren. "You did good. All but one, far better than I expected. Hopefully, most of them make it out there with night coming."

"I couldn't clear the lock out, it was caked in there too tightly." His expression showed shame. "I was going to keep trying, but the woman forced me to go. Said it was alright so long as everyone else got away."

"She was smart then," Auska told him firmly, trying to catch her breath as she looked down at her side. It was oozing blood and badly. She would have to clean it up soon... somehow. They had no supplies. "You wouldn't have gotten any more time and then more people would have died or been captured again."

Jennifer could hear distant shouts in the distances, but the gunshots had ceased. "We need to find the others and get regrouped."

Auska shook her head. "We don't have time for that. It'll be dark soon. I know this area. There will be infected swarming the woods, cannibals, and slavers searching for us. If we try and find everyone right now, we will all likely be killed. We need to get moving. There is a small city just through the woods a few hours away. We can hole up there for a few days, then we can see if we can track down some of the others if they haven't made their way there already."

"A few days?" Jennifer gasped. "You can't expect them to survive a few days on their own!"

"They are going to have to!" Auska snapped back. "They don't and we don't have much of a choice."

"She's right you know," Kalvin stepped in. "It'll be dark soon. There is far too much noise and enemies about for us to be able to do anyone but ourselves any good right now. They are smart. I saw them run off in small groups. They will be able to watch out of one another until we find them, sis."

Auska started walking as quickly as she could bring herself to.

"Where are you going?" Wren called to her.

"I told you what I am doing, what the only logical thing to do is right now. I helped you free them, what you do with that is up to you."

Wren and Jennifer shared a look.

"I'm going with her, she's right," Kalvin said, jogging after Auska like a scared pup.

"She's not wrong," Wren said watching Auska leave. "As shitty as it is."

Jen spat bitterly. "I know, it's just how she says it. Let's go. This night is going to get a lot uglier before it starts to get pretty again."

Time seemed to slow for the small group as the last few hours of dusk lingered in the sky, giving them faint light to see by, pushing as quickly as they could through the edge of the forest.

Auska was slowing desperately, her oozing wounds draining what little strength she had and making her stumble and her feet drag tracks through the forest floor. *"You are leaving tracks even a blind woman could follow."* His words prodded her resolve, but to little use; she couldn't lift her feet any higher.

"They are getting louder," Kalvin said, his eyes looking back every few moments.

Wren grimaced. "That's because they are getting closer."

"We need to find someplace to hide soon." Jen looked back and thought she could make out silhouettes in the trees. "How much further?"

Auska forced herself to stop and lean up against a tree. She hadn't the strength to keep walking and talk at the same time. Wiping the sweat from her eyes she looked around. It had been so long since she had been here last, and even then she had been a child and hadn't paid much attention as they had run for their lives. "There should be an old work site around here soon."

"I don't see anything in any damn direction!" Jennifer growled at her, fingering the rifle she hadn't given back to Wren.

Auska had to restrain herself from yelling; it would only waste energy she didn't have. "I was fucking twelve."

"We need to keep moving either way," Wren urged them, knowing this wasn't going to get any better. "Let's move further out of the trees. Maybe we will be able to see this worksite."

"If she dropped that stupid skull she'd have less to carry and maybe she'd be able to stop leaving such an easy to follow trail," Jen muttered coldly.

Auska pushed off from the tree she was bracing herself on. "If it wasn't for this skull, you three would be fucking dead already. Now let's go."

Another hour rolled by, the demonic sounds of the infected howled throughout the woods like a pack of dogs. But soon they found the rusted chain-link fence that led into the old construction yard. Not much of the fence remained; a decade longer had seen most of it taken down and used for whatever its scavengers had needed it for.

"This… this is what cities look like?" Kalvin and Jen both gasped in awe as they moved their way through the broken yard towards the looming skyscape ahead. Both had been born in Sanctuary; neither had ever been this far from home nor seen the world for what it once had been.

The years had taken its toll on the old buildings. Few windows remained undamaged. Many of the buildings looked as if they were ready to crumble at the slightest disturbance, others were encased in Mother Nature, who was fighting back to take what was once hers. It was a breathtakingly beautiful sight to behold in its macabre way, but Auska also knew what dangers would lurk within.

Stopping again, they caught their breath. They had been able to stay ahead of the infected hordes. They suspected the infect would have been more interested in the noise from the cannibals' lair than anything they had done.

Looking up at the old loader, tears stung Auska's eyes. It was the same one, the same one that he had hidden them in while he had saved their lives yet again.

"You okay?" Wren asked, seeing the tears streak down her dirt and blood-stained face.

Sniffing them away she nodded. "The past brings back cruel reminders. We need to keep going, we are almost safe for the night."

A scream from the right drew their attention and weapons were raised and ready.

"Where is Kalvin?" Jen cried out, forgetting

anything else and rushing to the screams.

"NO!"

Before Auska or Wren could clear the corner two-gun shots sounded. When they finally reached the spot, Jen was pulling the bodies of two infected from her brother. His arm was bleeding badly.

"No, no, no!" Jen cried pulling him up into her arms. "What were you doing?"

"I... I... had to piss," Kalvin muttered, shock and confusion plain on his face. "They came out of... nowhere... I didn't even have time to..."

"He's been bitten," Wren whispered.

"Shut up!" Jen hissed back. "He hurt himself when he fell, right?"

Kalvin looked from her to the others, knowing the truth, but not knowing how to say it. "I... I..."

"Hurt yourself when you fell damn it!" Jennifer screamed, pulling him up to his feet. "Now we need to keep moving so we can find somewhere to hide and look after your cuts!"

Wren and Auska exchanged glances. This was bad, really bad, but they both knew it wasn't the time to deal with it. The sounds of gunshots would have been heard for miles, and trouble would be coming, either in the form of the infected or people, possibly both.

Auska grunted and lead the way, her mind racing with how this would now play out. This changed things, this made things a lot harder...

"You brought someone in to see her!" Tonka raged, the veins in his arms and neck bulging with fury as he paced the empty cell room.

Everett felt like a child being scowled by an angry parent, except this parent was a cannibal leader and this conversation could quickly turn into his untimely death. "She wanted to fuck. Fearing it might be her last time before she died. A simple request, one we all would be so happy to receive if we knew we might die soon."

Tonka turned a violent eye on him. "Have you fucked today?" The question was dripping with intention. "Because you might very well die this day, too!"

Everett wanted to rebut, to not cower away, but to do so would be certain death right now. He had to be calm, play the fool, and play the smaller man if he wanted to see the light of day again. It was daunting and cut his pride deeply, but survival was more important than pride. "It was clearly a mistake but an honest one."

"Clearly!" The cannibal leader snapped turning his attention back to his guards. "Who allowed Everett to bring this man in?"

A nervous man stepped forward. "I... I did sir. I thought no harm in it since we often allow our slaves to fuck as a reward."

"In the cell."

The guard's eyes widened. "Sir?"

"Get in the cell, or I will kill you where you stand," Tonka replied with a frightening calm. "You will fight in her stead until she is returned and finished what she started! If you are still alive by the time she is back, then you will have your freedom. If not, then you will continue to fight until you die or win your freedom in my eyes."

The guard looked for a moment like he would argue, but quickly thought better of it and slowly entered the cell where he was locked in.

"This deal has turned very poorly, Everett," Tonka said, glaring at the man in the cell. "Six of your men are dead, eleven of mine, not to mention all but one of your slaves are gone. Your fighter has fled and you stand here before me with empty hands for a deal we shook upon."

"I will find her, and bring her back here," Everett said evenly, "and I will collect the runaway slaves as well. Give me a day or two and all will be put right."

Laughing, Tonka shook his head. "No, this will never be made right, but it will be made acceptable!" He turned his fierce gaze upon the slaver. "Six of my men with go with you and your men to collect this bitch! The rest of your men stay here, under my protection, while my men collect the runaway slaves. The slaves are mine now! You bring me the woman and she fights once more, and the deal will stand with half the supplies promised!" He moved impossibly fast and clenched Everett's throat. "And each year you will trade me half of your new stock and this is the only deal you will get that doesn't involve you being my fucking dinner!"

"Deal!" Everett choked out, knowing he had no

other options.

Tonka shoved him back. "Now go and bring me back my property, and so help me if you think to run from me, Everett, I will send my hordes swarming through this wasteland to bring you back kicking and screaming!"

The slaver straightened himself and met the cannibal's eyes. "I'm not so foolish as to think of anything that stupid."

"I should hope not," Tonka's eyes showed his distrust. "My men will meet you outside in twenty minutes, be ready to go. We already know the direction she and her little friends went. The trail they left is easy enough to follow."

Everett stocked from the room, his rage seething out of him, as two of his men followed in behind him. "We need to get the cunt back and now and be away from this place!"

Vincent finished cleaning the floor as best as the mop would do on the aged linoleum. Pushing the bucket back into the closet, he closed it and turned back to face Kelli, who had her back turned to him as she finished setting out some of the things they would need tomorrow morning.

The last twenty-four hours they had said very little to each other. He was still hurt deeply by her words. He had told her nothing of Preston's and his conversation, as it would only further their argument and things were already tense enough. He had even spent last night sleeping on the floor; the thought of sharing the same bed angering him.

Vincent grabbed his coat and was about to leave when suddenly he felt a fool. Was this worth fighting over? What was happening, he would figure out and expose and then it would get better. But to be mad at Kelli for something she had nothing to do with was foolish, regardless of her opinions about it.

Grabbing her coat, he went to her, her back was still to him. "Let's go home and relax on our stupid little deck with a cup of tea and put this shit behind us, okay." He placed her coat over her shoulders when he noticed a piece of paper poking out of her jacket pocket.

"I would like that. I would like that very much." Smiling, she turned to face him, relief on her face.

Vincent pulled his eyes from the paper. It was paper, nothing more. Grinning he held out his arm. "Then let me walk you home, my lady."

Vincent finished pouring the two cups Earl Grey tea. Stolen tea. He didn't care; he took very little 'extra' ever for himself, but every now and then something would find its way into his pocket.

He went and sat beside her on the little bench they had set up outside their storage container. They both cuddled up under the thin blanket as they sipped their tea, enjoying the crisp fall air.

"I missed this," Kelli told him, "more then you know."

He kissed her head. "I missed it, too."

Just then they saw torchlight coming from the direction of the old water tower; something was being carried on a stretcher.

"What the hell is going on over there?" Vincent wondered.

"Not our problem," Kelli said. "Maybe we should go inside, it's getting cold."

Vincent put his drink down and stood. "It looks like someone is hurt or something."

"We are cooks, not doctors." She grabbed his hand. "I've missed you, let's go get 'warm'." But he wasn't listening as he started to make his way down the ramp. "Where are you going, Vincent?" She called to him desperately, not wanting him to get involved in anything else.

"I'll be right back. Just going to see if they need a hand or anything," he called back.

Vincent quickly cleared the distance to the men. "What is going on? Is someone hurt?"

Two of the men were from the First Division and quickly intercepted him. "Nothing to see here. Just an accident."

A sheet was pulled over the body. "Looks more like death than an accident."

"Yes, well. An accident that led to a death, sadly."

Vincent tried to look past them. "Who died? How? What happened?"

"Step back, Vincent!" Decan growled, pushing him back a step. "This isn't anything to do with you. The council will address what happened and to who in the morning. Until then, let us do our job."

Vincent watched them go, noticing a hand slip out from the sheet. A hand with a bold ring on it... he knew who it belonged to. His heart sank and his blood ran bitterly cold.

He turned and walked back to the house, each step darkening his mood.

"What happened?" Kelli asked. "Is everything alright?"

Vincent ignored her and walked into their house and straight to her coat. He searched the pocket and pulled out the piece of paper. *Meet me at the water tower at midnight, P.*

"What the fuck is going on..." he whispered.

"You weren't supposed to see that."

"What is going on, Kelli, why would you hide this from me?" He turned around and Kelli was standing in the doorway, her revolver pointed at his chest. "What the fuck are you doing?"

Tears streamed down her face. "Why couldn't you just accept it and let it go! Auska wasn't meant to die, she just got caught up where she shouldn't have been! Why couldn't you just leave it alone, damn it!"

Her words stole his breath and he stumbled back a step. "You knew... you knew this whole time what they were doing."

"Not the whole time," she countered, as if it would somehow make things okay. "Only the last few years. I was brought into the secret because I came across the tunnel they use. They almost killed me, but I told them I'd never tell. Then they told me they are thinking of adding someone else to the council! Me, Vincent! Me, so long as I reported to them, told them what was happening, what the people were saying, doing. Do you know what that would do for us? The life we could finally enjoy?"

"You knew, you knew and you let it happen." He had never felt so sick and betrayed in all his life. "We could have stopped it, could have made things right."

"No, Vincent, I couldn't have," she countered, her tone darkening a little. "Neither could you, neither could Preston. No one can. Things are too hard, supplies too thin, people too crowded. This makes sense, this works. It's not perfect, but it works. It keeps the balance. All those traded are those who weren't pulling their weight, were causing problems, stirring the pot. They weaned out the weak and dangerous to make sure the strong and faithful survived, Vincent. This is about survival."

The note slipped to the floor. "I can't believe this. I can't believe you. That you would allow this, be alright with this, even embrace it." His eyes hardened. "What now, now that I know the truth?"

"You forget it," she told him, desperation in her voice. "You pretend you never figured it out and you let it go. We go on living a good life, and everything returns to normal. Can you please just do that?" Her eyes were begging. "For me, for us?"

"And if I say no?"

Kelli's lips quivered as she blinked away several

more tears. "Please don't."

"If you truly loved me, you wouldn't be pointing a gun at me, nor would we need to be having this conversation," he told her, knowing full well he was about to die.

"Don't make me do this Vincent. Don't throw away the last ten years." The gun shook dangerously in her small hands.

Vincent's eyes were distant and emotionless. "Kelli, I'm not making you do anything."

"Just let it fucking go, Vincent!" she screamed. "Just forget it all, just accept it and let's move on!"

"I can't…" he whispered, "… I won't."

Kelli's eyes hardened. "Then you leave me with no choice. You did this to yourself." The gun raised to his heart for a brief moment then lowered again. "I… I can't"

"It's okay," a rough voice said from behind her as Marshal, the captain of the First, stepped into the house, his gun drawn. "No need for anyone else to die tonight." He glared at Vincent. "But you will be coming with me and you will do so quietly and calmly, or unlike her, I will shoot you, but I won't make it quick."

Vincent held up his hands in surrender. "So how many people are in on this?"

"Enough," the captain replied. "Now let's get going. Put your arms down and act natural."

Vincent walked passed Kelli and stopped, his eyes looking into hers, disappointment and resentment clear on his face. With a shake of his head, he left.

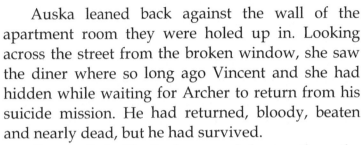

Auska leaned back against the wall of the apartment room they were holed up in. Looking across the street from the broken window, she saw the diner where so long ago Vincent and she had hidden while waiting for Archer to return from his suicide mission. He had returned, bloody, beaten and nearly dead, but he had survived.

She smiled. He had seemed larger than the world, stronger than the gods, and harder to kill than death itself, yet he had been just a man. If she could have relived those days again with him, she would have, all of it, every second, right up until the end.

"So, what are we going to do?" Wren whispered, breaking her concentration.

Auska rubbed her eyes. She was tired, so very tired. She had cleaned her wounds as best she could with the stale rainwater they had found and wrapped dirty curtains around the wounds. It would work for now until something better could be done. "We hide here for a few days, then move out." She shrugged. "See if we can find some of the others. Then you guys make a plan on what you want to do."

"That's not what I was talking about. I am talking about him." He pointed to the back room where Jennifer had put her brother after cleaning his wounds, which she still claimed were from falling. "And wait, what? 'We' make a plan? You make it sound like you won't be here."

"I'll stick around until I make a plan, then I am gone. What the others choose to do doesn't matter to me. Then can try to go back to Sanctuary or try to make a go for life elsewhere. Either way, it won't include me."

Wren looked at her strangely. "You really don't plan on sticking around with people, do you?"

"Not if I can avoid it," Auska replied. "At least not yet. I'm not ready for that. Don't know if I ever will be."

"Guess it's pointless for me to ask if you want a tag-along," he grinned sheepishly.

Auska chuckled slightly, making sure not to hurt her side. "And if I told you no, would you believe it was because you'd be better off with others than the world I will live in?"

"I'd believe it," he replied. "But would you believe that I'll likely just follow you anyway? Which will make thing a little awkward, but I can accept that if you can."

This time she couldn't stop herself from laughing and grabbed her side. "You are a strange little man, you know that, Wren? But I like you all the same."

"I take that as a compliment, since from what I have gathered you don't like anyone."

She forced a small smile. "It's not easy for me."

A moan from the other room drew both their attention back to the next real problem they faced. A dangerous and trying problem, one with a ticking time limit.

"So, what are we going to do about that?" Wren whispered again. "He's been bitten, he's going to turn... I've seen people turn within hours, sometimes it takes almost a day. But they always turn and it's always bad news."

"Jennifer isn't stupid, she knows what will happen. When the time comes, she will do what needs to be done."

Wren stared at the closed door to the room. "I'm not sure I share your optimism."

Auska tapped the rifle beside her. "If it comes to it, I'll kill him." Resting her head against the corner of the wall, she yawned. "We should all get some rest. Tomorrow we will need to see what we can find for food and supplies, or we are all dead anyway."

"So, what are you going to do?"

Auska sighed, wondering where she'd open her eyes to this time. Who would be dead, or dying? What traumatic scene would be burned into her memory from the past?

"For once, it's peaceful," Archer told her, knowing her inner thoughts.

Opening her eyes, she was almost happy to see he wasn't lying to her. They stood on top of the old hospital, where they had stayed for several days while Archer had been near death. It was where they had met Kelli and got the first real taste of what life could be like when people worked together towards a common goal. It had been beautiful, peaceful and everything young Auska had ever wanted.

"Had we not had that psycho Blare hot on our tails, this might have been a good place to stay," he told her as they watched the fish in the pond swimming.

Auska nearly laughed. "You would never have stayed."

Archer ran his hand through the water, scaring the fish to the far end of the pond. "Once I would have agreed with you, but truth be told this was a good place. The people were good. They weren't lazy, they weren't ignorant, they weren't pretending. They had a dream, a goal, and together they were seeing it through, making it real. Had it not been for us they might still be there, might have survived, grown, expanded." He shrugged. "It was a good place."

"Sanctuary is a good place, much the same as this had been." The words slipped from her.

Archer scoffed. "You hate it there, have said it aloud to me a hundred times or more by now!"

It was true, she did. She couldn't remember a time she had thought about it where she didn't get a feeling of anger. But now, now that the words had slipped out, she didn't feel so much bitterness, so much anger. "It's not perfect, never could be, but it could be better, a dream made real for people, to live, to really live."

"And how could that happen?"

"The cancer corrupting it needs to be removed."

"The council?"

"Yes."

Archer stared back at the pond. "That can't happen if no one ever knows the truth."

"I know."

"Someone has to give them hope."

"I know…"

A rage-filled scream broke through the early morning, snapping Auska and Wren wide awake.

"You fucking bitch!" Jennifer screamed from the room, kicking the door open, her rifle leading the way. "You fucking monster! You thought I wouldn't notice? That I wouldn't care?" A shot fired.

Auska had known by the way Jen was moving that she meant to kill her and had thrown herself to the side just as the bullet slammed into the wall behind her. She landed in a roll with her bad shoulder, fresh agony ripped through her and instead of rolling onto her feet she crashed into the rotting couch. Her rifle slipping from her grip and skidded against the wall.

"What the fuck are you doing, Jen!" Wren cried out, scrambling to his feet.

Jen fumbled with the bolt, trying to empty the casing and load another. "She killed him! She fucking killed my brother in the middle of the fucking night like a coward!" Seeing Auska recovering, she dropped the rifle and pulled the glass knife she had made the night before and charged.

"What the fuck are you talking about?" Auska cried back, dodging several wild swings, knowing she was running out of room to back up.

"Don't you dare try to deny it!" Jen hissed,

scoring a light hit across Auska's forearm.

Wren wasted no more time and grappled Jennifer from behind, pinning her arms to her sides. "Calm down Jen!"

"Let me fucking go, you piece of shit!" Jen screamed. "You would protect a murderer!"

"Jen, Jen!" Wren cried out, struggling to contain her. "He was bitten! He would have turned! It needed to be done!"

"Fuck you!" she screamed, finally struggling free, turned and slashed at him, but Wren was nimble enough to jump back in time. She twirled back around, ready to launch an attack back at her target. But Auska was right there and a fist slammed into her midsection. She buckled back and a knee caught her face throwing her back to the ground.

"Didn't touch your fucking brother!" Auska spat going to retrieve her lost rifle when another gunshot ripped into the floor beside it.

"Don't you even think about touching that gun."

Auska's heart sunk knowing the voice. "How the fuck did you find us?"

Everett, his two men, and six cannibals entered the apartment, armed and ready to fight. "Well, your stupid friend here firing her rifle and screaming like a banshee was like a dinner bell for these fine gentlemen behind me."

Glaring at Jennifer, Auska stepped back from the rifle as Everett moved closer. Already Wren and Jennifer were being bound. "I was really hoping I wouldn't have to see you again."

Everett slapped her across the face with enough force she crashed into the ground. "You've caused me a lot of fucking trouble with this bullshit little stunt!"

"I'll try to feel bad for you," she spat and got another slap for her effort.

"Enough talk!" one of the cannibals, a thin, wiry man said. "Tonka wants them back."

Auska glared at Everett as he pulled her roughly to her feet. She could never hope to fight this group and win, not in her condition and not like this. She would have to find another way.

Jennifer and Wren were already being pushed out the door, as both Everett's men and one of the cannibals stayed to bind Auska.

"I would have given you your freedom, you know," Everett muttered taking the leather cord from one of his men. "You just had one more fight and everything would have been perfect. Now you are fucked, I am fucked! Your friends in Sanctuary are fucked! All because you just couldn't do as you were fucking told!" He pushed her up against the wall and grabbed her arms, ready to tie them behind her back.

"Doesn't have to be," she whispered.

"What?" he asked, keeping his voice down moving closer.

"Doesn't have to end like this, for either of us. Let me go, let the others go. We kill the savages and go our own way."

"Then all my men die, and I lose everything," he

snapped. "I'm not so stupid as to allow that. You have no idea how long it's taken me to build what I have!"

"Or you can gain everything and more."

"The fuck are you talking about?"

"Hurry up!" the cannibal barked, watching them closely.

Auska turned her head and looked at him. "What if I could give you Sanctuary? You could be a king there, have your own little realm. Once the people know what the council is doing, they will latch on to the first person who frees them and promises them better."

"I'm not that stupid, girl." He shoved her to the doorway, his men flanking her.

"Well, that was fun, for a few hours," Wren muttered as Auska was forced in beside him and Jen.

Jennifer glared hatefully at her. "This isn't over between you and me."

Auska just shook her head and looked at Wren, waiting for him to say something. He quickly looked away.

Four of the cannibals led the way through the outer ruins of the city, their eyes vigilant as they gripped their weapons. Cities were dangerous; infected ruled and bands of survivors seldom were any kinder to newcomers. Everett and his two men guarded the rear while the two other cannibals guarded each flank.

The city was eerie. The creaking of old buildings rotting at their seams, sections of roofs or walls crumbling, echoed off every building and each time the group stiffened, expecting an attack or a horde of infected to clamber out of their hiding spot.

Within an hour, they had made it to the cities edge and back to the construction yard without incident. Shoulders sagged and tensions faded a little, knowing the most dangerous part of the trip was over.

"We will stop for a few minutes," the leader of the cannibal group told them, "and scout back to make sure we are not being followed by anyone. Joshua, Mickel, go make sure we are clear. If you see anyone, report back and we will deal with them together."

Auska, Wren, and Jennifer were forced to sit, while the other cannibals looked around for hidden enemies or things they could use. Everett talked quietly to his two men; his eyes continued to look over at her and she glared at him.

A shout from the side alerted them all to an issue.

"Infected! Come help me!" one of the cannibals called out and the sound of a fight could be heard.

"Go!" Everett told the other cannibals. "We'll keep watch on the prisoners.

The cannibals wasted no time in running to aid their comrade.

Everett dropped down beside Auska and pulled her face to look at him. "Swear to me you will help me take Sanctuary, and you will have your freedom and whatever supplies you can carry when it is done!"

"Done. Now hurry up before they get back!" Auska urged him.

His grip on her jaw tightened violently. "Fucking swear it to me, cunt!" He pulled Archer's skull from his pack. "Swear it on whatever the fuck this means to you, or so help me I will take you back to the cannibals and you will know true suffering!"

Auska's eyes lit up; she had thought the skull left behind. "I swear it to you on the greatest man I ever knew, I will help you take Sanctuary."

"No!" Jen gasped in surprise. "How the fuck could you sell everyone out like that, you piece of shit!"

"Boss, we better hurry. It sounds like they took care of the infected."

Everett moved in closer. "I swear if you betray me, I will peel the flesh from your body and force you to eat it!" He cut her binding. "Let's go!"

Auska got to her feet. "Not without them, too."

"What!" he hissed, rifle in hand, knowing trouble would be upon them soon.

"We'll need them."

"I'll not fucking help you!" Jennifer spat.

Auska turned a deadly stare on her. "You will unless you want to become food tonight!"

"Hurry up!" Everett tossed her the knife and Auska quickly cut their bindings. "But I swear to either of you, betray me or try to run, you will die!"

"What the fuck is going on here?" one of the cannibals bellowed out, coming around a massive stack of rock.

"Change of plans!" Everett growled, his rifle bucked, and the cannibal was thrown back, a gaping hole in his chest. "Move!"

Within moments, the sound of gunfire purged the world around them. Bullets whizzed by, striking the ground by their feet or punching holes in whatever they were near.

One of Everett's men turned and fired two rounds before he was shot in the thigh and fell to the ground. "Help me!" He tried to stumble out of the way.

No one stopped; to stop was to share his fate. Several more shots fired from his gun before he was easily overtaken.

"Give me a damn gun!" Auska screamed over the noise as they rounded the shell of a gravel truck.

"Not on your damn life!" Everett replied, checking to see how many rounds he had left.

"Then we will all fucking die here, you idiot!" she screamed, another bullet ricochet above their heads.

"We're fine!" he growled. "There are only three left!"

Auska turned to Jen, who was huddled near Wren. "Jen, you and me, circle five!"

Jen's eyed her with resentment but nodded, knowing if they didn't help, they would be gunned down. "Fine, but this doesn't change what is going to happen between us."

"Give us cover fire," Auska ordered, "now!"

"Where the fuck do you think you are going?"

Everett called out as both women ran from the cover of the truck into a maze of debris. He and his remaining man fired several rounds in the direction they had last seen the enemy. "Get back here!" he screamed. "Damn it!"

The two moved in perfect union through the piles of garbage and rubble that made up a good portion of the construction yard. The sound of gunshots lessened, as bullets were drying up, and shots needed to count.

Jen grabbed Auska's arm and pointed to her eyes and then to the left where she had seen someone duck down behind a large cement mixer. She hefted up a metal pipe she had found along the way and nodded.

Nodding back, Auska slipped off ahead and circled back around to await the signal.

Jen watched her go and almost turned her back to leave. Why should she be doing any of this? She could easily slip away right here and now. But she couldn't; something inside her refused to leave. She would see this through, and then she would get her revenge for her brother and stop what was being planned for her home! Yes, she could play this out, wait for the perfect moment before the strike.

Jennifer caught sight of Auska in place, and banged her pipe on everything around her, making as much noise as possible. She heard the shuffling of feet on the dusty ground and quickly found cover.

The cannibal rounded the corner, his handgun leading the way. "Come out, come out, wherever you are! Come out nicely and I won't kill you... at least not yet," he snickered.

Jen's heart was pounding in her chest; he was getting close, too close. Had Auska abandoned her? Set her up to be killed so she would no longer be a threat? The bitch was cold-hearted and malicious, it should come as no surprise.

"Fine!" the taller woman whispered. "I'll deal with this myself!"

She shot straight up, pipe back ready to strike, blood sprayed across her face as a knife blade tore through the man's jugular.

Auska snatched the gun before he hit the ground. "Why the fuck would you stand up?"

"I thought you left me to die."

Walking right up to Jennifer, Auska pressed a finger into her chest. "Keep up this bullshit and I will. I need you to fucking trust me in this and know I have a fucking plan to see everyone out of this, hopefully alive. Now let's go, we got two more."

"I'll never trust you. You killed my brother. I won't let that go unpunished."

"I didn't kill your damn brother!" Auska roared. "I would have when he turned if you were too much of a coward to do it like you should have done after he was bitten. But I was leaving that to you, hoping you'd have the balls to do what needed to be done! If I would have killed him, I would have come to you and told you, not done it in secret in the dark like a coward!"

"You bitch!" Jennifer screamed, swinging the

pipe for her head.

Auska quickly sidestepped the deadly blow and fired.

Jen froze, shock upon her face, staring wide-eyed with fear at Auska. A grunt and the sound of someone collapsing behind her shook her out of her daze. She looked back and saw one of the other cannibals in his death throes in the dirt. Quickly, she checked herself; she hadn't been shot. "You... you didn't shoot me..."

Stepping in Auska thundered a left hook into the taller woman's jaw-dropping her to the ground. "Attack me again, I fucking dare you!" She grimaced; throwing that punch had flared the pain in her side and shoulder but she threw another one anyway, knocking Jen further into the ground. "This isn't going to work if I have to fight you, too!"

Before Jen could spit back a reply, Wren, Everett and his man came around the corner. "There you are! Tried to run, did you?"

The handgun came up again and the dull click was heard by all. Auska shrugged and tossed it to Everett. "You got lucky. I had to waste a bullet on this piece of shit." She kicked the dead cannibal.

Everett finally noticed the two corpses and lowered his weapon. "Don't do that again."

"Do what?" Jen spat, pulling herself off the ground, wiping the blood from her split lips. "Save everyone's lives? I'll pass on listening to that advice, idiot."

The slaver stepped in close to her. "It's not

advice, it's an order. Or a threat, however you choose to take it." He looked at both sternly. "You are both still MY property, and until the bargain is fulfilled it will remain so."

Jen was about to speak when he slapped her hard enough to knock her off her feet and into the dirty ground once more.

"Don't fucking test me." Then he reached over and grabbed Auska by the throat and pulled her close. Looking down at the empty gun, he squeezed her neck harder. "Pull that shit again and I will snap your fucking neck!"

"Can't blame a girl for trying." She tried to grin.

"Boss, we need to get the fuck out of here," the other man said. "That one that got away, he'll be running right back to his friends and then we are fucked."

"We need to get back to the Abyss and quickly," Everett told them, starting to lead the way.

"What? Boss why?"

"You and I, Boras, can't take Sanctuary by ourselves. We need others or as many as we can save."

"Jesus Christ, boss, going back there is suicide!" the burly slaver said, fear gripping his every word. "We should just run, we can get far enough away. Tonka's grasp only goes so far. He won't give chase more than a hundred miles before giving up."

"What makes you think you'll get a hundred miles before he finds you?" Wren asked.

"Shut up slave!" Boras snapped back.

"He's right, Boras. If we are going to do anything, we need the men back, and hopefully some of the gear, maybe even a trunk."

"I don't like this. Not one fucking bite, boss," Boras grumbled.

"Neither do I, but we are fucked right now. We've got nothing. We lost everything." He turned a bitter glare towards Auska. "But this 'arrangement' could turn out very well for us, so long as we do it right."

"You know this bitch is going to betray us, right? Or try to kill us or run." Boras shouldered his rifle.

"Stop treating us like property and the chances of me running a knife across your throat lessen drastically," Auska snapped back. "Besides, this one," she pointed to Jen, "wants to go home and he wants to find a home. Promise them that and I am sure they will lessen in the attempts on your lives, too."

"And what about you?" Everett asked. "What do you want?"

Auska's eyes burned with purpose. "The council dead, and Sanctuary the way it was promised to be."

Jen rolled her eyes. "And you think a slaver will be a better choice for leadership?"

"I'll have no need to be a slaver once I rule my own community," he replied, the idea growing more and more on him. "Now let's get going. We will come up with a plan on the way."

———◦———

By the time the small group had reached the Abyss again, dusk was setting in. They had come across the cannibal survivor of their fight: he had been taken by surprise by the infected and torn to pieces. It had been a gruesome sight, but a welcoming one, ensuring the group that no one would be on alert yet and their betrayal was still unknown. A slight chance that this would work was still within their grasp.

"Good, they haven't locked them up within the mine," Everett whispered as they watched his band of slavers milling around their small campsite, surrounded by enemies. From what they could see at least seven stood guard around Everett's men.

"I don't see any weapons," Jen said. "They must have taken them in fear of retaliation."

"That's going to make things harder," Auska muttered. They themselves only had a few weapons and only eleven rounds between them. She glanced at Everett. "You'll have to share those guns if you want this to work."

"So, you can shoot me and run off?" he scoffed. "Not likely."

"There are at least seven or more armed men guarding your men. You think you and your man are going to be able to take enough of them down before bullets are flying everywhere and everyone gets killed?" Auska reasoned. "Besides, you are the least of my issues right now. Getting caught here again is worse for my health than being stuck with you for a week!"

Everett stared into her eyes for a moment, then nearly laughed out loud. "Almost made me want to believe you." He looked back to his men. "They aren't without weapons. See how they are all stationed around the trucks and trailers? We have some hidden. When shit starts, they will know what to do."

"Don't think I am going to risk my neck helping with this madness if I am unarmed," Auska growled.

"I would never dream of sending you in unarmed," he handed her the hunting knife, "see?"

Auska resisted the urge to lunge at him with the blade, knowing he was expecting it. "Fine, let's do this."

"Not yet. We will wait until it grows a little darker..." Everett began to tell them when Auska darted forward ignoring him.

"Keep trying to tell her what to do," Wren chuckled. "Working out really well."

"Stupid bitch!" Everett growled nodding to Boras. "Open a path, get one of the trucks, drive north! The men will follow!"

He nodded and moved forward.

"You two, stay near me, and stay alive!" he grumbled.

Auska glanced back and saw the others finally moving up. Not that it mattered; she needed a gun and if he wouldn't trust her with one, she would get her own! Sticking to the shadows but moving far faster than she normally would to remain stealthy, she cleared the distance to the first sentry.

"Whose there?" the man called out, looking around.

Auska wasted no time playing games and sprung out of the bushes she was hiding in. With all the strength she could muster she launched the hunting knife, her side and shoulder roaring at her in agony, nearly stealing her breath as she did so. The moment the blade left her fingertips she was running with it, watching her target's eyes widen with understanding, lifting the shotgun up in her direction just as the knife slammed home in his chest.

There was no time to swerve or roll. Auska just kept running as the gun went off, the sound near deafening as she closed the distance. She felt a burst of heated air by her arm as she leapt forward and speared into the falling man. If the buckshot had hit her, she didn't have time to worry about it.

Auska's hand wrapped around the hilt of the knife twisting savagely, tore it out and slammed it down into her enemy's throat, before rolling off and picking up the shotgun. Already she could hear calls for help, angry voices and boots getting closer. "Fuck it, who wants to live forever anyway!"

Someone stepped around the knot of trees, handgun leading the way. Her knife laced up into his groin as she sprang up from her knees, with trained reflexes her free hand pushed the handgun up under the cannibal's chin. Twisting the hunting knife at the same time, the enemy couldn't help but pull the trigger on themselves.

Instantly all around her gunfire and screams

erupted, some in the distance, some striking the ground and trees around her. She watched Everett fire twice and then move into the opening, yelling orders to his remaining men who quickly realized their leader was there to help them. A truck roared to life and she knew it was time to go. She was in no condition to fight or run from an army of cannibals.

Checking the handgun, she grinned. Seven bullets would be helpful if she could manage to keep it. She tucked it away in her boot; hopefully, they wouldn't search her too closely. Cocking the shotgun, she jumped out into the confusion and fired into the chest of the first person she saw; whether he had been a slaver or cannibal she didn't know, nor care. The truck was already starting to move, and she needed to get on it or be left behind.

Running by another truck, she fired taking out the radiator. Hopefully, the others thought the same and dealt with the trucks. If not, the chase would be on in short order.

Wren was holding onto the back of the truck as it slowly moved through the camp and towards the grown-in road. "Auska, come on, hurry!"

Twenty feet to go! Already her lungs were burning, her side screamed at her and she could feel fresh blood trickling down her leg. Worry about that later! Flowing blood means you are still alive!

Ten feet! But the truck was picking up speed, and she was slowing down. Others were running past her, jumping into the open doors or grabbing hold of rails and steps, holding on for dear life as a war zone opened around them.

"Behind you!" Wren screamed.

Auska registered it too late as something slammed into her back causing her legs to buckle beneath her. She ate dirt as she crashed into a roll, bringing the shotgun up to block a steel pipe that came thundering down at her.

The impact of the blow made her elbows buckle; the next one nearly snapped her wrists. She kicked out, catching her attacker in the knee and quickly rolled to the side as another blow struck where she had just been.

She aimed the shotgun and fired, but nothing happened. The two blows had bent the chamber and destroyed all hope of it ever firing again.

"Gotcha now!" the cannibal roared, preparing for another mighty swing.

Suddenly his knees gave out, his eyes wide with surprise. Auska didn't question her luck and kicked up into his chin, snapping his head back as a knife slashed across his neck and gushes of blood sprayed out.

"Get up!" Jennifer screamed at her, her eyes dangerous. "You'll not die like that!"

They scrambled for the truck which had slowed only slightly; for them or the last of the other men who ran for it, they didn't know, nor cared. But soon they were holding on for dear life as the truck sped away into the growing darkness and the sound of fighting died away. But it would follow them... none of them had any disillusion that this would be over that easily.

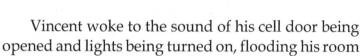

Vincent woke to the sound of his cell door being opened and lights being turned on, flooding his room with blinding white light. He flinched and covered his eyes, allowing them to slowly adjust after the last two days of almost pure darkness.

Blinking away tears, he tried to focus on the open doorway and the three people who entered. He knew instantly one of them was Kelli; the others were Conwell and Murphy, captain of the First.

He had been held down here in his cell, wherever here was, for what he had to guess was four or five days now. It was hard to tell time underground and often in pitch blackness. And calling it a cell wasn't a fair description, for as far as imprisonment went it was the nicest cage he'd ever found himself in.

It was an empty room, with a cot, blanket, bucket and empty faded grey walls of concrete. The floor was cracked white tile that likely hadn't been cleaned since before the virus spread. The room was at least ten feet by twelve, and only had the slight lingering musky smell of feces and urine.

"Good, you are awake," Conwell said, standing just inside the doorway, the other two flanking him on either side.

Vincent blinked away the burning tears as he tried to stare up at the older councilman. "You here to finally kill me, or you just going to let me rot down here like an animal?"

"Kill you?" Conwell gasped in dismay. "Nothing could be further from my mind. I am here hoping you are finally going to see reason and accept things for what they are."

Vincent's chuckle dripped with slight mania. "And what would that be, that you sell well-bred and well-fed slaves to the outside world?"

"To put it simply, yes," Conwell replied. "But let us be real, you aren't an idiot. Kelli surely tried to explain it to you and surely, with all the time in the world lately to think it over, you can see the reason behind it." Conwell stepped closer. "I'll not lie, Vincent, it is a cruel and horrible thing, sickening really, and took us years of hard discussions. But after seeing dozens die from starvation, overpopulation, and sickness each year, we realized it was the only way to keep the majority alive and well."

Laughing, Vincent forced his eyes to lock on his. "The fact that you have so easily justified it, your tone so devoid of any real emotion. A decade or more of doing it and you haven't even tried to change things, to expand Sanctuary or set up a new location... nothing... just acceptance of what you are doing. What happens when things beyond the walls get even worse? Do you really think these slavers just 'find' these things? You know as well as I do they kill innocent people for them. Steal, cheat, murder, whatever it takes."

"Hence one of the reasons you are still alive,

Vincent," Conwell replied. "New insights, new ideas, new motivation. Yes, we could still use you as our chef, for the last few days your poor wife has been run ragged with your absence and in no way is as good as you. But in the end, she will do if she must. We made do before you and we can manage without you if it comes to that."

"So, I can cook and plan meals, so I get to live? I earn a safety net here? I won't be dragged from my bed and sold like fucking livestock?" He spat on the floor. "How bloody delightful!"

"Because of you, several less people each year have to be "sold," Murphy replied. "Think about that before you make your decision."

"That is just one of the reasons you have been granted safety, Vincent. The other is you are a smart man. You have survived out there, you know what it is like. Most of us behind these walls only got a taste of the world beyond. Ignorance keeps us safe, keeps us from being able to see past what we know and how we do things. But that doesn't mean there isn't room to grow, to change, as long as the right perspective is there."

"What are you trying to say?" Vincent asked with growing unease.

"Accept what is happening, allow it, for the time being, keep the secret, keep the peace, go back to work. In the Spring, we will bring you on as part of the council and you can help us slowly make changes."

"You've got to be fucking kidding me!"

"Vincent, just accept it!" Kelli blurted out.

"Thought Kelli was to get a seat on the council, for her 'service' to your secrets!" he spat again.

Conwell sighed. "She was, but she forfeited it to you if you'll only take it. Frankly, Vincent, your time runs short. I can see you'll need a few more days to think this over." He stood again. "After that, you'll be free of this cell, either in a bag or as a high citizen of Sanctuary." He went to the door. "The choice is yours to make. We have been more than fair in this."

"Yeah," Vincent coughed out, "fair... like that's even a word you should be able to say."

"May I have a moment?" Kelli asked Conwell.

"Make it quick," Conwell replied, annoyance in his tone. "Murphy stay here and lock up when she is done."

Kelli cleared the room and knelt beside him. "Just say yes, Vincent! Don't be a fucking idiot, not over this! Dying isn't going to change anything, no one will even know why. But accepting and living offers you the chance to change everything in time! Don't throw everything away for some stupid pride or moral that doesn't apply to this world anymore."

Staring at her with pained eyes, he whispered, "Why do you even care?"

"Because I love you! If I didn't, this conversation today wouldn't have happened and you'd be dead right now!" Her eyes glistened with fresh tears. "Don't throw it all away! What we have, what we might still be able to have, what Sanctuary can still have and become!"

"Leave me alone, Kelli," Vincent muttered moving away from her. A small amount of him wanted to attack, to see if he could take Captain Murphy and fight his way out of here. Another part didn't even care at this point. What was the point? Everything... every single thing was broken, the world lost to anyone with any desire to see good in it still.

Sighing, Kelli stood. "Well, think long and hard, Vincent, because when that door opens again, it'll be do or die. If not for me, think of everyone out there and the good you could still bring them."

The door closed and he could hear the faint footfalls as they walked away from wherever he was. He could also hear them talking vaguely and knew Kelli was being asked if they thought he would commit to their ideal, or if the next time that door opened, he'd be a dead man.

He laughed to himself. "I wish I knew the answer to that myself. What would you have done, Archer?" He asked the empty room. "What a dumb question that is... You'd never have stayed here long enough for this to happen, and if it had happened you would have just fought your way out of this room with a shoe or something stupid like that because you were fucking fearless!" He banged his head on the wall behind him. "And I am not. I don't want to die... not yet and certainly not like this. But I don't think I can live with this secret." He cursed. "Why'd they have to give me options..."

Finally, the truck sputtered, the last gas fumes forcing the engine the last twenty meters before giving up and coasting to a stop. They had gotten further than they had expected and easily put nearly thirty miles between them and the cannibals. A good head start, but with the death of the truck and few weapons, a sense of foreboding was already lingering in everyone's eyes.

"Everyone lineup!" Everett called out with brisk authority as he climbed out of the backseat of the truck. "Discussion time ladies! Big news, big things!"

The men almost looked confused by this turn of events but followed protocol and lined up along the side of the truck anyways. Some weren't looking well; wounds that needed looking after bled and dripped from more than a handful of them. On the drive two men hadn't been able to hold on and had fallen off, to stay where they landed.

"Fuck, boss, it is good to see you again!" one of the men said with a black toothy grin; a bloody cut had dried just above his left eye.

Another was checking to see if a bullet had gone through or was stuck in his shoulder. "Almost thought you might have left us for dead. Glad I was wrong. Though if I had been you, I wouldn't have come back like a hero."

"That's why he's the boss," another man said.

Everett walked up and down the line of the nine men he had left. It was a small group, but the ones here were tough, hard men who would listen and follow him… or so he hoped. "Our lives have been turned upside down this fucking trip! Worse than ever before, much worse, and I promised you a grand payout for riding with me."

Several voiced their agreement, their eyes staring hatefully at Auska, Jennifer and Wren, who stood up against the truck, uneasy.

"It's because of that bitch!" one of the men growled and others quickly agreed, the air of danger quickly taking over.

Everett held up his hands and silenced them, knowing if he let the anger build too much, he'd have no control. "You aren't wrong, it is entirely that bitch's fault. Since the night at the pump house, she has caused us nothing but grief."

"Let us have some fun with her and cut her throat after!" Several loud cheers came from this.

"Enough!" The slaver leader roared out. "Hours ago, I would have agreed with you. Hell, I would have been the first to push her over a log, but the situation can change quickly and new outcomes have been presented."

One of the men limped forward a step. "And what could have possibly happened to spare that bitch's life after all the shit she has caused us? All the lives lost because of her! Our supplies and wares have gone! We are fucking ruined boss!"

"Sanctuary," he told them with a grin.

"We are going back?" someone muttered.

"We have nothing to trade now."

"We aren't going back to trade with them, we aren't going back to seek safety." He grinned. "We are going back to take over and claim it as ours! Then the men we lost, the supplies we lost, will be worth it. We will have our own kingdom to rule!"

The men began talking amongst themselves; some were happy with this news, others confused, others not sold at all.

"And how the fuck do you think we are going to take a place like that with a tiny handful of us, against hundreds of them?"

"With their help." He pointed to Auska and Jen.

Now the man that stepped forward truly started to laugh. "Have you lost your fucking mind, Everett?" He turned to look at the others. "Do you really think you can trust the word of those two? More so, to help us take over their home?"

"You mean the home that sold us like cattle to you pricks?" Auska snarled, meeting his gaze with her own. "Or the one that has been doing this for years and will continue to do it unless it is stopped?" She stepped forward threateningly, feeling the handgun still wedged into her boot. Would she be fast enough if needed? "Is that the fucking home you are referring to? Because that's not a home I hold a lot of care for anymore."

"Who the fuck are you to open your fucking mouth to me, you stupid wench!" hissed the man raising his hand, but Everett placed a hand on his chest and pushed him back a step.

"She is right," one of the others said in the group

and got a lot of stares. "No guys, think about it. What does that place have for her now? They cast her out for sale. Why would she have any good feelings for them?"

"Don't overthink this, Derek," Everett told the man. "We aren't going in there for slaughter, we are going in to kill the council and the soldiers who would stand in our way. The rest go unharmed," he grinned again. "Can't rule a kingdom if all the subjects are dead."

"And how the fuck are we going to manage that?" the first man growled again. "Just storm the fucking wall? We'll be shot down before we even reach it."

"You aren't thinking clearly, aren't seeing the golden key we have right fucking here!" Everett growled pointing to Auska and Jen again. "A plan is in the works, one that, if all goes well, will see none of us dead! But before anything else is done, who is with me and who is not? For if you are with me then we shall march on our new kingdom! Those who are not may take what they can from the truck and fuck off. I'll give you twenty mins to decide, then we march."

Auska, Jennifer and Wren were set into the middle of the camp; all around them were Everett's men, watching them closely. They were chained to each other by the ankles, not the throat and not to trees. There had only been the one chain in the truck and not enough to do it the way they had before. So, this was settled upon, regardless of Auska's and Jennifer's protests that they wouldn't run off or attack anyone.

It was fine. Auska knew she could leave whenever she wanted. They hadn't searched her and found the handgun, even though they had searched every inch of Wren and found all his hidden pins. There would be no lock picking to free them, but a bullet thought the lock would work just fine if it was needed; then she would have six more, to kill who she had to.

After Everett's little pep talk, all his men had finally agreed to follow him, though it was clear a few of them had their doubts. They had walked for nearly an hour before things had become too dark and they had made camp. No fire was permitted; they were in too open terrain to allow such a thing. It would be seen for a score of miles in every direction and the threat of Tonka and his army was still large.

The night was chill and crisp; every step they took north would bring them back into the coming of winter's grip. Frost would already be seeping into the ground and snow would begin to fall any day now. If this plan didn't work, it would be likely most of them would die from the cold alone before anything else would end them.

"So, what's the escape plan?" Wren whispered, looking around to make sure no one was paying attention. "Cause unless one of you has something to pick a lock with, I'm not much help right now. They got every one of them when they searched me."

Jennifer glared over at Auska. "Yes, please enlighten us as to the escape plan now, or are we all on our own again?"

"There is no escape plan. We follow through with this," Auska replied coldly. "We follow through with this because it is what needs to happen. The council needs to be stopped."

"Of course, there is no escape plan because you are practically one of them now." Jen hissed. "You are a fucking coward and a traitor! And to think all I wanted was to be your fucking friend!"

Auska shrugged. "And I told you from day one I didn't need nor want friends and for you to fuck off." She glared at the taller girl.

"Guess I should have listened to you," the taller girl muttered. "Might have saved a whole lot of grief."

"Well, this is going to be a pleasant adventure I can just tell," Wren groaned.

"I'll not let that bastard and these pricks to overtake Sanctuary," Jen said coldly. "I don't care what you've promised for yourself. It's still my home and I'll not have it ruled by worse men then it already is."

"I need you to trust me, Jen."

"Like my brother did when he chose to follow you, just for you to put a knife in his heart?"

"Hey, you three shut the fuck up!" one of the men growled from the dark.

Auska looked at Wren and sighed, pulling the tattered blanket around her. This was stupid, the whole thing was stupid, her plan was so full of fault that it was clearly stupid. She should just wait an hour, shoot her lock off, kill Everett and run and never look back. That is what she should do, what she would have done only days before... until she had witnessed her younger self screaming at Archer in her dream about not wanting to survive but to live. Something inside her had changed, an old wire reconnected in her... a sudden need to see to a wrong being righted, no matter what that meant.

Sanctuary was meant to be a safe place, not what it had turned into. She would see to it that new management would be put in place. It would work, she just needed to hold strong and play this out until the end. It would work, she would see to that.

Auska looked over at Jen, who seemed to have fallen asleep. "Don't hate me for what will happen, just have faith that I know what I am doing," she told herself before sleep slowly crept into her.

Three days of travel had worn the small group down. They were up before first light and pushing hard well after dusk, trying to cover as much ground as they could before winter took hold and they were caught in the first snowstorms. They were ill-prepared for this kind of weather and it was sapping their strength and morale quickly.

They had about two full days of hard travel left before they would reach Sanctuary. Then a day of planning and set up, and then the attack. It would either go brilliantly or fail miserably. There would be no middle ground, and everyone was aware of it. If they failed to take Sanctuary, any survivors of the attack that escaped would be hunted down easily by the defenders or freeze to death in a matter of days.

Either way, it was a win or die situation and they had already crossed the threshold of no return. Supplies were nearly gone, food rations dwindled to a few bites each a day. The cold was sapping their strength at night and even with the small fires they were allowed now, it wasn't enough when you were sleeping on the frozen ground.

"What will be the best way to close the last distance to Sanctuary?" Everett asked, walking beside Auska.

"Northeast. They will have done their checks and scouting a few days ago and be working through other sectors, giving us a clear sheltered run within half a mile from the wall."

Everett kept his eyes forward as they walked. "So, tell me exactly how this is going to work, how you plan on getting us in there and taking over so easily?" His tone had an edge of violence to it. Everything was riding on this single plan and if she fucked him over, he would strangle the fucking life from her here and now.

"Do you know where the tunnel is that they use to transport..." her tone turned ugly, "...people, out of?"

"Yes, but there is no way to get in from the outside, it's locked up tight from the inside," he replied. "Believe me, we looked at it once before. It'd take a week to break through by hand, and that's if we had the tools, which we don't. Not to mention it's guarded closely. Even when we looked around there was always at least three guards around the area. Short of blowing a hole through the entrance, that way isn't going to work."

"It'll work if someone opens it from the inside," she assured him.

"Yeah, you just know someone inside that knows where the secret tunnel is that will be willing to open it for us?" Everett scoffed. "Pray tell me who this person is so that I can shake his bloody hand, not to mention how you are going to relay that information to them?"

Auska turned and looked at Wren. "He's the guy to open the door. And I'm the one who will sneak in and find it."

"Me?" Wren stammered. "Me, what now?"

"Him? Are you fucking serious?" Everett snapped.

Shrugging, Auska picked up the pace. "He's the only one we got that can pick locks, you got a better idea?"

"And what makes you think I am going to let you two sneak over the wall? Do you think I am fucking stupid? I allow that and that's it. Next thing I'll have to deal with is an army."

Auska stopped dead in her track and spun around on him, her eyes burning with hatred and contempt. "You're a piece of shit and I would gladly watch you die with a smile on my face." Her voice quivered, "But the council in there is selling people like fucking cattle, sold ME like fucking cattle! I have a bigger score to settle with them than I do with you! And I can't get to them without you! So, you see where my dilemma is?"

"Everett!" Jackson cried out rushing up to the group. The wound above his eye still looked bad, but there was nothing they could do about it. "They're still following us!"

"What?"

"The cannibals," he wheezed. "Fucking cocksuckers are only about a day behind us and gaining fast!"

"Fucking Tonka just won't quit!" Everett growled, staring the way they had come, almost expecting to see the enemy. "How many?"

"Twenty, twenty-five," he shrugged, "give or take. Armed to the teeth and looking for a fight."

"The fuck we going to do boss?" a different man said, gripping the long-handled axe tighter.

"We need to keep fucking moving!" Auska barked at them.

All eyes were upon her then.

"This is all your fucking fault, cunt," the beady-eyed man named Rik hissed out, "so you'd best keep your trap shut!"

Auska went face to face with him, her anger

getting the better of her. "You going to make me? Cause I'd like to fucking see that, little man!"

He lifted a fist to strike her but before he could her knee connected with his groin and a left hook spun him back around and to the frozen ground.

Instantly Everett's men surrounded her, weapons brandished for a fight. Auska noticed Wren edging closer, but Jennifer just glared over a man's shoulder at her, no intention of helping in her features.

"Kill me and you are all as good as dead out here," Auska said calmly, knowing it was true. They needed her now more then they needed any of each other.

Everett pushed his way through the tight circle. "Stand down, stand down! We have more important issues to worry about than her." He stared down at his man, who was just starting to recover then back to her. "You attack one of my men again and I'll hobble you for it. We need each other, remember? But that doesn't mean you need to be able to walk without a limp."

Auska stepped forward and pushed a finger into his chest. "And you just came to need me a lot more. Because I have a better plan now that we have cannibals to worry about." Her eye glimmered with excitement. "One that might just make this all a lot easier."

"What are you plotting?" Everett asked, almost worried.

"Tell you on the way. We need to get to my stash

spots."

—————————◦•◦—————————

Vincent heard the footsteps and voices outside the door again. So, it had been two days already? Felt like four at least, but he knew that wasn't right. Food had been slipped under the door twice, so he knew when dinner was at least. He could only imagine what they were discussing outside; it sounded like a mixture of anger and hopefulness.

Soon the door creaked open once more. Light flooded in, but the main lights stayed off this time, making the pain in his eyes not nearly as bad.

Conwell stepped in, flanked by two men of the First Division, who were armed with rifles and looked ready to execute him at a moment's notice.

Vincent pushed himself off the cot and stood tall. If he was about to die, then he planned on doing it on his feet.

"What is your answer?" Conwell asked. There was no give in his tone this time, no remorse, no pleasantries; it was business, cold and calculated.

His insides felt like water and his knees began to quiver. This was it, after everything, this was how he was going to die. In a dark room, where no one knew where he was, and no one would know the truth. So be it then.

He took a deep breath, knowing this would be the last words he ever uttered. "I agree," he paused, the words sounding like someone else, "I will keep quiet about everything, you let me help fix things in time on council." Jesus Christ! What the hell just happened?

Conwell smiled and waved his hands to the guards, putting them at ease. "You made the right decision, Vincent." He moved in closer. "But know this: you will be watched, closer than you can imagine, and if we get the slightest hint you might open your fucking mouth, we will peel the flesh from your bones."

Vincent nodded, his guts twisting to the point he was sure he would vomit. Not for the threat, that meant nothing to him, but because of the words that had so involuntarily slipped from his mouth. He had been prepared to die, accepted it, stood by it, with what he knew now, almost wanted it. But his survival instincts had betrayed him.

"What am I to tell people," he asked, "about where I have been?"

"That's already been taken care of. You've been sick, a bout of pneumonia, but you pulled through and will be back to work tomorrow. So, I suggest you get rested up." Conwell nodded to the two guards.

"Where am I to stay now?"

"Nothing out there changes Vincent." The council man's tone was dangerous. "Put aside whatever chip you have with Kelli, for you two had better be as lovely and cute as ever. Do I make myself clear, Vincent?"

"Yes."

"Do not make me regret this. Your usefulness

can easily be dismissed."

Vincent nodded, following them out into the hallway. They were in a basement and down one side of the hallway was the tunnel! The tunnel they had used to sell people without anyone noticing. His heart raced, but he kept his face passive.

"Take him up and make him bathe and change, then lead him to Dr. Brown's office. Make sure the doctor fills him in on everything he needs to know about his 'sickness'. I want it well-rehearsed for when he is asked questions. Also, make sure you have two trusted men watching him at all times. If he even remotely looks like he is doing anything he shouldn't... you know what to do."

"You got it, boss."

"So, I am to be a dog on a leash then? I sniff the wrong tree and I'll be put down?" The words just escaped him as he felt his anger rising. Death might have been better.

Conwell looked at him stone-faced. "Until we can be sure you are onboard, yes. Now get him out of here. We have wasted enough time with this."

***

The group had traveled long and hard into the night, the threat coming behind them, urging their steps faster, their breaks shorter. The cold seeped mercilessly into their bones anytime they stopped, and for the few hours they did allow themselves sleep, everyone slept close together, staving off the worst of the cold with combined body heat.

The first flakes of winter had begun to descend upon them and the mood darkened further. They were ill-prepared for winter, none of them dressed for its wicked bite.

Food had run out and one of Everett's men had shot a wolf that had wandered too close to the run-down group. The man had been scolded bitterly, for the gunshot could be heard for miles and was a dinner bell for the enemy and infected alike. Yet the scolding had been short-lived as everyone ate their meager share of the tough, stringy, overcooked meat. A fire to cook it had been unavoidable, and needing energy and warmth Everett had allowed it, had even allowed the fire to burn until everyone had eaten before it was snuffed out.

Their scout Tyler had reported back that Tonka and his group were less than half a day behind them, and they themselves were only half a day from Sanctuary. The clock was ticking. Even with full stomachs, the slavers were exhausted, worn out, and many still carrying grievous wounds from their escape from the Abyss. If Tonka caught up to them before they reached Sanctuary, they were all dead men.

"We can do this, men," Everett announced boldly, though even he was feeling ready to give up. "We have come this far, and we are now hours away from our goal!"

There was a grumble from the others, who looked defeated already.

"I promise you!" Everett barked out, feeling new strength course through him as he thought of it. "By this time tomorrow, we will be warm, full and in control of Sanctuary!"

This stirred the men a little more, the dead light in their eyes burned a little brighter, the energy seemed to flow a little more eagerly.

"Now let's get this over with!" He turned to Auska and muttered, "This fucking better work."

———◦———

Auska halted them and moved off to a fallen log, Everett with his rifle was quick to follow her, his finger never far from the trigger. She suspected he figured she was wearing them down until they were too weak to be much of a threat. He wasn't entirely wrong, but she still needed him and his scum.

"Hold on!" he barked, seeing her reaching for something.

Auska raised her hands and stepped back. No point getting shot this close to the finish line. "It's just one of my stash spots. We need what is in it."

Everett pulled the scrap metal top off the hole and peered inside at the array of hidden stuff. "I see nothing of use in here."

Rolling her eyes, Auska reached back into the hole, retrieving a length of rope and crudely fashioned grappling hook. "We'll need this to get over the wall. Can't exactly knock on the front door, now can we."

"No weapons?"

"All my fucking weapons were lost when we attacked the pumphouse and you pricks showed up." Auska glanced back at Jen, who was leaned up against a large pine. The taller girl has said less than a dozen words to her in the last day and a half, but her eyes always lingered on her with intent. It was only a matter of time before she tried something stupid. Auska just hoped Jen would hold off until they had taken Sanctuary.

"How does any of this help us defeat Tonka and his men?" Everett growled, starting to feel a fool.

Auska shouldered the rope. "You're just going to start the fight. Sanctuary will finish it. But none of this works if I don't get inside and talk to those I need to. And I need to do it before Tonka gets here, so we don't really have time to have a vote."

"Fine, you can take your little lover, but the other girl stays with me."

"Fine."

Everett grinned. "And Brock goes with you."

Violence burned in her eyes. "No."

"Yes."

"Anyone else but him."

But he was shaking his head. "No, he is the only one I can fully trust still. He will keep an eye on you two and make sure you get the job done in one piece."

"He's just as likely to beat and rape me as he is to actually do anything helpful."

"Lucky for you. That's a chance I am willing to

take."

"We're wasting time we don't have. The sooner this is done, the sooner we are either all dead or victorious," she snarled and stalked away.

By the time they were within sight of Sanctuary's walls, it was already dark. Auska had to guess most of the residents would be in the feasting hall eating whatever Vincent and Kelli had come up with for that night. The thought of real food made her stomach twist, but she forced the thought away; there were more important things to worry about. This was the ideal time to sneak over the wall.

Their scout had returned minutes ago informing them Tonka and his crew were a little over an hour behind them. The fight would happen tonight; there was no escaping it now. Half the stage was set; now all that was left was to try and get the key players into place.

"The guard has left, now is your chance," Everett told her, putting down the binoculars.

Auska nodded grimly and motioned for Wren to follow her, her eyes stopping on Brock; his grin was wicked knowing she wasn't happy about this. "Let's go." Before she could move, Everett's hand was gripped around her arm painfully.

"I better see you at the tunnel." His tone was distrusting.

Auska shrugged her arm away. "Either I'm there

or I'm not. The moment I'm over that wall, whatever happens, happens."

With that, she was off, Wren and Brock in tow. Each second in the open was grueling and she expected to hear the shouts of alarm or the sound of bullets raining down on them. But soon their backs were pressed up against the sheet metal section as they fought to regain control of their labored breathing.

Brock started the way they had come when a quick flash of light informed them that the guard was gone again.

With a soft grunt, Auska let the grappling hook fly and was pleased when she tugged the rope that the hook had found something solid.

"I'll go first, then Wren. Brock, you bring up the rear."

"Not a chance, bitch," Brock replied. "I'm not that stupid. You'll leave me down here or cut the rope while I am climbing. Your boyfriend can go last."

Auska shrugged. "Have it your way. Just be fucking quiet when you get up there. We'll have maybe two minutes to get up and find cover before the guard is back." Without another word she was climbing, her mind racing a million miles. Brock had been right; she would have cut the rope once he was almost at the top, but now her plans needed to change.

Gripping the side of the wall she peered over, hoping to catch sight of who was on patrol. She saw nothing and swung herself over and motioned for Brock to climb up as she kept her eyes peeled for movement around her.

"This place looks better than I could have ever guessed," Brock whispered, stepping in front of her to get a better look. "I'm going to like it here, I think."

Auska did her best to control her breathing. "Remember what I told you in the tunnel?" She watched him stiffen as she pressed a blade to his throat.

"You think now is the time to try and live up to such threats?"

"Yes," she hissed, clapping her free hand across his mouth and slashing the knife across his jugular.

Leaning back, she felt him struggle and try to twist free, but each second stole that much more of his strength until finally, she laid his limp form down on the wooden walkway. Her hands were slick with warm blood and she was brought great joy watching the last of it spill from his neck.

"Certainly not what I was expecting to climb up and see," Wren whispered behind her.

"He had it coming since the last time we were here."

Wren looked around nervously, watching the glow of a torchlight slowly get closer. "We've got about a minute to clean this up."

"No, I want it found. Let's go, we need cover. Things are about to get dangerous."

Wren followed in behind her. "Maybe next time we do something together it can just be a nice romantic walk or something casual, with a little less escaping or breaking into hostile places."

Auska grinned as she led the way through the shadows and down from the wall rampart. It wouldn't be long before the body was found, and then things would get interesting.

———————◦◦◦———————

Staring down at the counter, Vincent tried to scrub away a stain that had been there for as long as he had. It was a dark grey blotch that he had tried to remove a hundred times before, but it had never gone away. Tonight, he scrubbed at it with a bitter disdain; not for the stain itself, but because of the guilt and turmoil that boiled within himself.

After his visit with Dr. Brown, he had been allowed to clean up and dress but had had little time to do anything else before he was ushered back here to start dinner. His two guards had watched his every movement, and even now one guarded each doorway into the kitchen.

Vincent wasn't even sure what he had even made for dinner that night; he had simply gone through the motions, his mind a million miles away. Kelli had assisted him and talked to him the whole time, her features and tone betraying nothing of what had happened. It was like everything was as it always had been. It made his guts twist violently just thinking about it. Being here in the same room as she now made him ill. All he wanted to do was scream and yell and destroy this place in a fit of rage, but he remained calm and passive.

Dinner had gone off well. When the food had been brought out and was being served, everyone was happy to see him back. It had almost lifted his heart, but then he wondered how many knew the truth as they came through the line. How many eyes stared at him with a false innocence to the horrendous crime being committed here? How many of them were wolves mingling with the sheep?

He had gone through the motions, played his part, smiled, and chatted, and acted like everything was fine now. He had told them of the illness and all the lies the doctor has told him to tell. It had been easily believed.

The warning siren sounded throughout the building and all of Sanctuary, and he could hear the sudden commotion out in the hall as everyone stood and lined up. Those who manned the wall or were part of a Division had their meeting places and were quick to leave. The rest were to return to their homes and await further instructions.

"Wonder what that's all about?" Kelli asked drying one of the large pots she had just cleaned, truly unfazed by the sudden alarm. "Wonder if it's a false alarm and someone hit the button by accident?"

Vincent watched the two guards glare in at them as if somehow the alarm going off had something to do with him; as if somehow he had been able to orchestrate some great plan in the short-guarded hours he had been out of his cell. He shrugged at them, not sure of what else he should do.

Normally they would be escorted back to their place, but the kitchen was a priority for two reasons. It wasn't allowed to go uncleaned; too many sicknesses had spread throughout the years due to lack of timely cleaning. Plus, the food was always to be guarded in lockdown events.

"Hopefully they figure out what it is and deal with it quickly," Kelli said, moving around him to pack some dishes away, "I don't want to be stuck here all night. It's been too long, and that bed has been lonely by myself."

Vincent chuckled in bitter disbelief at her words. Did she really expect him to share a bed with her after all of this? If it wasn't for the guns that followed him, he wouldn't even be here or within a thousand feet of her ever again.

"You're so quiet tonight, my love. It's making the night drag by."

"Fuck off," he growled, just loud enough for her to hear him.

Kelli stopped right beside him and stared up at him. "Things go back to the way they were before. You know the rules. Accept them and this will all be a lot easier... for both of us."

Glaring at her, he stopped scrubbing. "We can play pretend when the spotlight is on, Kelli, but when we are alone you are dead to me. Do not think anything is going to be okay between us every again. You are a fucking disgusting monster in my eyes now."

Scorn flashed across her face. "Best be careful what you say to me, Vincent. Your life hangs in the balance."

He smiled maniacally at her. "I don't fucking care. I get to be miserable with this 'arrangement', I'm going to ensure you are just as miserable."

"Oh really?" She eyes were as cold as ice. "Tavish."

One of the First Division guards stood in the doorway. "Yes?"

Kelli turned back to Vincent. "I think Vincent might need to be reminded of what rests in the balance here for him if he doesn't play ball."

"And what might that be?" But the voice wasn't Tavish's.

"Auska!" Vincent gasped wide-eyed. "You're… alive!"

Kelli spun around and saw Auska peering out from behind Tavish, a pistol pressed up under his chin. "Auska! We thought you were dead!"

"I'm a lot harder to kill than that."

"What the hell is going on in here?" Rogan asked turning into the kitchen from his post by the second door. His eyes widened at the sight of Auska. "Holy shit!" He went to reach for his gun, but he stopped himself, shoulders slumped.

"What… what are you doing Rogan!" Tavish whimpered. "Fucking help me!"

Rogan unstrapped his gun belt and dropped it onto the floor. "No. Whatever revenge she has planned now, she's earned for what we did to her and the others."

"The fuck is a matter with you!" her prisoner shrieked. "She's going to kill us!"

"Auska put the gun down!" Kelli cut in before anyone else could say anything. "You are making a big mistake here, let's talk this out before anyone gets hurt."

Auska ignored her. "Vincent, how are you?"

His eyes were wide with wonder. "I can't believe it... I watched them hang you... I watched you die..."

"No..." Rogan muttered, shame coating his every word, "you watched Cindy Smith die that day..."

"Jesus Christ..." Vincent whispered in more shock, "...what have we become..."

Auska pressed her mouth close to Tavish's ear. "...you should have stayed in bed tonight..."

"Please don't!" he begged, his knees giving out as he slumped to the floor. "I was only following orders..."

"It's just survival... survival is always hard." She pushed her knife through his back into his heart. "Wren, get in here!"

Wren stepped around the corner and rolled his eyes. "Everywhere you go there just seems to be more bodies piling up."

"Go get Rogan's gun belt," she ordered him, still holding her gun at the second in command of the First Division, though it seemed apparent he had surrendered.

Kelli moved with a viper's speed and grabbed hold of Wren as he walked by, a small knife pressed up against his throat. "Drop the gun, Auska! Now!"

"What the fuck are you doing?" Auska asked, the pistol up and aimed as she looked for a clean shot. "I am here to save everyone from the council."

"You should have just stayed away!" Kelli snapped back nervously, her head staying tucked behind Wren's. "We had things under control now, things were going to get better! Go back to normal, before you fucked it up with your bullshit!"

"What the fuck are you talking about?"

"She knew Auska," Vincent replied solemnly. "She's known for years what the council was doing."

Auska's eyes burned with new hatred as she stared at Kelli in a new light. "How could you?"

"Not everything is so black and white!" She licked her lips nervously.

"You're just as bad as they are!" Auska hissed, tightening her grip on the gun.

"Last chance Auska! Drop the gun or I kill your friend!"

"You forget so easily Kelli," Auska replied, her face void of emotion, "I don't have friends remember?"

"Maybe you could make an exception this time?" Wren asked, feeling the blade bite into his neck and a warm trickle of blood dripped down.

"I won't ask aga…" Kelli's voice stopped; the knife slipped from her hand as she stumbled back into the counter. Wren needed no more opening then that to bolt out of the way of trouble.

Vincent's face was pale, his grip absolute on the twelve-inch blade he had rammed into Kelli's side, up into her lung.

Blood trickled down her lips. "You... you... killed me..." Her eyes glistened with sorrow at his betrayal.

"No," he sniffed away the tears that threatened him as he twisted the blade, "you killed yourself, Kelli, when you forgot what this place was meant to be for everyone... for us."

Kelli crumbled to the floor, the life slowly fading from her eyes as they remained locked on Vincent's. "I... st...ill... lov..."

Vincent let the blade dropped to the floor.

Auska ran over to him and pulled him into a tight embrace. "I never thought I'd see you again!" she whispered in his ear, breaking him from the scene he had just committed.

Vincent hugged her back, hugged her with all the love and strengthen he had saved throughout the years for a moment just like this. "I thought you were dead... had I known I would have come for you!"

"I know," she told him and pulled away, finally hearing distant gunshots. "But that can wait. Tonight, Sanctuary will be freed from the council once and for all!"

"How? They are well protected, more so now than ever before," Vincent explained.

Auska turned a violent eye on Rogan. "You deserve to fucking die for what you've allowed to happen!"

He nodded. "I do."

"But maybe there is still a chance you can make things right before judgement is passed."

"Anything."

"There is a small army of cannibals attacking another small group right now just about half a mile away from the walls. Get the First and every other fighting man out there and put them down! Before they finish up and attack here!"

Rogan looked confused. "But there is no way they could get in."

"I'm not worried about them getting in," she replied coldly, "I want as many guns as I can get out there and not in here."

Finally, understanding hit him. "You'd trust me to do that and not betray you?"

"You gave up without even an attempt of a fight just now." She shrugged. "If you wanted to you could have tried, or even ran and gotten help. I truly believe you want this to stop and this is your chance to see that happen." She took a step closer, her mood darkening. "But this doesn't forgive the sins you've already committed. I would suggest once the fight out there is finished, you don't come back."

"Understood," he replied, his voice wavering. "I will get as many of the First and every other Division as I can out there." With that, he slipped out the side door.

"Do you think we can trust him?" Wren asked.

"Probably not," she turned back to Vincent.

"They have a tunnel, they used it to transport the 'sick' out to the slavers. I need to find it and I don't have a lot of time."

"Then it's good for you that I know where it is as of this morning," he told her, his face a torrent of emotions as he looked down at Kelli's body.

Auska gripped his shoulders and forced him to look at her. "I need you to trust me, trust me like you never have before. I am doing something that is going to save Sanctuary and turn this place into what it should have always been. But I need you to trust me."

"Of course, I trust you, Auska, I've always trusted you."

"Good. Lead the way."

"The stairway down to the tunnel is through the infirmary," Vincent explained as they moved through the hallways unhindered, with everyone fighting or hiding in their homes.

Auska nodded. "Makes sense. One of the hardest places to get into and easy to transfer the 'sick' without anyone ever seeing."

"This place is amazing," Wren whispered as he tried to take it all in as they sped past everything.

"It'll be better once tonight is over," Auska told him.

Wren grabbed her hand and stopped her. "Are you sure you want to do this?"

"Of course, I am!" Auska stammered. "The council needs to be stopped."

"I know that but letting Everett and his goons in to take over. You know they're not going to be any better."

"Whose taking over?" Vincent asked, suddenly worried.

"I don't have time to explain this all to you both." She looked from Vincent to Wren. "I just need you both to trust me. I know what I am doing, I swear it."

Wren took her hand in his and kissed the top of it. "Okay, I trust you. Let's get this finished so I can take you on a date that doesn't involve killing people."

They stopped in front of the infirmary doors.

"Date, eh?" Vincent winked at her.

"Don't start with me on that," Auska muttered, feeling almost embarrassed by it. She tried the door, but it was locked tight.

"I have a plan." Vincent grabbed Wren and smeared the still damp blood over his face. "Play hurt and badly."

Auska stepped out of the view of the bulletproof glass window on the door.

Vincent banged on the door frantically. "Open up! Hurry!" He cried. "We got someone who has been stabbed! Hurry, damn it!" He pounded harder.

Finally, Tony from the Eight looked out, Dr. Brown and Nurse Whitney peering over his shoulder.

"What's wrong?" Tony asked, staring out at

them.

"Open up!" Vincent barked, doing his best to hold a limp Wren up. The man's face was hidden so they wouldn't be able to know it wasn't one of theirs. "He's been stabbed. There is fighting outside, someone got in!"

"The door's not to be opened during a lockdown," Tony called out apologetically.

"Are you kidding me? He's dying, Tony! Just open the doors and get him in, then lock them again!"

Tony turned to the doctor and things were whispered before finally the doctor nodded and ran off to get supplies.

"Okay, I will open the door. We will get him on a bed, then you have to leave again, quickly!" Tony explained, unlocking the door.

The moment the door open, Vincent hauled Wren within and Auska was right behind them.

Tony turned back to the door to see a handgun pressed in his face. "What the hell? Auska, can it really be you?"

Auska's eyes burned with betrayal. "Did you fucking know?"

"Know?" Tony asked confused.

"Did you fucking know, damn it!" She grabbed his weapon and pressed hers further into his face until he was up against the wall. "Don't you fucking dare lie to me, Tony. Did you know what they were doing?"

"He didn't know." Dr. Brown said from the other side of the room where he and Whitney had been prepping a bed.

"Then why is he here?" she questioned, her gun not dropping an inch.

"I just got here, was told to make sure the medical supplies were safe during the lockdown," Tony explained, his eyes still staring at her in wonder. "I watched them kill you... how can this..."

"You can ask these fucking pieces of shit!" Auska growled, finally lowering her gun and pointing to the doctor and nurse. "How they have been helping the council sell people to slavers!"

Tony's eyes went wide.

"So, what happens now?" Dr. Brown asked. "I'll remind you, Whitney and I are the only real trained medical professionals here."

"You think that will save you?" Auska walked up to them, her gun leading the way.

"Auska, he's right!" Vincent cut in. "I don't like it any more than you, but after what goes down tonight, we are going to need their skills more than ever before."

Auska glared at the doctor hard. "This is far from over, you piece of shit. Tony, I need you to watch these two and don't let them go anywhere."

"What's happening?" the veteran asked, taking his gun back and training it on his two charges.

"The council is going to topple tonight for their crimes," Auska told him, then followed Vincent to the back where the door led to the basement.

Everett cursed while staring at the hidden tunnel door from their hiding spot. Out of his eleven, only eight were still with him. Brock was already over the wall, and two others had been shot down when the fight with Tonka had started.

Gunshots, screams, and fighting could be heard clearly almost all around them as cannibals and Sanctuary fighters engaged. It had been an uplifting sight watching the gates of the walled compound opened and three dozen or so fighters pour out in trained fashion.

It had been then Everett had ordered his men to disengage to retreat to the tunnel entrance. They had done their part out here, and it appeared Auska had done hers inside. Now it was just a matter of getting in and finishing this dangerous game before the fight was over.

"Fuck, she left us to die, I just know it!" someone grumbled from behind him.

It was hard to think otherwise as he glared at the locked doorway and the battle raged closer. If that door didn't open soon, they would have to fight again, and this time it would be with both Tonka and Sanctuary troops.

"Boss, we are sitting ducks out here if we get cornered."

"I am well aware of that," Everett replied, doing his best to keep the fear from his own tone.

"We should accept the fact that she screwed us and try and make a run for it."

"Brock is with her; he will see she sticks to the

plan." Though deep down he wondered if Brock had been smart enough to keep himself out of trouble. If Auska pissed him off bad enough he might have easily killed her and now be wandering around aimlessly within. It wasn't a favorable thought, given the likelihood of it.

Seconds dragged by like minutes; minutes felt like hours. The smell of gunpowder and blood was thick in the air. Hoots and howls of nearby infected were drawing closer at the sound of the dinner bell.

"You really think she could be trusted?" Jennifer asked, moving closer to the large man. "After everything she has said and done to prove to you she is a snake."

"Shut up, girl," he growled. "I trust her no more then I trust you right now."

"You know if those doors do open, I will kill her before this is over."

"What you and she do once this is over is none of my business." He turned a sharp eye on her. "But if you try and kill her before this is done, then I will ensure you suffer dearly for it."

Jennifer grinned. "Funny thing is you think you'll still be alive at the end of this."

He was just about to order the retreat when a crack of light appeared from the heavy steel door and Wren poked his head out.

"Time to move!" Everett ordered and his remaining men followed in a line behind him across the open ground and into the safety of the tunnel before the door was closed once more.

"I was beginning to think you'd fucked me over, girl!"

Auska ignored him. "Come, we need to take the gateway so the others can't be let in!"

Everett grabbed her arm and spun her around. "Where is Brock?"

"He didn't want to listen, so he's dead now."

He cursed and stepped in closer. "You are testing my patience, girl."

"I guess it's a good thing in another few hours we will be free of one another, then, isn't it?" She pulled away. "Now, follow me and let's finish this."

"What do we do about these two?" one of the slavers asked, looking at Wren and Vincent.

"You do nothing." Auska snapped. "They have their job to do."

"And what's that?" Everett asked as they moved down the tunnel. Wren was a coward, but this other man he knew nothing about, and there was a hardness to him. He could be dangerous.

"Someone needs to explain to the people what the council has been doing and that they are being put down and new leaders put into place." She pointed to Vincent. "Who better than the person they all love, the cook." She pointed to Jennifer next. "And who else better than someone they all have been told I killed because of all this mess."

They reached the end of the tunnel and into the hallway below the medical facility, kitchen and mess hall. It was quiet down here, eerily so. But everyone would be outside the walls fighting, manning the walls or safely tucked away into their homes.

Soon they were at the exit of the building. A small handful of people were walking the perimeter of the wall, their eyes staring outward, bows and rifles trained on the open ground for enemy movement. Auska was pleased to see far fewer soldiers on the walls then she had suspected. Due to where the fight was taking place, only three men were watching the gate.

"I don't suspect we will have very long before they begin to return," Auska whispered. The gunshots were few and far between now, the battle coming to an end. They would stay out there another half hour maybe longer, ensuring the enemy was dead and to strip them of their gear. Then they would be left for food for whatever infected would find them. Tomorrow, what was left would be cleared away and burned. "You, me and one other will head for the council's quarters and put an end to them. The rest of your men need to take the gates. Then slowly spread out along the wall and subdue the others, without killing them!"

"That might be hard," one of his men replied.

"Be a lot harder convincing these people you are their saviors if you've killed their friends and family."

"She's right," Everett told them. "Subdue, do not kill, unless you have no other choice."

Auska turned her attention back to Vincent, Jennifer, and Wren. "You three need to sneak around to the homes, let everyone know what is happening, get them gathered. Make them aware of the truth." She looked at Jen, who still wore an expression of hatred of her and everything that was happening. "I would think seeing Jennifer alive and being able to account for all that has happened should be enough proof they need."

"I don't know how many of them are in on it," Vincent told her.

"If they expose themselves, do what you feel you must. We don't have the pleasure of handpicking."

With that, the group split into three, all going to execute an important role in the task at hand.

Auska stopped a little way from the council's apartment complex. Likely the others that lived in there were corrupted as well, but that meant little to her. She didn't need them, she needed to get to the council. Only once the four of them were either dead or dragged out in front of the town would a new start begin to happen.

"There will be guards inside, men from the First Division, well trained and well-armed. We will need to move fast and strike hard." She pulled the gun she had taken from Brock from behind her back; she still had hers hidden in her boot and wanted to keep it that way.

"How many do you figure are in there?" Jarrod asked.

Auska shrugged. "I don't know, I've never been in there before. Could be as few as three, could be as many as a dozen."

"That's not very promising," Jarrod muttered.

"If I were to guess, I would say five, maybe six."

"Guess we should go and find out," Everett said but placed a hand on Auska's shoulder so she would look at him. "It's almost done. I am surprised you've actually kept your word on this."

She pulled herself away from his touch. "You're just lucky I hate them more then I hate you. But you better do right by this place when they're gone, or I'll be coming for you next."

Everett nodded. "I think I will. I think I will like it here."

Quickly they dashed across the open ground and flanked either side of the double doors. Auska checked and was surprised to find them unlocked. The sudden alarm must have caused those who left or entered to be forgetful.

Slowly she pulled the door open and slipped inside; Everett and Jarrod followed. The small mildly furnished lobby was empty of people, but the lingering smell in the still air showed that people had been there not long ago.

Likely the first-class citizens quickly returning to their roomy apartments as soon as the alarm sounded. They would be locked safely indoors, enjoying whatever luxuries were hidden behind those doors until they were given the all-clear that it was safe to come out. The thought sent a ripple of anger through her, but she pushed it aside. They were not her focus; they were merely pawns of the council. Cut the head from the snake and the body would wither.

The elevator shaft was wide open; the box within had been taken out long before she had arrived, now the cables and pull system had been modified to hoist supplies up to one of the four floors. Glancing up the shaft, she wondered if they would be able to make the climb unheard, but a flash of her last time in an elevator shaft quickly dismissed the idea.

The trio moved for the stairwell. Auska cracked the door and listened.

"What the fuck are you waiting for?" grumbled Jarrod. "Let's get this shit done!"

Everett flashed his man a glare that shut him up quickly.

"It's clear." Auska moved her way up, climbing the stairs on the far side, giving her the greatest view of what was in front of and above her. Her movements were near silent as death; she could not say the same for the two bulky men following her.

"Someone's coming!" Jarrod whispered to them and they all crouched down and listened.

It was coming from below them; someone had entered the building and they could hear the front doors being locked. Two sets of voices could be heard, chatting to each other as they made their way to the stairwell.

Before Auska or Everett could say anything, Jarrod charged down the stairs, pulling a large hunting knife as he went. He bulled through the swinging door and crashed into a well-dressed man and woman.

The woman cried out as she was thrown to the

hard-tiled floor. The man crashed into a large planter, shattering the porcelain pot and destroying the poor plant within, but was just able to keep himself on his feet.

"What is the meaning of this!" he barked out, turning to see the stocky man approaching him with a knife. "Who... who are you?" He tried to back up but was met with the wall.

"Jarrod, don't hurt them!" Everett commanded as he stepped out, Auska in tow.

"We've come too far and are too close, boss." Jarred replied, flipping the knife between hands as he eyed the pathetic man. "They will ruin everything if we let them live."

"It wouldn't do to kill the people I am here the liberate from corruption," Everett reminded him sternly.

"What... what are you talking about?" the woman asked as she pushed herself up onto her knees. "Who are you? What are you doing here?" She spied Auska and her face betrayed her knowledge. "Auska? What... you... you were killed..."

Auska pushed herself forward, knowing full well they knew what had happened. "Mrs. Augustine," her eyes were cold, "the news of my death was greatly exaggerated it would seem."

"But... but... we saw you hang..." Mr. Augustine sputtered out.

"So, who did you sacrifice to keep that secret?" Auska pressed, her body shakily with fury.

"I have no idea what you are talking about." Mrs.

Augustine replied, her eyes downcast.

"How long have you known?" Auska pressed. "How fucking long have you two known what was happening?"

"Please, we don't know what you are talking about," Mr. Augustine announced. "Just don't hurt us."

"Boss, we are wasting time," Jarrod growled licking his lips. "Time we don't have much of right now!"

Auska's boot lashed out, catching the woman in the face, throwing her back to the ground as she pounced on her, the blade pressed dangerously to her throat. Her husband tried to step in to intervene, but Jarrod was there to stop him.

"I will ask you one more time, how long did you know about it?" A thin line of blood began to leak down her captive's slender neck.

"Four years!" Mr. Augustine blurted out. "We've known about the deal for four years."

"Who else knows?" Auska snarled, the blade not leaving the woman's throat.

"Everyone within the building and all of the First Division," he sighed in defeat. "We were all brought in on it slowly. It didn't sit well with most of us, but what choice did we have?"

"Plenty!" Auska plunged the knife into Mrs. Augustine's throat, twisted and stood watching the woman's eyes as she realized death was upon her.

"NO!" Mr. Augustine made a move, but Jarrod lanced his knife up under the man's chin into his brain.

"Care to explain how that was fucking helpful to my cause!" Everett growled.

"Anyone who knows has no right to draw breath!" Auska hissed in reply. "You want to win these people, then those involved in this will need to be put to death!"

"I was involved in this, remember."

"I would suggest you keep that part out of your welcoming speech," was all she said before making her way to the stairs again, a trail of blood dripping from her blade.

They reached the second floor and it took every ounce of strength for Auska not to start kicking down doors and butchering the bastards inside. There would be time for judgements later. Right now, the four council members needed to be dealt with.

Soon they were outside the stairwell door leading to the fourth floor; it was locked. Beyond this door was where all that Sanctuary should have been had been corrupted, where the sick minds of four had doomed countless lives with lies and decent, all for the sake of not losing their grip of power.

"We should grab Wren," Everett whispered. "He can pick the lock."

"No time." Auska grabbed her hidden pistol and fired, blowing the lock to pieces before kicking the door in.

"What in the heavens is going on!" Mr. Greenfield gasped from behind his desk within the small lobby. His eyes widening terror as he saw

Auska charge straight for him.

Auska knew this man. This was the lackey the council used for all their work; he ran errands and gave orders around Sanctuary by word of the council. "Surprised to see me, Greenfield!"

"Shit!" He fumbled with a drawer at his desk, pulled it open and raised a small revolver.

Auska was quicker and slapped the gun wide. A shot went off into the drywall as it was knocked from his hand. She pressed the gun barrel under his fat chin. "Where are they?"

"You'll never get to them," he whimpered, his eyes filling with tears of terror, "and I'll not help you!"

Everett grabbed the short, fat man away from her and slammed him against the wall, putting half his body through it. "You want to live to see tomorrow? Start fucking talking."

"You... you don't scare me, Everett!" Mr. Greenfield blabbered out. "It will be you who won't see tomorrow!"

"Don't be stupid, fat man." Everett sneered. "Everything outside this floor is mine already."

"You... you lie!"

"I could use a man like you, someone who knows what's what," Everett told him. "Just tell me where they are."

Suddenly the double doors on the far side of the room burst open. Two of the First Division guards stepped out, both with rifles ready.

"Kill them!" Mr. Greenfield bellowed out as he

was swung around as a human shield.

"Put the guns down, gentlemen," Everett told them firmly, his own handgun poised at them.

"What the fuck is this about Everett?" one of the guards growled, taking in the scene before them.

Everett grinned. "Just need to have a little chat with your bosses about something quick."

"You were paid the body count you asked for, there is nothing more that needs discussing until next year."

"That's not why I am here."

"Kill them, damn it!" Greenfield cried out, warm piss soaking his leggings and filling his fine slippers.

"Only reason you'd be stupid enough to come here is to die," the second guard snarled.

Auska rolled her eyes as she hid behind the deck; she was sure they hadn't seen her. This conversation made her blood boil and was getting nowhere. There was no reasoning here, only death.

She sprang up and fired, her aim off in her haste. The bullet bit into the wooden door an inch from its intended target. Then bullets were flying.

Everett ducked behind his whimpering captive as two bullets punched into Greenfield's chest. He fired two rounds as he backed up; where they landed, he didn't know. His shield had gone limp; either he had passed out or, the more likely, he was dead. Either way, the dead weight was near impossible for him to hold with one arm. As soon as he was near, he threw himself over the wooden bench in the room and took cover.

Auska watched Everett get to cover. Each second, she had hoped a bullet would find him and at the same time knew he was still needed to finish this. Jarrod was pinned at the stairwell door; every time he tried to get his rifle round to fire, a bullet was quick to keep him in place. From here she couldn't be sure, but it looked like he was bleeding already from a wound in his arm.

Reaching under the desk, Auska recovered Greenfield's fallen revolver. She would need this... she tucked it away into her boot. Five bullets were left in her pistol... she had to make them count.

Springing up again, she fired. Her targets were doing their best to stay close to the door frame while still controlling the attacker's movements. Again, she had missed.

"We need to all fire at once!" Auska called out as another bullet tore into the wooden desk. She didn't wait for an answer. "On three! One... two... three!"

Thankfully, Everett and Jarrod both sprang up and began firing. A bullet ripped into Jarrod's side and another into his thigh as he let out three shots of his own. A bullet hit Everett low in the shoulder but still, he fired on.

After the first seconds had passed, Auska finally sprang up and over the desk. Her first shot took one of the guards in the guts. His rifle dropped and another round was quick to find him as he stumbled into better view. Her second shot sent a spray of drywall into the face of the second guard, who was turning his aim on her. A third round took him in the knee and he pitched to the carpeted floor.

Everett wasted no time seeing the attack Auska was going for and he cleared the bench and followed, knowing one guard was down. He watched the blood spray from the second guard's knee and fired as the man fell, taking him in the head.

Auska scrambled to get to one of the fallen rifles, but just as her fingers reached for it a fist connected with her face and she was spun around and crashed into the wall.

"Everyone go on three, eh?" Everett yelled, kicking her in the ribs and grabbing the rifle near her and kicking her handgun away. "Trying to get me killed in the process?" He levelled the gun at her. "Give me one fucking reason why I even need you anymore, you stupid bitch!"

Auska coughed and rolled onto her back and stared up at him. "If I wanted you dead, I would have killed you a hundred times over with that pistol I had hidden in my boot for the last several days. They had us pinned down. There was no way to distract them where we would have clear shots unless they had their attention elsewhere. You two were elsewhere, and it worked." She coughed again, feeling her side and knew the cracked ribs from the Abyss were now certainly broken. "As for still needing me, if you kill me Vincent will make sure you don't live long enough to see the sunrise."

"You are playing a dangerous game with me, girl." Everett snarled. "This is almost over, don't fuck with our agreement now or you will fucking regret it."

Auska pushed herself to her knees and slowly stood. "Wouldn't dream of it."

"Jarrod, time to go," Everett called, knowing more men could be coming at any moment. He could already hear movement and cries for help down beneath them and had to assume the residents were fleeing the building after hearing the gun battle.

"Boss..." Jarrod groaned, using the wall to brace himself as he stepped around the corner. "...I'm not doing so... great." Blood seeped out from at least three bullet wounds and had stained most of his right side already.

"Fuck sakes!" Everett growled. Before he could make a move towards him, a bullet punched through Jarrod's chest and he collapsed to the carpet.

Everett dived behind the door frame as another bullet sank into the wall behind him.

Auska flatted herself to the wall and peered down the hallway and caught sight of two figures she had only seen in the flesh a handful of times. Bruce Harlow and John Conwell.

"Leave now and all will be forgotten!" Conwell yelled down the hallway.

"Fuck you!" Auska screamed back and a bullet hit where her head had been a second before. "Kick me a rifle!" She heard a sound she had trained herself to know by heart.

Everett looked down at the second rifle beside him and then back at her. "If only I trusted you."

"NOW!" she yelled at him, refusing to let the

opportunity go.

Instinctively, he kicked the rifle across the floor, his foot betraying his brain.

Auska pushed off from the wall and dived into a roll, ignoring the torrent of agony that swept through her body from her ribs. She snatched up the rifle as another bullet sounded from somewhere. If it hit her, she didn't feel it.

She was on her feet running down the hallway at full speed, the rifle already up and aimed. John Conwell dropped his jammed gun and fled as Bruce Harlow took aim again. But he was too slow as she pulled the trigger first.

Everything went in slow motion as the spark flared from the gun barrel. She swore she could see the bullet soar through the hallway, Harlow's eyes widening a moment before the lead blew out the back of his head, spraying the wall with blood and brains.

Auska forced herself to slow to a stop as she reached the corner, not knowing if Conwell was hiding around it ready to attack. Everything in her wanted to just give chase and attack, but common sense prevailed this one time.

A gunshot sounded beyond the doors.

Instantly Everett was beside her; his shoulder looked bad, as blood oozed from it. "You are just full of daredevil surprise, girl." He grinned. "A shame we got off on such a bad foot, you and me. We could do great things together."

"Get fucked," she muttered, turning the corner,

her rifle leading the way. The last twenty feet of the hallway was empty, and there before them stood a set of polished double doors. "Let's finish this."

Auska kicked open the door and at the very same time threw herself against the wall as several bullets hissed by, sinking into flesh. She spun back and fired her aim true as Conwell was thrown back into the large office table. He sunk down, the handgun lost and forgotten to him as he stared down at the blood oozing from the wound in his side. The body of Patricia Thornhill was a dozen feet away, blood dripping from the ceiling where she had stood before she pulled the trigger. Coward.

"He...lp... me!" Everett gasped, sinking to his knees, two bullet wounds in his chest.

Auska kicked his fallen rifle away and glared down at him. "Guess I forgot to tell you to move." Her grinned was wicked. "Or maybe I didn't forget."

Blood trickled down his lips as he wobbled, fighting to stay on his knees. "We... had a... deal."

"I know we did." She moved close to him. "But not the deal you are thinking. Remember that first night when I told you to release me or I would kill you before this was over?" Her hand plunged forward, burying her knife into his chest. His eyes bulged. "You ignored my deal. Your mistake." She twisted the knife and kicked him back to the floor, relishing it as his chest fell for the last time.

"I... I knew we should have... just killed you," Conwell muttered from the floor behind her.

Turning her attention back to him, she grinned.

"You should have. I, for one, will not be making that mistake with you."

The older man chuckled coldly. "You have no idea what you are doing. You are going to ruin this place. We had a system… it worked. Kept the majority alive… you have ruined it all with your reckless sense of moral justice."

"No old man, you ruined it when you thought you could sell me like cattle to that piece of shit." She pointed to the slaver's body.

"Then be done with it, Auska," he groaned. "Kill me and have your revenge."

Auska smiled wide. "Oh, I thought about that, but see you owe a lot more people than just me. I think my revenge will best be served watching you be torn apart by the mob… now that they know what you've done."

Conwell's eyes widened and he reached for his revolver but Auska quickly knocked it aside.

"Auska?" a familiar voice said from behind them.

"Barry, kill her!" Conwell screamed with newfound enthusiasm.

Auska straightened, keeping her weapon down as she turned to face her Division leader.

"By the gods, it is you!" Barry gasped, his gun lowering a little. "I watched you get hanged! How… how is this possible?" He looked from her to Conwell. "What is happening here?"

"You watched an innocent girl get hanged so these pieces of shit could cover up the truth of what they have been doing for over a decade." She kicked Conwell hard. "Selling people off to slavers for supplies."

"I command you to shoot her, Barry! Look at what she has done! She's come back to finish us all off!"

Barry's gun came up again as he fought some inner turmoil of what to do and who to believe.

"Barry, you once asked me to trust you," she stepped towards him arms wide. "I am asking you to do the same for me now. I am not the enemy."

Barry looked around the room and back out in the hallway at all the carnage, then back at her. With a deep sigh, he lowered his rifle. "I trust you."

"Did the Eight go outside to fight?"

Barry shook his head. "No, we were to stay behind with the Sixth to patrol the streets."

"Then let's go for a walk. We have news to spread."

Vincent stood at the head of the growing group in the courtyard where they had all watched Auska hang only weeks before. He and Jennifer had gone door to door talking to people, doing their best to explain what was happening. It hadn't been long before the gunshots within the compound had stirred a greater number of people much faster.

Word spread much quicker that way, and soon nearly everyone left in Sanctuary was milling around, awaiting some truth and clarity to what was really happening. Many had gathered meager weapons as they realized that a handful of the men on the walls were not their own.

Soon those of higher standing had rushed out to join them, screaming about murder and carnage that was taking place within the council's apartments. Vincent had made sure these new arrivals were herded together and under watch. There was something about the way they moved, talked, and how their eyes seemed more nervous and concerned than the others that bothered him. *How many of them knew the truth that had been happening for years?* he wondered.

Vincent had been surprised that those upon the walls had been subdued so easily by the slavers. With their attention out into the trees, they had been easy pickings for the crafty invaders.

Now, it was a waiting game. The gunshots from beyond the wall had ceased some time ago, and already a handful of soldiers had returned and were calling to be let in. The gunfire within the apartment complex where the council resided had also ceased several minutes ago.

Vincent felt a tightness in his chest. Auska was strong, smart and dangerous, yet fear gripped him. And he prayed she was still alive. He had already lost too much lately. To lose her again after just finding out she was still alive would break him beyond repair.

From everything Jennifer and Wren had told

him, the man she was with, this Everett, was just as likely to kill her as the council and their guards would be. It did not sit well with him. Not much of any of this did, but Auska was alive and that was something in this horrible nightmare his life had been of late.

He looked around and noticed both Jennifer and Wren weren't with him anymore. He wondered if they were keeping an eye on the crowd or hiding. It didn't matter.

"Let our soldiers in!" someone cried out, and several others shouted their agreement.

"What's going on?"

"They can't be trusted!"

The shouts and murmurs were getting louder. The energy in the courtyard was building dangerously.

"PEOPLE!" A booming voice cut through the crowds.

The crowd turned towards the steel walkway where the council gave their announcements. There walking across it was Barry, Auska, two other Eight Division soldiers, and the battered and bloodied form of John Conwell.

"People, people, listen to me!" Barry called out to them, gathering everyone's attention. "You need to listen! A terrible discovery has been brought to light tonight!"

"Where the fuck is Everett!" one of the slavers on the wall called out.

As if on cue, Tony and a score of others from the

Eight Division swarmed the wall from the sides and below. Before anyone could comprehend what was happening, shots were fired and the last of the slavers were dead before they had a chance to react.

Auska pushed Conwell forward and onto his knees. "Tell them the fucking truth!"

Gasps and more murmurs erupted from the crowd at seeing Auska alive.

"People help me!" Conwell called out to them. "They are traitors! Trying to kill us all!"

"Wait!" someone yelled. "How is she still alive?"

More murmurs.

"Because he lied to you!" Auska called down to them. "Because the council has been lying to you for years. The 'sick' that they claimed died were sold year after year! To slavers!" She shoved Conwell. "Tell them," and she leaned down close to his ear, "and I will grant you a quick death, prick."

Now the shouts and cries were angry as full realization began to take over the mob.

"Tell them!" Auska slashed her knife down the side of his face, taking his ear clean from the side of his head.

Conwell screamed in agony, tears streaking down his blood-splattered face. "It's true!" He cried. "It's all true! But we…" his voice was cut short as Auska kicked him down into the mass of people below.

The people of Sanctuary were mad, filled with violence at what they had heard. Their fists and boots rained down endlessly on the frail body of John

Conwell until finally there was little more than a pulpy mess.

"Things are going to change for the better!" Auska proclaimed after Conwell's screams ceased. "The council is no more! A new age has come to Sanctuary, where we no longer will have those who are privileged and those who are not! We can all strive for the same dream, the dream of a better life for all of us!"

A cheer went up from below as the people began to finally understand.

"This is for my brother!" Jen cried from behind.

"Jen, no!" Wren cried as he ran across the walkway trying to catch her in time. "It was me, Jen!"

Auska turned and caught sight of the raised handgun. Before Auska could act the gun went off...

⸻◦⸻

Auska opened her eyes, confused to see the dream world where Archer had died before her once again. As horrible of memories that she had of this place, this time it held a strange and majestic beauty to it.

The grass was no longer dry, brittle clumps as it had been, but rich and vibrant. Long lush stalks waved in a fresh, sweet-scented breeze that caressed grass and skin alike. The forest surrounding the glade no longer felt foreboding and dangerous, with the promise of a hidden death from monsters both human and fiend.

The sky was full of wonderful vibrant colors; pinks, purples, oranges, and reds mingled together in the most tranquil harmony she had ever seen before as the sunset in the distant mountains. Yet even with the slow consuming of shadows making their way across the landscape, there was no fear, no quickening of heart with the perils night could bring.

Auska inhaled deeply, as if for the first time in her life, the serenity of the place absorbing into her every fiber. All her worries, hatreds and fears disintegrated with each passing moment.

Never in her life had she known such peace.

"Am I dead?" she asked aloud.

"Not yet," came a familiar voice in reply.

She turned to the spot where she had last seen Archer, where he had died saving her, where she had collected his bones years later. He stood there now in the exact spot, smiling at her as a father would their child.

"I was shot," she told him. "Jen shot me."

"She did."

"Is this the afterlife?"

Archer shook his head. "No, this is the same as it's always been. A dream inside your own mind."

Her face screwed up a bit. "But it feels different, everything feels more alive, more welcoming, safer... peaceful."

"Because, in a sense, it is."

"You said I was not dead yet, but if I am here that must mean that I am dying then?" She was surprised that her tone held no fear or concern at the question.

"You are dying, yes."

Auska took another deep breath, savoring the sensation that filled her whole being. "That's it then. At least I was able to free Sanctuary."

Archer's smile was warm and saddened. "It doesn't

have to be it."

"But you said I was dying."

"You are," he replied, "but dying is not dead. You can go back. You can fight to survive."

The thought shifted conflict within her that surprised her. "There's nothing left for me to do now. I accomplished what I set out to do."

Archer scowled at her and ran a hand across her cheek where he used to slap her. "Don't be daft, girl. There is always more to do, more to see... more to feel."

Flashes of Vincent, Jennifer, and other faces assaulted her for a moment, then Wren's face hung in her mind's eyes for a long moment before it too disappeared. "I don't know if I want to go back now."

"You don't have to, but you do have to make up your mind now," he replied as he sat against the fallen tree where he had died.

"Does it have to be now?" she asked. "Can I not stay here a while longer with you?"

"It has to be now. Too much longer and the decision won't be yours to make."

"What are my options?"

Archer smiled at her. "You can come sit here with me and we will watch the sunset together, or," he pointed behind her to the trail she had taken so many years before with Vincent and Kelli, "you travel the way you once did and find your way home."

Home.

The word sounded as sweet as the air tasted here and her heart fluttered with something she had never felt before.

"I've never known a place I felt I could call home," she

whispered.

"It's not too late."

"What would you have me do?" she asked desperately, seeing the cool shadows looming closer.

"The decision is yours, kid," he told her softly. "But remember the little girl you once were, what that young girl once defiantly told me."

I don't want to just survive; I want to live!

"Would you hate me if I stayed here with you?" Tears began to seep down her cheeks.

"I could never hate you, kid. But I will be here still when the time comes. We can watch the sunset together another time."

Auska closed her eyes and took a steadying breath before opening them again. "Then I will see you later, and we will watch it together then."

He smiled at her as she turned towards the forest path.

"…she is coming to…"

Epilogue

Auska entered the clearing holding her new rifle tightly. It was how she had remembered it the last time she had been here in real life when she had retrieved Archer's bones. Yet the sensation she felt here now was peaceful, like it had been months before in her dream.

Making her way to the fallen tree, a few tattered remains of his clothing still remained, but all other signs that a great man had fallen here were dust in the wind.

Dropping her pack to the ground, she opened it and removed a bundle of cloth. Carefully she unwrapped its contents, letting the cloth drop to the earth as she held the sun-bleached skull before her.

"You've saved me more times than I can count." Her eyes misted with tears. "But this final time has truly given me life. I will be back one day, and we will watch the sunset together one last time."

Placing it on the ground by the log she positioned it so it would face the sunset, which was just starting over the distant mountains.

"Auska," a pleasant voice called to her.

Turning, she smiled as Wren made his way over to her. "I am done here."

"Are you sure?" he asked.

"Yes," she took his hand in hers and he kissed it softly.

"I wish I could have known him."

She smiled at that thought. "No, you don't, he would have hated you."

They shared a chuckle.

"We should get going. It'll be dark soon and we've got a good trek back to camp," Wren told her.

"We best not keep Barry and the Eight waiting then."

They made their way back to the trees.

"I am surprised Jennifer let you carry your pack here."

Auska rolled her eyes. "She has her own to carry. Besides, I need to build up my strength."

"She'll never forgive herself for shooting you."

"She will, and it better be soon," Auska grumbled. "I don't need a nanny anymore."

"I heard that Vincent and the other council members want to make a new Division, one to go out into the world and find other decent people. They want to make a new settlement so we can expand next year."

Auska smiled.

~Fin~

Made in the USA
Columbia, SC
09 October 2020